The Inventor's Secret

The Inventor's Secret

Andrea Cremer

PHILOMEL BOOKS

An Imprint of Penguin Group (USA)

PHILOMEL BOOKS

Published by the Penguin Group
Penguin Group (USA) LLC
375 Hudson Street, New York, NY 10014

USA | Canada | UK | Ireland | Australia | New Zealand | India | South Africa | China
penguin.com
A Penguin Random House Company

Library of Congress Cataloging-in-Publication Data
Cremer, Andrea R.
The inventor's secret / Andrea Cremer. pages cm
Summary: In an alternate nineteenth-century America that is still a colony of
Britain's industrial empire, sixteen-year-old Charlotte and her fellow refugees'
struggle to survive is interrupted by a newcomer with no memory, bearing secrets
about a terrible future.
[1. Science fiction. 2. Survival—Fiction. 3. Refugees—Fiction. 4. Amnesia—
Fiction. 5. New York (State)—History—19th century—Fiction.] I. Title.
PZ7.C86385Inm 2014 [Fic]—dc23 2013018111
Printed in the United States of America.
ISBN 978-0-399-15962-6
1 3 5 7 9 10 8 6 4 2

Edited by Jill Santopolo. Design by Semadar Megged and Amy Wu.
Text set in 11.75-point Sabon MT.

FOR MY TEACHERS

British
Territory

Disputed
Western
Territory

Mexican
Territory

Pacific
Ocean

Indian
Territory

Mississippi
Trade
Zone

Amherst Province

Cornwallis Province

French
Territory

Arnold Province

Spanish Territory

Atlantic
Ocean

Disputed British/French
Caribbean

Did I request thee, Maker, from my clay,
To mould me man? Did I solicit thee
From darkness to promote me?

John Milton, *Paradise Lost*
(quoted by Mary Shelley in *Frankenstein*)

1.

EVERY HEARTBEAT BROUGHT the boy closer. Charlotte heard the shallow pulls of his breath, the uneven, heavy pounding of his footfalls. She stayed curled within the hollows of the massive tree's roots, body perfectly still other than the sweat that beaded on her forehead in the close air. A single drop of moisture trailed along her temple, dripped from her jaw, and disappeared into her bodice.

The boy threw another glance over his shoulder. Five more steps, and he'd hit the tripwire. Four. Three. Two. One.

He cried out in alarm as his ankle hooked on the taut line stretched between two trees. His yelp cut off when his body slammed into the forest floor, forcing the air from his lungs.

Charlotte lunged from her hiding place, muscles shrieking in relief as they snapped out of the tight crouch. Her practiced feet barely touched the ground and she ran with as much silence as the low rustle of her skirts would allow.

The boy moaned and started to push himself up on one elbow. He grunted when Charlotte kicked him over onto his back and pinned him against the ground with one foot.

His wide eyes fixed on the revolver she had aimed at his chest.

"Please," he whispered.

She adjusted her aim—right between his eyes—and shook her head. "I'm not in the habit of granting the requests of strangers."

Charlotte put more weight onto her foot, and he squirmed.

"Who are you?" she asked, and wished her voice were gritty instead of gentle.

He didn't blink; his eyes mirrored the rust-tinged gleam of the breaking dawn.

"I don't know."

"Say again?" She frowned.

Fear bloomed in his tawny irises. "I . . . I don't know."

"You don't know," she repeated.

He shook his head.

She glanced at the tangle of brush from which he'd emerged. "What are you running from?"

He frowned, and again said, "I don't know."

"If you don't know, then why were you running?" she snapped.

"The sounds." He shuddered.

"Sounds?" Charlotte felt as though frost had formed on the bare skin of her arms. She scanned the forest, dread building in her chest.

The whistle shrieked as though her fear had summoned it. The iron beast, tall as the trees around it, emerged from the thick woods on the same deer trail the boy had followed. Imperial Labor Gatherers were built like giants. The square, blunt head of the machine pushed through the higher branches of the trees, snapping them like twigs. Two multijointed brass arms sprouted on each side of its wide torso and its long fingers were spread wide, ready to clutch and capture. Charlotte's eyes immediately found the thick bars of its hollow rib cage.

Empty.

"Who sent a Gatherer after you?"

His voice shook. "Is that what it is?"

"Are you an idiot?" She spat on the ground beside him. "You must know a Rotpot when you see one! Everyone out here knows how the Empire hunts."

The screech of metal in need of oiling cooled Charlotte's boiling temper. A horn sounded. Another answered in the distance. But not nearly distant enough.

She didn't have time to mull over options. She lifted her foot from the boy's chest and offered him her hand.

The only advantage they had over the Rotpots was that the lumbering iron men maneuvered slowly in the forest.

"We need to leave this place. Now."

The boy gripped her fingers without hesitation, but he shot a terrified glance at the approaching Gatherer. They were partially concealed from view by a huge oak, but the machine was close enough that Charlotte could see its operator shifting gears from within the giant's iron skull. She watched as the man reached up, pulled down a helmet with telescoping goggles, and began to swivel the Rotpot's head around.

Charlotte hesitated a moment too long. And he saw her.

Cranking hard on a wheel, which made steam spout from the machine's shoulders, the operator turned the iron man to pursue them.

"Go!" Charlotte shoved the boy away from her. "Run east! I'll catch up."

"What are you—" he started to ask, but began to run when she pushed him so hard that he almost fell over.

When she was certain he wasn't looking back, Charlotte reached into her skirt pocket. Her hand found cool metal, and she pulled a small object from within the folds of muslin. It only took a few winds of the key before sputters and sparks leapt from her palm. She sighed and regretfully set the magnet mouse on the ground, pointing it at the encroaching machine. The little creature whirred and skittered away, its spring-anchored wheels accommodating the rough path she'd set it upon.

"Come on."

When Charlotte caught up with the boy, she ignored the puzzled look on his face and grasped his hand, forcing him to run with her into the dark western wood, away from the now bloodred haze of early sun that stretched through the forest canopy.

Between gasps of breath, his fingers tightened on hers. She glanced at him.

His tawny eyes had sharpened, and he peered at her like a hawk. "What's your name?" he asked.

Charlotte dropped his hand and gathered her skirts to accommodate her leap over a moss-covered log.

"Charlotte."

"Thank you for not leaving me back there, Charlotte."

She looked away from him, nodded, and ran a bit faster. Behind them she heard the explosion she'd been waiting for. Though they were hardly out of danger, Charlotte smiled, feeling a surge of triumph. But a moment later, a single thought chased her giddiness away.

Ash is going to kill me.

2.

THE LAST BEAMS of sunlight were cutting through the forest by the time they reached the tree.

"Bloody hell!" Charlotte groped through the tangle of roots in search of subtle tactile differentiation. Her companion gasped at her outburst, and she spared him a glance. Not that he could tell. She'd tied a kerchief around his eyes when the sounds of the Gatherers seemed far off enough to risk slowing down.

The boy's face scrunched up, as if he was thinking hard. After a moment, he said, "Girls shouldn't use that kind of language. Someone told me that . . . I think . . ."

Though he appeared to be running from the Brits, she couldn't risk letting a stranger learn the way to the Catacombs. The Empire's attempts at finding their hideaway had been limited to Gatherer sweeps and a few crow-scopes, none of which had been successful. It wasn't out of the realm of possibility that they'd stoop to sending a real person out to hunt for them. And someone like this boy, who seemed so vulnerable, would be the perfect spy. If he was and this was a trap she'd sprung, Charlotte would never forgive herself.

"Well, you may not know who you are, but apparently you were brought up in polite society," Charlotte said sourly, her mood darkened by new suspicions about who he might be. "If you're planning on sticking around, you'll find girls here do a lot of things they aren't meant to do."

He simply turned his head in her direction, puzzled and waiting for an explanation. Charlotte's answer was an unkind laugh. Perhaps she should have been more compassionate, but the consequences of revealing their hideout were too dangerous. And Birch was almost too clever with his inventions. She'd never been able to locate the false branch without effort, and delays could be very costly. The Rotpots might have been stopped by her mouse, but nothing was certain. A slowed Gatherer was still a threat.

"I . . . I . . ." Beside her the boy was stammering as if unsure whether to apologize.

"Hush," she said, keeping her voice gentle, and he fell silent.

Her fingers brushed over a root with bark harder and colder than the others.

"Here it is."

"Here's what?" He waggled his head around point-lessly.

"I said hush." Charlotte stifled laughter at the boy's bobbing head, knowing it was cruel given his helpless state.

She found the latch on the underside of the thick root, and a compartment in the artificial wood popped open. Quickly turning the crank hidden within the compart-ment, Charlotte held her breath until the voice came crack-ling through.

"Verification?"

"Iphigenia," Charlotte said with a little smile. *Birch and his myths.*

The boy drew a sharp breath. "Who is that? Who's there?" He sounded genuinely afraid.

"It's all right," she whispered, and leaned closer to the voicebox. "And there are two of us, so you'll need to open both channels."

There was a long pause in which Charlotte's heart be-gan to beat heavily, once again making her question the decision to bring the strange boy with her.

"The basket will be waiting," the voice confirmed, and a little relief seeped through her veins.

The pale boy was still twisting his neck, as if somehow doing so would enlighten him as to the origin of the voice despite his blindfold.

"What's happening?" he asked, facing away from Charlotte. Rather than attempt an explanation, Charlotte grabbed his wrist and tugged him toward the roaring falls.

As the pounding of water on rocks grew louder, the boy resisted Charlotte's guidance for the first time.

"Stop! Please!" He jerked back, throwing her off balance.

"Don't do that!" Charlotte whirled around and grabbed his arms. "We're about to cross a narrow and quite slippery path. If you make me lose my footing, we'll both be in the drink, and I don't fancy a swim, no matter how hot the summer air may be."

"Is it a river?" he asked. "Where are we?"

Charlotte couldn't blame the boy for his questions, but she was close to losing her patience. Hadn't she already done enough to help him? All she wanted was to get inside the Catacombs, where they would be hidden from any Gatherers that might still be combing the forest. What did Meg always say when she was fighting with Ash?

Meg's warm voice slipped into Charlotte's mind. *Try to see it from his point of view. It's a horrible burden, Lottie. The weight of leadership.*

Charlotte looked at the pale boy, frowning. His burden wasn't that of her brother's—a responsibility for a ramshackle group aged five to seventeen—but this boy bore the weight of fear and, at the moment, blindness. Both of which must be awful to contend with. With that in mind, Charlotte said, "I'm taking you to a hiding place beneath the falls. I promise it's safe. The machines won't find us there. I can't tell you more."

The boy tilted his head toward the sound of her voice. He groped the air until he found her hands.

"Okay."

She smiled, though he couldn't see it, and drew him over the moss-covered rocks that paved the way to the falls. As they came closer, the spray from the falls dampened their clothing and their hair. Charlotte was grateful the boy had decided to trust her and ask no further questions because at this point she would have had to shout to be heard.

When they passed beneath the torrent of water, the air shimmered as the native moss gave way to the bioluminescent variety Birch had cultivated to light the pathway into the Catacombs.

Charlotte wished she could remove the boy's blindfold. Entering the passageway that led into the Catacombs delighted her each time she returned. Not only because it meant she was almost home, but also because the glowing jade moss gave light that was welcoming. Seeing it might ease the boy's mind, reassuring him that she led him to a place of safety rather than danger.

She turned left, taking them into a narrow side passage that at first glance would have appeared to be nothing more than a shadow cast by the tumbling cascade. Within the twisting cavern, the shimmering green moss forfeited its place to mounds of fungus. Their long stems and umbrella-like tops glowed blue instead of green, throwing the cavern into a perpetual twilight.

The boy remained silent, but from the way he gripped her fingers, Charlotte knew his fear hadn't abated.

"We're almost there," she whispered and squeezed his hand, garnering a weak smile from him.

The passage abruptly opened up to a massive cavern—the place where the falls hid its priceless treasure: a refuge, one of the only sites hidden from the far-seeing eyes of the Empire. While from the outside the falls appeared to cover a solid rock base, several meters beneath the cascade, the earth opened into a maze of caves. Some were narrow tunnels like the one from which they'd just emerged. Others were enormous open spaces, large enough to house a dirigible. Far below them, the surface of an underground lake rippled with the current that tugged it into an underground river. A dark twin that snaked beneath earth and stone to meet its aboveground counterpart some two leagues past the falls.

They were standing on a platform. Smooth stone reinforced by iron bracings and a brass railing that featured a hinged gate. On the other side of the gate, as had been promised, the basket was waiting, dangling from a long iron chain that stretched up until it disappeared into a rock shelf high above them. The lift resembled a birdcage more than a basket. Charlotte opened the gate and the basket door, pushing the boy inside and following him after she'd secured the gate once more. The basket swung under their weight, and the boy gripped the brass weave that held them.

"You put me in a cage?" Panic crept into his question.

"Shhh." She took his hand again as much to stop him from ripping the blindfold off as to reassure him. "I'm here too. It's not a cage—it's an elevator."

With her free hand, she reached up and pulled the wooden handle attached to a brass chain that hung from the ceiling of the basket. Far above them, a bell sounded; its chiming bounced off the cavern walls. A flurry of tinkling notes melded with the roar of the falls for a few moments.

Charlotte shushed the boy before he could ask what the bell meant. Now that she was out of the forest, away from the Gatherers and a short ride from home, she was tired and more than a little anxious about what awaited her on the upper platform. Not so much what as who, she had to admit.

As the clicking of gears and the steady winding of the chain filled the basket, they began to move up. The swiftness of the lift's ascent never failed to surprise Charlotte slightly, but it caught the boy completely off guard. He lurched to the side, and the basket swung out over the lake.

"Stop that!" Charlotte grabbed him, holding him still at the center of the swaying basket. "If you don't move, the lift won't swing out."

"S-sorry." The boy's teeth chattered with nerves.

Peering at him, Charlotte felt a creeping fear tickle her spine. She'd assumed his awful colorless skin had been a result of his fear, but looking at him closely, she thought it might be the natural state of his flesh. And it struck

Charlotte as quite odd. Flesh so pale it had an ashen cast. She forced herself to hang on to him so he wouldn't unbalance the lift again, but she now worried his wan quality was a harbinger of illness. And that it might be catching.

Her nagging thoughts were interrupted when they passed the lip of the upper platform and the gears slowly ground to a halt.

The first sight that greeted her was three pairs of boots. The first was black, thick soled, and scarred with burn marks. The second pair was also black, but polished and trimmer of cut and heel, showing only their shiny tips rather than stretching to the knee like the first pair. The third pair made her groan. Faded brown and featuring an array of loops and buckles that held knives in place, this pair was soon joined by a grinning face as their owner crouched to peer into the basket.

Jack, clad in his regular garb of leather breeches and two low-slung, gun-heavy belts, threaded his fingers through the brass weaving of the basket, rising with it until he was standing. "Well, well. What a fine catch we have today, mateys."

"Cap it, Jack," Charlotte said.

He pushed stray locks of his bronze hair beneath his tweed cap and continued to smile as he opened the platform gate. "A mermaid and a . . . what?"

Jack's mirthful expression vanished as he stared at the blindfolded boy.

Charlotte swallowed the hardness that had formed in her throat. Jack turned to look at the wearer of the polished boots. Charlotte was looking that way too.

The boots were mostly covered by black military pants, close fitting with brass buttons from knee to ankle and looser to the waist, where they met with a band-collared white shirt and burgundy vest with matching cravat. The owner of the boots carried an ebony cane tipped with a brass globe.

Ashley wasn't wearing his usual black overcoat, but its absence did nothing to impede his air of authority.

"Pip called in that two were arriving instead of just one," he told Charlotte.

She glanced over to the wheelhouse, where a slight girl wearing goggles was mostly hidden by pulls, levers, and cranks. Pip gave Charlotte a quick, apologetic wave and then ducked out of sight.

Throwing her shoulders back, Charlotte exited the basket, dragging the boy with her.

"The Rotpots were after him," she said, meeting her brother's stern gaze. "I had to help him."

"Of course *you* had to." Ash tapped a shiny boot on the stone platform.

She didn't offer further explanation but refused to look away. Charlotte didn't want to quail before her brother because rumors of her unexpected guest seemed to have spread throughout the Catacombs. From the mouth of the caverns that led to their living quarters, half a dozen little faces with wide eyes peeked out, watching Charlotte and Ashley's exchange. The children should have been at their lessons or chores, but Charlotte knew well enough that when something this unusual took place in their mostly cloistered lives, it was irresistible. When she'd been younger, Charlotte had snuck away from her responsibilities many a time for events much less exciting than the arrival of a stranger. Ash had always chided her for her impetuous behavior. Her brother had been born a leader, all sobriety and steadfastness. He was never tempted away from duty the way Charlotte so often had been.

Ash frowned and walked up to the blindfolded boy.

"And what do you have to say for yourself?" Ash asked him. "Who has my sister brought us?"

"I . . . I can't . . ." The boy strained toward the sound of Ash's voice.

Ash put the brass tip of his cane beneath the boy's chin. "I know you can't see, boy. If you'll tell me how you came to be in the forest, perhaps we can show you a bit more hospitality."

Charlotte stepped forward, hitting the length of the cane so it thwacked away from the stranger. She jerked the kerchief down so the boy blinked into the sudden light.

"Leave him be. You weren't the one being chased by an iron beast with a cage for a belly."

Ash stared at her, his dark brown eyes full of incredulity and budding fury. He didn't speak to Charlotte, though, instead turning his hard gaze on the faces peering out from the cavern opening. Ashley didn't have to say anything. The children bolted away, the pitter-patter of their speedy steps echoing in the cavern like sudden rainfall.

"Do you know if he's hurt, Charlotte?" The boy wearing the burn-scarred black boots scampered forward, peering at the new arrival.

Jack, who'd taken a few steps back as if to survey the unfolding scene from a safe distance, answered as he threaded his thumbs into his wide belt loops. "He looks fine to me. Are you sure he was really running from them?"

Charlotte ignored Jack, instead smiling at Birch, who trotted over to the boy's side.

"Let's have a look." The boots weren't the only pockmarked part of Birch's wardrobe. From his thick apron to his elbow-length gloves, the tinker's brown leather clothing boasted enough black marks to rival a leopard's spots.

The boy was shivering, but he nodded and didn't object when Birch inspected him.

"No injuries I can see. He's not feverish. If anything, I'd say he's a little clammy." Birch scratched his thatch of wheat-colored hair.

A tiny head capped by large round ears peeked around one side of Birch's neck. Its wide black eyes stared at the strange boy. The boy stared back as the bat climbed from Birch's neck onto his shoulder. Its minuscule claws fastened to one of the straps of the tinker's leather apron, never losing its grip as Birch moved.

"There's, there's something on you," the boy said, his tone wary but also curious.

"What?" Birch glanced at the shoulder the boy pointed to. "Oh. That's just Moses. He's usually crawling somewhere on my apron. Doesn't like to roost anymore, understandably. Fell when he was just a baby and broke both wings. I found him floating in the river one day when I was collecting guano to make gunpowder. Had to rebuild his wings myself."

Birch coaxed Moses onto his hand and then gently stretched out one of the bat's wings, which produced a soft clicking sound as the appendage unfurled. The underside of Moses's wing glinted with silver.

"The key was creating a new bone structure using hollow tubes," Birch explained. "Light enough so he could fly."

"What proof do you have that he was trying to escape?" Ash was still watching Charlotte instead of looking at the boy.

Charlotte's charge seemed content conversing with Birch, so she gave Ash her full attention.

"Only that he was alone in the forest and running from Rotpots." Charlotte thrust her chin out. "That was good enough for me."

"How reassuring," Ash said. "And you failed to notice that he's dressed in clothes from the Hive?"

Charlotte's eyes went wide. She turned to look at her

companion, feeling blood leach from her face. Her brother was right. While the trio waiting to meet them wore a mishmash of clothes cobbled together into outfits favored by each, the boy wore gray tweed pants and a matching fitted jacket with button and chain closures. His wardrobe marked him as belonging to the Hive: the artisan caste of the New York metropolis.

Ash released her from his glare, but before he said anything more, the strange boy jerked hard to the right. The sudden movement pulled his hand free of Charlotte's grasp.

Until that moment, the boy had been leaning close to Birch's shoulder, examining Moses's mechanical wing. Now he stood straight as an iron rod, gazing at Birch.

"Maker. Maker. Maker," the boy said. His limbs began to shake violently.

"What the—" Jack leapt forward, drawing a knife from his boot and holding it low, putting himself between Charlotte and the now flailing boy.

"Maker! Maker! Maker!" the boy cried. His shouts bounced off the cavern ceiling and walls, filling the air with a haunting chorus of echoes: *Maker! Maker! Maker!*

"Rustbuckets. He's having a fit." Ash raised his cane. "Easy, Jack."

"Grab him, or he'll go right over the edge," Birch warned, but Ash was already moving. While the boy's arms lashed, Ash slipped his cane through the stranger's belt and hauled him away from the precipice. With another deft movement, Ash freed his cane just before the boy flopped to the ground, lolling about with no control of his body's violent movements.

With a horrible shudder, he gave a slow, whining cry and went still.

"Oh, Athene, he's not dead, is he?" Charlotte's hands went to her mouth.

Birch knelt beside the boy and laid his head on the prostrate figure's chest. With a sigh, he said, "I don't hear a heartbeat, but . . ."

The boy moaned. Birch frowned and sat up quickly.

Charlotte gulped air in relief. "What happened? Did Moses do something to scare him?"

"Why would anyone be frightened by Moses?" Birch asked. Hearing his name, the bat peered toward Charlotte, as if daring her to answer.

Charlotte ignored the question, knowing that pointing out to Birch that most people considered bats frightening little creatures would only provoke an endless debate with the tinker about fear and rationality.

Jack returned the knife to his boot.

"You've brought home a strange pet. I definitely prefer the bat," he said to Charlotte, earning an elbow in the ribs. "Ouch!" Jack rubbed at his side. "Now you have to kiss me so my feelings aren't hurt."

"I meant to hurt your feelings," Charlotte said.

"I guess that means I'll have to kiss you myself so I feel better."

Charlotte jumped out of his reach. "Don't you dare."

"Jack, get over here," Ash said. He was leaning over the boy, who, despite making a sound, still appeared to be unconscious. "Help Birch take him inside. Then get Meg. Between the two of them, maybe we can sort this one out."

Birch grabbed the boy around his shoulders, while Jack grabbed his legs. His body swung limply between them as they carried him off the platform. Charlotte began to inch away from the basket.

"And you're going where?" Ash blocked her path with his cane.

"With them," she declared, hoping her confident tone would get her out of any punishment Ash had in mind.

"Not until we've had a chance to discuss your heroic exploits of the afternoon," Ash said. "Come with me."

Charlotte stood up tall until her brother turned away. Then her shoulders slumped and she reluctantly followed him into the Catacombs.

3.

WHOEVER HAD DISCOVERED the system of caves known as the Catacombs and why they were named thus had been lost or forgotten. The current inhabitants' best guess was that the twisting labyrinth of stone chambers and passages had reminded those first people of the sacred resting places of the dead hidden beneath churches in the Old World. Or perhaps the intrepid explorers had enjoyed an overdeveloped sense of irony, forecasting that anyone forced to seek out refuge beneath the falls might be better off dead than alive.

Charlotte trailed after her brother as he led her past smaller chambers and through tunnels until they reached the refectory. An oblong room not far below the earth's surface, this cavern served as a gathering place and dining room. The first group of refugees who'd inhabited the Catacombs had drilled narrow fissures through the rock, allowing steam and smoke to escape in small amounts. Birch's workshop was riddled with such fissures, which provided a bountiful source of energy for his experiments. The Catacombs might have resembled a place belonging to the dead, but within these tunnels, Nature had offered a perfect place in which they could live safely out of reach of the Empire.

Ashley pulled a wooden cup out of the cupboards and went to a tall cask, turning the spout until fizzing amber liquid poured out. He walked to the long table in the center of the room, sat down, and began to drink his cider. He didn't offer any to Charlotte, nor did he ask her to sit down. He waited for silence to flood the room so Charlotte would know just how furious he was, as if the telltale twitching beneath his right eye hadn't already told her so.

She spread her hands pleadingly. "There were *two* Rotpots after him."

"I see." Ash's ability to speak through clenched teeth was impressive.

"He's just a boy," she said, casting her lot with a play for his sympathy.

"He's at least as old as you, Charlotte. Do you consider yourself a child?"

She fisted her hands on her curving hips. "I've been a woman for over three years now."

He smirked. "Lord, spare us all."

"Oh, hush." She gave up her attempt to win him over. "I blindfolded him."

He took a gulp of cider and let his cup clatter onto the wooden table. "At least you were sensible enough to think of that. Anything else about this encounter you'd like to share?"

"I had to use one of the mice." Charlotte looked away when he shot her a stony gaze. "Two Rotpots. What choice did I have?"

At last he sighed. "At least you made it back here safely. Pip says all the scopes are clear. You weren't followed. As for the mice, Birch has almost finished another batch, though we'll be desperate for parts soon enough."

Her breath caught with excitement. "When do we have to go?"

"Tomorrow morning," he answered, showing the first hint of a smile since Charlotte had returned from scouting. "You know it might be healthier if you didn't look forward to being in danger."

"It might be." Charlotte smiled at her older brother. "But it might also bore me to death. I'd better not risk it."

A polite cough sounded behind Charlotte. "I don't want to intrude."

"Come in, Birch," Ash said.

Birch offered her a sympathetic smile before looking at Ash.

"The boy is awake again and seems harmless enough," Birch said. He went to the cask and drew himself a cup of cider. "Though I'm a bit worried he might be ill."

Charlotte cringed, remembering her own fears when she took a close look at the boy's odd complexion.

Ash's eyebrow shot up. "How's that?"

"He doesn't know his name or where his home is or why he was even in the forest. All he can come up with is that the reason he's here is grave." Birch took a seat at the table beside Ash. After he'd had a few sips of cider, he put his cup down. Moses scrambled along Birch's arm and onto the table. The metal of his wings clacked as the bat hooked himself around the cup and tipped his head in to lap up cider. "That's his new favorite word. *Grave*. And on top of that, he just looks a bit . . . off."

"Speaking of off," Charlotte replied, giving Moses a pointed look, "I thought we agreed that he wasn't allowed to drink from our cups anymore."

"But he likes it." Birch's gaze flicked from the thirsty bat to Charlotte. "Did you notice how odd the boy's skin color is, or rather, how odd the lack of color in his skin is?"

"I, um . . . ," Charlotte mumbled.

Ash glared at his sister.

She took a step back. "We had to run. I didn't have time for a lot of questions."

"So you brought a potentially disease-bearing stray with amnesia here?" He drummed his fingers on the table.

"Would you have preferred I let him be taken?" Charlotte snapped.

He frowned at her.

"Like I said," Birch interjected, running a nervous hand through his pale hair, "I don't think he poses a threat. Poor boy is terrified as a snared rabbit. And it looks like he hasn't eaten for days. It could be that whatever happened to him in New York gave him enough of a fright to take his mind for a bit."

"Like Pip was when she first arrived?" Charlotte asked.

Birch nodded. "A good three days passed before her memories came back. There are awful things in the city. Sometimes the mind retreats to protect itself."

"Who's watching him now?" Ash asked.

"Meg and Jack."

Ash nodded. "Good. Meg's got the gentlest nature around here."

Charlotte ignored the meaningful look he threw her way.

"And Jack . . . well, there's no help for Jack," Ash finished, and Charlotte laughed drily.

"If Meg stays with the boy, will she have time to attend to the other children?" Birch asked Ashley.

With a slight frown, Ash replied, "It's time Meg passed those responsibilities to some of the older children. She's almost eighteen."

Birch nodded, but Charlotte looked at her hands. *She's almost eighteen.*

The room grew stale with a somber mood until Birch glanced at both of them and asked, "Are you still planning on making the run tomorrow?"

"Of course," Ash said. Charlotte perked up, letting anticipation of an imminent adventure chase away the sour thoughts that had filled her mind.

"Oh, good." Birch smiled, and his fingers began to twitch as if tinkering with invisible machinery. "There's much to be done, and I don't have half the materials I need to do it."

Moses noticed the tinker's fidgeting and abandoned the cider cup, returning to Birch's arm and crawling his way into one of the leather apron's chest pockets.

"We'll leave at dawn." Ash drained his cup. "Provided there are no unforeseen repercussions from grave boy's arrival."

Charlotte snorted, but when Ash looked at her, she asked, "If we're leaving at dawn, might I be permitted to seek my bed? No matter what you think of it, my day was exhausting, and I'd rather not nod off on dear Pocky tomorrow."

Birch's mouth twisted. "Oh no, that would be disastrous."

"I was joking about the gun, Birch." She offered him a kind smile before narrowing her eyes at her brother. "But not about being knackered."

"Go to bed then." Ash went to draw himself another cup of cider. "It's not as if you care what I have to say anyway."

He sounded so tired that Charlotte felt a pinch of guilt. "I didn't mean any harm, Ash."

"I know that, Charlotte. Get some sleep." He threw a brief smile at her before tilting his cup at Birch. "Cider?"

"Not for me," Birch said as he adjusted his goggles atop his forehead. "I've many hours left in the workshop tonight. We can't have the *Pisces* breaking down on your run."

Ash coughed up a mouthful of cider. "No. We wouldn't want that."

Stifling a giggle, Charlotte slipped out of the refectory. She took a sloping tunnel to her right until she reached her door. The round wooden door was set within an iron frame that had been fitted to the small cave's opening. Once inside, she shrugged off her coat and tossed it onto her bed, happy to let the cool cavern air brush across the bare skin of her arms. Though they worked with the original shape and composition of the caves, the Catacombs hadn't been left without improvements over the years.

Charlotte's favorite remained the tangle of pipes that slithered out of the rock wall, their nozzles dropping into small basins that had been carved from the rock itself. Placing a stopper in the drainage pipe that channeled water out of the Catacombs and into her bedroom, Charlotte let warm water fill the basin and went to her wardrobe. She opened the door, smiling as always as the clockwork gears sprung to life. On the inside of the door, a mirror descended. Metal stars swirled around its perimeter, shifting into the patterns of diverse constellations as they circled the mirror. On the inside of the opposite door, a whimsical melody ebbed out as steel pins struck a turning metal cylinder. In front of the device, two tiny mechanical dancers spun to the allegro from E. T. A. Hoffmann's Quintet for Harp. The wardrobe had been a gift to Charlotte from Ash, Jack, Meg, and Birch on her sixteenth birthday. Its arrival had rendered her speechless and made her wonder even more than usual about Jack, though speculating about him was a regular pastime for Charlotte.

Jack had arrived suddenly a little less than a year before, returning with Ash, who'd been on a scouting run. Thinking of that day, Charlotte made a mental note to remind Ash that he was the one who had set a precedent of bringing home strays.

Of course, it had been different with Jack. She couldn't deny that. While the boy she'd found today claimed to have no memory of his former life, Jack had been running from his. He'd shown up in the hard, scorch-marked leather uniform of New York's Foundry laborers. When Jack had begged for asylum, Ash had welcomed him in without question. The two boys had become fast friends, which meant Jack was constantly within nagging distance of Charlotte.

For the first two weeks, Jack and Charlotte had been at each other's throats. Her brother instantly had a new confidante, which left Charlotte feeling excluded and unimportant. When she'd complained to Ash, he had told her that Jack was a welcome addition to the Catacombs, an asset in ways she couldn't appreciate, so she'd better get used to him. Naturally she'd retaliated by hazing Jack relentlessly. She gave him incorrect directions so he'd get lost in the tunnels. She sent him to Birch's workshop when she knew the tinker was working on the most volatile and incendiary experiments.

But Charlotte's efforts only seemed to invite more teasing and attention from Jack. Their banter would escalate to shouting and finally Charlotte's shrieked declarations that one of them would have to leave the Catacombs because she couldn't bear another moment of his presence.

When Ash determined that neither his friend nor his sister was going to back down, he declared that they must find a way to reach détente, or he would force them to share a room—permanently. Charlotte was aghast, while Jack merely laughed until his face went purple.

She'd fled to her room, hoping to wait out her brother's obvious bout of madness. Jack had surprised her by showing up the next morning with a peace offering. From within his long leather coat he produced a square steel box, its lid etched with flowering vines. Too startled to do anything but open the box he offered, Charlotte's breath was snatched away when music poured out, the tinkling sounds flowing all around her as she watched a tiny steel garden of leaves, shrubs, and flowers grow. The plants retreated when she closed the lid and grew once more when she opened it.

The song, Jack told her, was called the *Moonlight Sonata* and was by a German composer named Beethoven. One of the metalsmiths Jack had worked alongside in the Foundry kept the scraps of metal and had a secret craft of creating extraordinary musical devices that he sold on the black market. The man had given the piece to Jack to use for bartering when he'd fled the fires and smoke of the Foundry, but Jack had found Ash and been brought to the Catacombs before he'd had to trade the box.

Charlotte had been taken aback by the extravagance of Jack's gesture. With the music still chiming in her ears and metal flowers growing beside her fingers, Charlotte tried to refuse the lovely trinket, but Jack insisted this gift would be a peace offering.

From that moment, Charlotte had decided two things. One, that Jack was much more than he'd first appeared to be. And two, she could share the Catacombs with him after all.

They hadn't exactly become friends, but their rivalry had transformed from hostility to an unorthodox form of entertainment. The longer their banter went on, Charlotte discovered that as irksome as Jack could be, she missed him when he wasn't around to provoke her. And she enjoyed honing the sharpness of her tongue at Jack's expense.

She listened to the music in the box constantly, carrying it with her through the Catacombs' tunnels so she could hold it to her ear. The song haunted her as she tried to contemplate how the rippling notes could be so beautiful and so sad at the same time.

Ash, pleased that his insistence on a détente had worked, teased Charlotte about her sudden change of heart. He suggested more than once that the box was, in fact, hexed, and the more Charlotte listened to its music, the more she'd been under Jack's thrall. Though she wanted to prove her brother wrong, Charlotte loved the tinkling music too much to give up her habit of frequently carrying the box in her pocket when she was in the Catacombs so she could listen to it when she pleased.

Observing her delight in the contraption, Ash conspired with Jack to bring more mechanical music into Charlotte's life. The pair had found a broken-down, discarded wardrobe in the Heap during one of their scavenging runs. They'd dragged it back to the Catacombs in the middle of the night and stashed it in Jack's room, knowing Charlotte would never set foot there. Ash and Meg had refinished the wood surfaces, while Birch repaired the mechanisms in the doors.

On the morning of her sixteenth birthday Charlotte had awoken to a rippling melody, but not the one she'd grown so familiar with. All four of them were standing beside the resurrected wardrobe, waiting for her reaction.

Charlotte took in the scene and promptly burst into tears, horrifying them all. But her tears were happy ones, and they were reassured when she leapt from her bed and grabbed Birch, who blushed like a rose when Charlotte made him waltz around the room with her. Ash then asked Meg to dance, and the four of them spun around the room like the wooden dancers twirling in the door. Jack simply watched them and smiled.

Now several months gone, her birthday was the last truly happy day Charlotte remembered. Relative peace with Jack had given way to ongoing conflicts with Ash. Their fights had grown more frequent and gained intensity. And they both knew why, but neither was willing to speak of the matter.

Charlotte's sixteenth birthday had passed. That meant Ash's eighteenth birthday was approaching.

Charlotte sighed at the thought and left the wardrobe doors open so the music would continue. Taking a soft cloth from one of the shelves, she returned to the basin and turned off the taps. Her chest was tight with thoughts of Ash coming of age. When he turned eighteen, he would leave the Catacombs. Leave her. And no matter how often or how vehemently she pleaded, he wouldn't agree to let her go with him.

She moved the warm, damp cloth over her shoulders and down her arms, wishing that the soothing motion would wash away her anxious thoughts along with the grime of the day. Charlotte splashed water on her face, blotted away the moisture, and unbound her hair from its usual twist. Her russet hair reached to the middle of her back, and she used her fingers to work out the tangles.

Deciding that was all the effort her weary self was willing to put into grooming for the day, she reached around for the laces of the corset that bound her soft, sleeveless blouse to her torso. She loosened the stays and began the tedious process of freeing herself from the embrace of boning and leather.

Still working at the laces with her fingers, Charlotte walked back to the wardrobe and pulled open a wide drawer so she could return the corset to its place among its sisters. She ran her fingers over the varied textures of leathers that ranged in hue from the tawny shade of a fawn to embossed leather as dark as obsidian.

A sudden voice behind her made Charlotte give a yelp of surprise.

"Getting ready for bed, are we?"

4.

CHARLOTTE WHIRLED AROUND to catch Jack staring at her from where he stood in the doorway.

Charlotte's hands froze on the laces of her corset.

"What are you doing here, Jack?"

He gazed at her for a moment and then said, "Your brother sent me."

She waited for the polite reaction, which would have been for Jack to apologize and leave or at least turn his back. Instead, he chose simply to lean against the door frame and let his eyes roam over her.

"Do you mind?" Charlotte straightened up.

"No, not at all."

She scowled at him. "I'm trying to get undressed."

"You know I'm quite good with knots." He lifted his eyebrows. "Need a hand?"

"No, not at all," she parroted. Charlotte stared him down and carefully worked out the tangle of lacing at her back.

Jack didn't balk, but remained perfectly still. A smile twitched at one corner of his mouth.

"I see you're good with knots too."

Unwilling to lose this dare, Charlotte pulled the corset away from her body and dropped it. The stiff boning clattered against the stone floor. When Jack still didn't move, Charlotte glared at him but determinedly moved her fingers to the buttons of her blouse. A ripple of satisfaction passed through her veins when his eyes widened ever so slightly. She knew it was hotheaded of her, but she couldn't resist the temptation of outdoing Jack. Though she wanted to laugh, it would ruin the moment, so Charlotte held her breath and slipped one button free, then a second. Jack's skin began to pale, then his cheeks started to go pink. His changing expression made her hesitate. His face was no longer full of mirth, but instead was fighting shock . . . or maybe horror. The thrill Charlotte had been feeling boiled up into anger.

How dare he! Thinking he could spend every other moment teasing her and making suggestive remarks, but when she took up the gauntlet, he looked at her as though she'd done something awful.

Her cheeks were hot, and likely redder than his, which

made her angrier still. She opened her mouth, ready to box his ears with her indignation.

"Holy Hephaestus!" Ash appeared behind Jack, who jumped at the sound of Ash's voice and knocked his head on the top of the door frame.

"Bloody hell." Jack rubbed the top of his head. "Can't we make the doors any taller? This happens to me at least once a day. I'm going to have a permanent lump."

Charlotte put her hands on her hips. "Bring the falls down on us so poor Jack doesn't bump his head? Don't you listen to anything Birch says?"

"Only when he's telling me how not to blow myself up," Jack quipped. "Or suggesting that he's going to teach that bat of his to scout for us during night patrols."

"I think you should keep up the head injuries. Horns would be a natural look for you."

Ash shoved Jack back from the door. "Why are you standing in front of Jack with only half of your clothes on?"

She blushed but said, "This is more than half. You can't see anything."

"And that's a good thing," Ash told her. "I'd hate to have to gouge Jack's eyes out. He'd be much less helpful in a fight if he were blind."

"Eye gouging? Really, Ash?" Jack laughed. "You know eventually someone's going to peruse the goods Charlotte has to offer."

"Peruse my what?" Charlotte began to look around for

something to throw at Jack's head, giving him a second bump to match the first.

"Jack—" Ash's voice made her stop her search for projectiles and gaze at her brother instead. She hadn't known Ash could growl his words, but apparently he could. And very well.

Jack continued without heeding Ash's tone. "You might want to rethink your position, because I'm sure it will be someone she likes, and if you blind the poor fool, she'll be cross with you."

"I will most definitely like him, and he will not be a fool." Charlotte rose on her tiptoes so she could glare at Jack over Ash's shoulder. "Which means it will *not* be you."

"Is that the reason just a moment ago I could see your—" Jack coughed, glancing at Ash. "Never mind."

"I expect more of you, Jack," Ash said. "She's just a girl."

"She's not just a girl—she's your sister. And that means you think she's five years younger than she really is. Wake up, friend." Jack laughed, but covered it with another cough when Ash glared at him.

"*She* is standing right here, and she does not appreciate being talked about like a child," Charlotte said, lifting her chin.

Ash turned to her. "I know Jack can be irritating, Charlotte, but you shouldn't let him draw you into his pranks."

"If he weren't so irritating, I wouldn't have been so tempted to give him a taste of his own medicine."

Jack returned to lounging against the door frame. "Ummm, irritating Jack is standing right here too." He fixed his eyes on Charlotte, mischief filling his gaze once more. "And is that what that was? My own medicine? Interesting."

"Shut it, Jack." Ash whirled on him. He grabbed Jack by the collar and shoved him down the hall. "The only reason you're not bleeding right now is that *I* know that *you* know better than to insult my sister."

"He insults me every day!" Charlotte protested.

Jack started to reply, but Ash cut him off. "You'll stay bruise free if you shut that trap of yours. Get down to the dock and see if Birch needs help getting the *Pisces* ready for tomorrow's launch."

For a moment, Jack's face twisted as if he would argue, but instead he mock saluted Ash, saying, "Whatever you think is best, sir," and walked away.

Ash sighed, shaking his head.

"You should have punched him," Charlotte offered. "He needs a good punch."

"I'm not sure what Jack needs, but I'm absolutely certain you don't know." Ash frowned. "Tell me again why you were undressing in front of him?"

The way her brother posed the question made Charlotte squirm. "I wasn't undressing in front of him."

His eyes narrowed.

"Well, if you have to be literal about it, I suppose I was." Charlotte spread her hands, exasperated. "But it was only because he walked in without knocking and then wouldn't admit he'd done anything wrong."

"So you decided the best thing to do was to keep taking your clothes off?" Ash asked.

Charlotte refused to give in to her brother's obvious attempt to shame her. "I know what you're trying to do, Ash, but it wasn't like that. You know how Jack is."

"Yes," Ash said. "I do know how Jack is. And I'm sure he was goading you one way or another. But, Charlotte, you must understand—no matter how well you think you know Jack, he's still a man."

"What is that supposed to mean?"

Her brother's voice faltered. "I mean . . . it's difficult to say. You don't know as much about men as you think you do. Mother hasn't been here to speak with you—"

"I know about men and women, Ash. I'm not a little girl, no matter how much you refuse to accept that. Jack was right. You do think I'm five years younger than I am."

Ash straightened, shaking a finger at her. "So you think young women of your oh-so-mature age have license to strip in front of any man who bursts into their room?"

"It wasn't any man, it was Jack!" Charlotte spat. "And it was just a stupid game."

"I don't know if it was only a game," Ash said coldly. "But it was most certainly stupid. And childish. If you want to prove that you're an adult, then act like one. I'm of half a mind to leave you here tomorrow."

Charlotte felt angry tears creeping into her eyes. "You

would never talk to Jack or Birch like this! They're always joking and pranking."

"Jack and Birch aren't my sisters." His voice was gentler. "I don't want you to get hurt."

"You think Jack would hurt me?" Charlotte blinked her tears away, looking up at her brother's face. "But I thought you trusted him."

"I do. And he wouldn't hurt you. At least not . . . purposefully." Ash choked a little on the words.

She was surprised to see crimson creeping up his neck, coloring his ears.

"I shouldn't be the one to—" He met her puzzled gaze and quickly looked away. "I'll ask Meg."

"Ask Meg what?" Charlotte crossed her arms, fully prepared to sulk. "Are you really not going to let me come tomorrow?"

Caught up in his own thoughts, Ash's reply was distracted. "No . . . it's just . . . never mind. I can't afford to leave you here. You're too good with the POC."

"*She's* called Pocky, and of course I am." Charlotte's anger withered, and she flung her arms around her brother, kissing him on the cheek. "And you'd miss me too much."

Ash tensed up for a moment, but his temper had cooled and he ruffled her hair.

Stepping back, Charlotte said, "What did you want anyway? Jack said you sent him to find me."

"I did." Ash's scowl returned momentarily. "And I came to find you myself because he was taking too long."

Not wanting to revisit their argument, she quickly asked, "Well, what do you need?"

"Meg came to the refectory," Ash said, looking tired. "Grave just woke up."

"Who?"

"Your stray."

"You're calling him Grave?" Charlotte asked.

"Birch is," Ash told her. "I guess I picked up the habit." Charlotte shrugged. "What about him?"

"He wants to leave the workshop, and we'd like to keep him there. We can't risk him wandering around the Catacombs."

"Do you really think he poses a threat?" Charlotte asked. If anything, the stranger Birch had christened Grave seemed sick or mentally unhinged, but not dangerous.

Ash shrugged. "It doesn't matter what I think. We can't be too cautious. Even if he's perfectly harmless, he'd get lost in the tunnels without a guide."

Charlotte nodded. New inhabitants of the Catacombs were required to have a seasoned resident with them until they could manage to navigate the tunnels on their own.

"Would you visit him and convince him that staying with Birch is the best option he has for now?" Ash asked. "Don't tell him too much about us. Just enough to keep him calm until we learn more about who he is."

"Why me?" It had been a long day, and Charlotte was feeling desperate for sleep.

"Because he trusts you, Lottie. You're the one who

saved him and all." Ash smiled. "This is a consequence of your action. Reap what you've sown. I'll consider it a mark of your newfound maturity."

"Don't gloat. I'll go." Charlotte swiped her corset from the floor. "Just let me get dressed again."

Ash turned to leave, muttering, "You shouldn't have gotten undressed in the first place."

He closed the door before Charlotte had a chance to reply.

5.

EVEN IF CHARLOTTE hadn't known how to get to the workshop, she could have found it by closing her eyes and smelling her way through the Catacombs. As she approached the tinker's den, the unmistakable odors of molten metals, sulfur, and charred leather filled the air. Though it was by far the most thoroughly ventilated of any of the caverns, the workshop never lost its haze of steam and smoke.

With a slightly wrinkled nose, Charlotte picked her way through the room. It was the most irregular cave in the Catacombs. Though long and wide, it featured an array of strangely shaped nooks and small chambers that Birch used to house his creations in their various states of completion.

She found Birch at his largest workbench tightening the gears on a conglomeration of mechanical parts that no doubt belonged in the guts of some machine. Moses was hanging from the ceiling above Birch, and Meg was perched on a nearby stool with a wooden cup in her hands.

"Ash said you needed me." Charlotte waved to Meg before she peeked over Birch's shoulder. "What's that?"

"Don't ask," Meg said before Birch could answer. "I did, and the answer took half an hour."

Birch gave her a sour look. "You can't understand how this part functions without conceptualizing the whole machine."

"Which is why you don't want to ask," Meg told Charlotte as she slid from the stool. Meg's hair, dark as a raven's wing, was piled atop her head and held in place by an engraved steel cuff. A matching steel cuff encircled her slender wrist, its bright hue accentuating the loveliness of her deep skin tone.

"Never mind, then." Charlotte smiled at her while Birch huffed, insulted.

Charlotte turned her smile on the tinker. "Don't be cross. Not all of us need to know how your inventions work. Just how to use them."

"No one appreciates my art," Birch said.

"Pip does," Meg countered. "She idolizes you."

"*Idolize* is a strong word." Birch brushed metal filings off his apron.

"Strong and accurate." Charlotte brought Birch a broom. "The moment she's out of the wheelhouse she'll be down here."

Birch coughed his embarrassment. "She's a fine assistant."

"I think the word you're looking for is *protégé*," Meg teased. "Or maybe *supplicant*."

"Another strong and accurate word." Charlotte laughed.

"If you're done." Birch snatched the broom and swept the filings into a corner full of metal scraps. Nothing that could be melted down and used in the future would go to waste on Birch's watch. "Can we turn to the pressing matter at hand? Grave is not adjusting well."

"He's only just arrived," Charlotte said. "Do you expect him to settle in like he meant to end up here?"

"People aren't like machines, Birch," Meg told him. "They aren't predictable."

"Since when are Birch's machines predictable?" Charlotte smirked.

Birch's mouth twitched into a wicked smile. "If you continue to insult me, I'll take the POC away and make you use another gun."

"You can never separate me and Pocky." Charlotte wagged her finger at him. "We were meant to be together. But you're right. I shouldn't insult you. Your eyebrows have grown back perfectly."

"As I was saying," Meg interrupted, "people aren't predictable, and your boy is . . ."

"A conundrum," Birch scratched at his temple beneath the leather strap of his goggles.

A new head appeared from around the corner, featuring sea-green pigtails that bounced like springs.

"A what drum?" Pip asked. "Does it need fixing? How can I help?"

"Why, hello, Pip." Meg winked at Birch, who turned away, but not before Charlotte saw him blushing. "What a surprise."

Pip bounced into the workshop. "Scoff's on the night shift this week. He should have been there an hour ago. But he was late. He claims he was this close to a breakthrough, but I think he was just making excuses."

"A breakthrough on what?" Birch asked, his eyes bright with interest.

"I don't know," Pip said, rolling her eyes. "You know how Scoff is. All secretive about whatever he's working on. I keep telling him he'd be better off watching you work, but does he listen to me? No."

"Excuse me." They all turned around at the sound of the unfamiliar voice.

Grave was standing at the edge of the workshop, looking just as odd and ashen as he had when Charlotte had found him. He'd emerged from the side tunnel that led to the infirmary, which had purposefully been placed adjacent to the workshop, since that was where most of the injuries happened. Usually to Birch.

Grave's eyes found Meg. "I tried to sleep, like you asked. But I couldn't."

Meg nodded, and her voice took on the tone she used with the small children who lived in the Catacombs. "That's understandable. You've had a difficult time. I made you a sleep draught."

She offered him the cup, but he stepped back into the shadows of the tunnel.

"It's meant to help you," she coaxed. "We want you to get well."

"You think I'm sick?" he said from the darkness.

Meg threw a questioning glance at Birch, who pulled off his work gloves.

"We're not sure, Grave," he told the boy. "But it's a bad sign that you have no memory, and your coloring—"

"What did you call me?" Grave asked.

"Oh . . . ummm . . . yes, the name . . ." Birch tugged at his shirt collar. "You kept talking about a 'grave time,' and so I started calling you Grave."

Charlotte chimed in. "He didn't mean any harm."

Grave shook his head. "I suppose I don't mind. It's nice to be called something."

Pip scooted forward, peering at Grave. "It's not a very nice name, though. I could pick a name for you. I'm very creative."

"Why is your hair green?" Grave asked.

"Scoff," Pip answered, without bothering to take into

consideration that Grave had no idea who Scoff was. "Shall I name you, then? Something dashing?"

"No," Grave said quickly. "Grave is fine. That's all I remember, after all."

"Please sit." Meg beckoned Grave from the shadows, inviting him to sit on the stool.

"Thank you." He smiled at her, but his eyes quickly fixed on Charlotte. "I'm glad you're here. I wanted to talk to you."

"About what?" Charlotte asked. "Ash said you were trying to leave."

"Who's Ash?"

"The boss of us," Pip answered as she hopped up on the workbench, letting her legs dangle off the edge.

"He's my brother," Charlotte cut in. "And Pip is right. Ash is in charge."

"I told him that you didn't want to stay in the workshop," Birch explained. "That's why Charlotte came."

Grave ducked his head, throwing an abashed look at Birch. "I'm sorry. I didn't mean to cause trouble. The children kept sneaking into the room to look at me. They whispered and giggled, but ran away if I tried to talk with them."

"They shouldn't have done that," Charlotte said. "But they didn't mean any harm. They're only curious about you."

"Neither did I," Grave told her.

"No trouble, chap," Birch said. "But you can't go wandering off in the Catacombs until you get to know the place. You'll end up walking till you reach the Worldclock at the center of the Earth."

"Very likely." Meg nodded. "We weren't trying to make a prisoner of you. Just to keep you safe."

"I understand," Grave said, turning his eyes on Charlotte. His tawny irises were the only feature he had that bore color and light. Their hue reminded her of amber reflecting sunlight—a striking contrast to his silver-white hair and ashen skin.

"I don't want to give offense," he said to Meg, though he was still looking at Charlotte. "But I wanted to talk to her because she saved me from that thing."

"And?" Charlotte asked.

"And I thought you'd be the least likely to lie to me."

"Pshaw!" Pip brandished a screwdriver at him. "We aren't a pack of liars."

"Hush, Pip," Meg snapped. "We're strangers to him, and this is a strange place. Have a little compassion."

Pip rolled her eyes and began sorting different-sized cogs into piles beside her on the workbench.

Grave offered Meg a shy smile. "I thought Charlotte would tell me where I am."

"You're in a place called the Catacombs," Charlotte told him. She waved her hand at her companions. "This is our home. There are about two dozen of us living in the caves at the moment, and there isn't a person among us you can't trust. The eldest—Ashley, Meg, Birch, Pip, Scoff, and me—keep the Catacombs supplied and secured so the younger children here have a safe place to grow up. This is a refuge for them—for us—from the Empire."

"Empire?" Grave sighed, his body wilting a bit. "There's so much I don't know. I wish I could remember."

"We'll help you," Meg said, proffering the wooden cup. "But you really should rest."

Grave looked to Charlotte, who nodded. He took the cup, swirling its liquid contents.

"Before I sleep, tell me why you're here." He looked around the group. "You're so young. I thought I'd be taken to the person in charge. An adult."

"The adults are doing the important work. Work that's far from here," Charlotte answered him, flinching a little at the thought of Ashley's reminding them that Meg's eighteenth birthday was drawing close. "And we'll be doing that same work when we're of age too."

Pip giggled. "Safe and cozy caves."

"Safe enough," Charlotte said. She frowned at Grave. "You don't remember anything? Just something about a 'grave time'?"

Grave nodded. "Sometimes when I close my eyes, I can see a man standing over me, and he whispers, 'A grave time, such a grave time.'"

"Do you remember anything else about the man?" Charlotte asked.

"Nothing," Grave told her. "I hear his voice, but I can't see his face. Just the shape of a man, like a shadow."

"You really should rest," Meg said to him, but she fixed a piercing look on Charlotte before she addressed Grave again. "I've made up a cot for you in the infirmary."

Charlotte returned Meg's gaze stonily. "Why don't I go with you?"

Meg wore a smug smile when Grave perked up.

"Thank you," he said, waiting for Charlotte to lead him out of the workshop.

On the short walk to the infirmary, Charlotte sternly shooed away a little flock of children who'd clustered outside the door, hoping to spy Grave. They gave her glum looks, but complied, and Charlotte led Grave into his accommodations. The hollow featured rounded walls, an apothecary's cabinet, and three cots—one of which boasted fresh linens, courtesy of Meg.

"Am I the only one who's staying here?" Grave asked as Charlotte turned a crank on the wall. A moment later, the glass globes that ringed the room began to glow, offering more light than the bioluminescent blue fungi.

"Be thankful for that," Charlotte said with a wry smile. "Anyone else stuck in here might keep you up all night with their coughing. Or their complaining about Birch blowing them up."

Grave shifted his weight uneasily.

"You'll have the room to yourself, but Birch sleeps in a room that's attached to the workshop, so he'll be close by," Charlotte said quickly.

"Where do you sleep?" he asked.

Charlotte startled a bit at his query. It was the sort of inappropriate question she'd come to expect from Jack, but not a stranger.

Grave made a choking, horrified noise and stepped back. "Argh. Please. I didn't intend . . ."

Seeing his distress, Charlotte caught her breath and said, "Of course. No harm done."

"I only . . . I feel so alone," he said, sitting on the cot. "And you were so kind."

"I wasn't kind," she told him. "No one belongs in the belly of a Rotpot."

He nodded, staring into the wooden cup Meg had given him. Charlotte's heart pinched, and she rested her hand on his shoulder.

"And you're not alone," she said. "I'm sure Meg will be checking on you all night."

"Meg?" Grave frowned. "Not you?"

"Trust me"—Charlotte laughed—"it's Meg you want. She's a healer and is quite the mother hen. Now drink that sleep draught she made you and get the rest you need. We'll talk more tomorrow."

"I'll go to sleep," he said quickly, "but I don't want to drink this."

When she balked, he said, "Please."

"Very well." She couldn't blame him for not wanting to drink the strange-smelling liquid.

Charlotte waited in the room until his breathing was slow and even. She stole from the infirmary and made her way to the workshop. She was surprised to find only Meg waiting for her.

"How is he?" Meg asked.

"Asleep," Charlotte told her. "Where are Pip and Birch?"

"At the dock, tinkering with the *Pisces*." Meg moved toward the passage from which Charlotte had just emerged. "I think I'll stay in the infirmary too. In case he wakes up and gets a fright."

"Good idea," Charlotte said, making to leave.

"Charlotte." Meg's voice made Charlotte pause. "Don't let Ash be too hard on you about Grave. Bringing him here was the right thing to do, and Ash knows it. He's just overly protective of all of us."

"That's easy for you to say." Charlotte grimaced. "He's never cross with you."

Meg laughed. "Good night, Charlotte."

"Night." Charlotte retraced her steps out of the workshop and toward her room. Her path took her past Ash's room. The door was ajar, and the voices within brought her to a halt.

"It will be there," Jack was saying. "Like we hoped."

"Intact?" Ash asked. "That's a big haul. How will we bring it back?"

"I'll take care of it," Jack told him. "As long as you're sure that cave you found is a safe enough place to stash it."

"It's the best we can manage," Ash said. "It'll have to do."

Along with their voices, Charlotte heard a strange buzzing sound. Curiosity made her peep around the door frame.

Ash was flopped across a chair, his suspenders hanging loose at his waist. Jack stood nearby. His hands were cupped, and a small whirring object hovered above his palms.

Charlotte gasped. "Hephaestus's hammer! Is that a homingbird?"

Ash jumped out of the chair. "Charlotte!"

The sight of the homingbird had so startled her that she'd forgotten she'd technically been eavesdropping.

She tried to cover her mistake by striding confidently into the room. Jack closed his hands over the tiny bird, and the whirring of its wings stopped.

"Don't hide it," she said. "I want to see."

"This is a private conversation, Lottie," Ash told her.

She put her hands on her hips. "Then why is the door open?"

"The door is ajar," Jack said. "Not open."

"And I presumed everyone was asleep, not haunting the passageways," Ash said.

"I was checking on Grave," Charlotte sniffed. "Like *you* told me to."

"Who's Grave?" Jack frowned.

"Charlotte's act of charity," Ash answered. "How is he?"

"Sleeping now," Charlotte told him. "But he's scared, so being a bit kinder to him wouldn't hurt."

"I'll find time for kindness when we know he isn't a threat," Ash said.

She scowled at her brother and turned to Jack. "Where did the bird come from? I didn't think Birch had figured out how to make them work."

He didn't answer, and she drew a sharp breath.

"It's not a message from *inside,* is it? From the Empire?" she asked. "Who sent it?"

Jack swallowed, glancing at Ash.

"I already told you this is a private conversation, Charlotte." Ash pushed her toward the door. "Now go to bed."

Despite her protests, Ash unceremoniously shoved her into the passage. When she whirled around to shout at him for his rudeness, he shut the door in her face. Charlotte considered banging on the solid wood until Ash lost patience and opened the door again, but she knew that wouldn't get her what she wanted. The only thing left for her to do was figure out how she would discover whatever Ash and Jack were scheming. That she should just leave it alone never crossed Charlotte's mind. Charlotte wasn't one to leave things alone, and Ashley would just have to accept that.

6.

CHARLOTTE CLOMPED HER way down the spiral staircase until she reached the dock.

"Morning!" Jack offered her a leather-wrapped steel flask.

"Ugh." She waved him off. "It's a bit early."

"It's tea." He smiled.

"Oh." She laughed. "Then yes, please."

He kept a cautious watch over her while she sipped the hot tea. Charlotte knew he was waiting for her to ask about last night and the homingbird, but she wasn't going to. If she'd learned anything about her brother and Jack, it was that being obstinate about the issue would get her nowhere. The more she acted as though she didn't care about the incident, the better her chances at getting what she wanted.

When she handed back his flask with a benign smile, Jack relaxed.

"Who's piloting today?" Charlotte asked.

"I am!" The shout came from above. Scoff's lavender hair was in its usual state of disarray. Though the purple hue was something new. Forgoing the last few stairs, he hopped over the iron rail and landed on the dock with the grace of a cat.

Jack frowned at Scoff. "Weren't you at the wheelhouse all night?"

Scoff bobbed his head. "I was, but I promise I'm perfectly alert. I am currently under the miraculous sway of my Perpetuation tonic. Keeps you going as long as you need."

He leaned toward Jack, whispering, "Plus, it enhances virility."

"And turns your hair purple?" Jack asked.

"A harmless side effect that wears off once you've stopped dosing yourself."

"Any other harmless consequences of this tonic?" Jack sidled away from Scoff.

"The smell," Scoff said.

Jack took another step away.

"I don't smell anything," Charlotte said.

"Sniff my hair." Scoff pointed to his head.

Though Jack drew a finger across his throat, Charlotte took a whiff of Scoff's purple tresses.

"Oh, that's lovely." Charlotte laughed. "It smells of lilac."

"Lilac being an essential component of Perpetuation tonic," Scoff pronounced.

"I don't want to look or smell like a lilac," Jack said. "No matter the benefits."

"Charlotte?" Scoff turned hopeful eyes on her when he produced a stoppered glass bottle from inside his long gray coat. "Purple hair would suit you. I would even go so far to say it would highlight those lovely green eyes of yours."

"Maybe later." This time Charlotte took a step back. "I'm quite awake. Thank you."

"It's too bad Pip isn't coming," Scoff mused. "I'm sure she'd try it."

"You've already turned her hair the color of Charlotte's eyes," Jack said. "Leave the poor girl be."

Scoff returned the bottle to his coat pocket. "She's perfectly happy with her green hair. And she no longer gets headaches."

"Good for her," Jack muttered.

The smart rap of a cane on the iron railing drew their attention. Ash paused on the last step of the spiral staircase, looking down at them.

"Are we ready to board?"

"Yes, sir." Scoff bowed.

"New hair, Scoff?" Ash raised a brow.

Reaching for his coat pocket, Scoff began, "As a matter of fact, perhaps I could interest you—"

"He's not interested." Jack pushed Scoff to the end of the dock.

Ash started along the dock, pausing beside his sister. "I trust you slept well?"

Like Jack, he waited for her to lay into him about tossing her out of his room. Charlotte offered him a serene smile instead, and his eyes narrowed in suspicion.

"Shall we away, dear brother?" she asked, taking his arm.

"Whatever you please, sweet sister," Ash said with a shake of his head. "I don't know what you're planning. But it won't work."

"Planning?" She fluttered her eyelashes at him. "Me?"

Ash grimaced, but didn't press her as they approached the gangplank.

The *Pisces* was half submerged to allow for boarding; only the curve of her back and the arc of her dorsal fin were visible. The rest of the ship's body was cloaked by dark water, but below the surface, her belly swelled, giving them plenty of room for cargo or passengers. Charlotte knew that Scoff had reached the bridge when a golden luminescence glimmered beneath the lake's gently rippling surface. She could just make out the shape of the *Pisces*'s smaller side fins and massive tail. The entire submersible was covered in hammered metal scales that shifted from bright gold to onyx as they opened and closed, channeling water that would help power the vessel.

With only his head and shoulders sticking out of the hatch, Jack called to Ash and Charlotte, "Are you having a family moment? Should I tell Scoff to shut her down?"

Charlotte said to Ash, "I expect you to hit him with your cane once we're aboard."

"Who am I to deny the wishes of my only sister?" Ashley winked at her.

Charlotte climbed the steep ramp to the hatch. The folds of her leather skirt beat against her ankles as she moved. The skirt was heavy but the best choice for a scavenging run as it offered better protection against cuts and burns than cloth.

She descended the ladder into the ship's belly, smiling at Jack as she passed him, and headed to the passenger seats at the rear of the bridge.

"What is that smile about?" Jack asked, watching her go by.

She didn't answer, but laughed a moment later when she heard the thwack of Ash's cane and Jack's shout.

Charlotte ducked her way through the narrow tube connecting the hatch to the bridge. She took her place in the row of seats behind Scoff and buckled herself into the leather harness.

"We all set?" Scoff asked without turning around.

Ash dropped into the seat beside Charlotte and pulled the harness over his shoulders. "In a minute. Jack's heading to the dorsal cannon."

"You think we'll need the cannon?" Charlotte asked.

"Not likely," Ash told her. "But he insisted. I think he's sore I hit him with my cane."

"Poor Jack." Charlotte grinned at her brother, and he winked.

Scoff pulled the navigator's helm down. Brass and leather covered his head and shoulders, and he adjusted the fit so the *Pisces*'s telescoping eyes matched up with his vision.

Jack's voice came piping into the bridge. "I'm strapped into the cannon."

Ash pulled a tube that dangled from the ceiling toward his face. "Thanks, Jack. We'll be off, then."

Scoff's hands began flying over the cranks and gears that formed a half circle around him. With a soft rumble, the *Pisces* came to life. Bubbles floated up around them.

"Here we go!" Scoff pushed two levers forward, and the *Pisces* knifed through the water. They dove down, and soon Charlotte's ears popped. With the crank of a wheel, two bright beams shot out from below the glass sphere at the front of the ship. The lights shone against rock as they descended, leveling out when they reached a gaping black hole in the wall.

The *Pisces* shot forward, and Charlotte gripped the sides of her chair. As much as she looked forward to any outings, she always hated this part. Fins all aflutter, the submersible raced through the underwater channel, which twisted, suddenly narrowed, opened up, and then narrowed again. Though she'd taken this trip more times than she could count, Charlotte always flinched and gasped along the way, certain that they wouldn't make a particularly sharp turn or that the ship was too large to fit through a narrow gap.

When Scoff dipped below a cluster of stalactites at the last possible second, Charlotte gave a little shriek.

Jack's voice crackled in the air. "Holy Hephaestus, Miss Charlotte! I heard you all the way back here. Ash, why don't you put that cane to good use and knock her out?"

Charlotte released her grip on the chair to snatch the speaking end of the voice horn as its tubing swung from the ceiling.

"Shut up, Jack!"

His tinny laugh came through the tube. "How many times have you done this? You always scream at the same place. But I think you're getting louder."

"Do you want me to come back there and knock you out?"

Ash grabbed the tube. "Ease off, you two. We're coming out of the tunnel."

Scoff hauled back on a lever, and the vessel pitched up, jetting toward the surface. He leveled the ship off so they were little more than a meter down in the river.

"Smooth sailing from here," Scoff announced.

Charlotte threw a sour look at her brother and then struggled out of her harness. "I'm going to get Pocky ready."

"Just don't shoot Jack."

"I make no promises," she muttered.

Ducking beneath metal tubes and air shafts, Charlotte progressed toward the rear of the hull. The weapons cache was housed below the cannon box at the end of the dorsal fin. She opened the metal cabinet and found Pocky waiting for her on the top shelf.

Taking the gun down, she began attaching the hooks on her vest to metal loops on the gun so its weight was evenly distributed across her body. She pulled a key from one of her vest pockets and inserted it into a lock on the gun's central chamber. When she turned the key, Charlotte was rewarded with a high-pitched hum that reverberated along the length of the weapon and made her skin tingle.

"Hey there, girl."

"You know that's a gun, right?" Jack's head poked down from the cannon box. "Not a sentient being?"

"Don't make her angry," Charlotte said, patting the wide double barrels of the gun. "You won't like her temper."

Jack climbed down the ladder. "This is why I keep telling Ash to get you a cat or a bird. Guns aren't proper pets."

"Says you," Charlotte told him. "Pocky has never let me down."

Jack looked admiringly at her weapon. "Polar Oppositional Carbine. One of a kind as far I know. I've never gotten to try it out." He leaned close and whispered, "Will you let me hold it?"

Charlotte stepped back. "It is a she, and no, you can't."

"Why not?" Jack sulked. "I won't hurt it . . . I mean her."

"You can't because Pocky is the only gun I'm carrying, whereas you have—" Charlotte examined Jack's double-layered belts and leather chest straps. "Six?"

He shrugged. "I never know what I'll be in the mood to use."

Charlotte groaned, turning away. The *Pisces* abruptly lurched to a stop, sending Jack sprawling onto the floor and Charlotte on top of him.

"Ouch!" Charlotte rubbed her elbow, which had banged against a metal grating. "Scoff could have given us a little warning. Pocky, are you okay?" She began to inspect the gun for damage.

"Pocky?" Jack grunted from beneath her. "What about me?"

"What about you?"

"You landed on me," he said. "Don't you care if I'm hurt?"

"Not particularly." Charlotte half turned to flash a wicked smile at him.

"Heartless," he said, but his eyes were laughing.

Despite Jack's accusation, Charlotte was suddenly too aware of her heart, which felt like it had taken on a stronger charge than the one powering her gun.

Jack seemed to notice the change too. The teasing light in his gaze faded, overtaken by something darker. Turbulent, but intriguing.

Charlotte felt his hand on her shoulder. He pulled her toward him.

"I could just take your gun," he said quietly.

"You could try," she whispered, because she couldn't find her breath. She didn't want to move away from him, but the strange push and pull of her body was unsettling. And she couldn't break her gaze from the shifting colors of Jack's hazel eyes.

He smiled slightly. "Trying would be the fun part."

Charlotte wasn't sure what he meant, but she had several ideas of what he might be suggesting, and she *was* certain that she wanted to know. She was about to suggest that he *should* try when Ash came barreling down the steps.

He stopped when he saw their tangle of limbs and guns. "What are you doing?"

Charlotte cried out in indignation as Jack dumped her out of his lap and stood up.

"Scoff didn't exactly pull off a smooth arrival," he told Ash. "We took a spill."

Ash offered Charlotte a hand, helping her up. "Are you all right?"

"Fine," she huffed, refusing to look at Jack. "So is Pocky."

Ash glanced at the gun. "Well, that's a relief. We're going to need her."

Jack was already making his way toward the front of the ship. "I'm going on ahead."

"Let me know what you find," Ash called after him.

"Will do!"

Charlotte frowned at her brother. "He's going without us?"

"He'll find us later, and Scoff's on lookout," Ash said quickly. "He sent out the decoy, so time starts working against us now. Grab a sack, and let's go."

She did as Ash asked, but the wheels of her mind were spinning. They never scavenged alone. Not ever. Why let Jack go off by himself now?

Charlotte forced the question away, knowing she couldn't afford distraction during this run. With a sack slung over her shoulder and Pocky resting against her waist, she followed Ash up and out of the hatch.

Scoff landed the *Pisces* close enough to the riverbank that Charlotte and Ash could jump into the shallows and wade to shore. Though she took a moment to search the river's edge, Charlotte didn't catch sight of Jack.

"The rats should be after the decoy," Ash said. "Let's head in."

The trees that lined the riverbank offered a thin barrier of nature before the Heap made its presence known. The smell of corroding metal made Charlotte's nose crinkle up as hills of industrial waste rose before them.

Since the Heap was a tinker's dream, Charlotte had always thought it a shame that Birch never came along on their scavenging runs. Of course, he sent wish lists with them and specific diagrams for the parts he needed, but he was too valuable to risk.

Ash held up his hand, and Charlotte stopped. They both went very still and listened for the telltale squeak and scrabble of rats.

"Clear," Ash said, dropping his hand. "Find what you can."

They ran side by side into the mounds of scrap metal and discarded machinery. Ash had Birch's list and began to search carefully through the rubble for specific items while Charlotte threw every piece of metal she could find into her sack. They worked quickly and without speaking for a quarter of an hour.

"Ready to drop?" Charlotte called to Ash and pointed to her bulging sack.

"Close enough," he answered.

They dragged their loot over the rough ground. The small wheels in casters that had been sewn over the surface of one half of the sack eased their burden, but they were still breathing hard by the time they reached the ship.

Several of the *Pisces*'s back scales flipped up, and a moment later, Scoff appeared standing in a lift. They shoved their full sacks into the elevator, and Scoff handed them two empty sacks in return.

"Ten minutes." Scoff tapped the watch face set in the leather cuff on his wrist. "No longer."

Ash nodded. He and Charlotte bolted back to the Heap.

This time Ash took less care in his choices, filling his sack at a fevered pace like Charlotte.

The sound of metal sliding down the side of a rubbish heap made them both stand up, searching for the source of the sound. Charlotte swung Pocky up, ready to fire.

"Ash!" Jack's voice rang out from behind a mound of brass bed frames.

"Here, Jack!" Ash answered.

Jack appeared a moment later, running toward them. When he was at their side, he bent over, putting his hands on his thighs and breathing hard.

"It's here," he gasped. "I found it."

"What's here?" Charlotte asked.

"Hush." Ash's glare startled her. He looked at Jack. "Where?"

"Not too far," Jack said. "I can do it."

"Can you do it in five minutes?" Ash asked him. "That's how long we have before the rats come back."

Jack paled, but he straightened, looking directly at Ash, and shook his head. "I'll need at least ten."

His eyes moved briefly to Charlotte, and his jaw clenched.

"I need you to buy me a little time," Jack said quietly to Ash.

"We'll draw the rats," Ash told him, and Charlotte's gut twisted. *Draw the rats?*

Jack glanced at Charlotte again. "No. Forget it. Let's just get out of here."

"This is important," Ash said. "Too important. We'll manage."

Charlotte couldn't find her voice. Jack drew a long breath and nodded.

"Go now."

Jack dashed into the rubble, turning once to wave at them, and then vanished behind the hills of refuse.

Ash dropped his sack and pulled out his cane. With a quick twist of its brass top, the metal came free of the ebony rod. A long silver blade slid out, and Charlotte gasped when he pulled his shirt sleeve up and drew the sword's sharp edge along his arm. Blood welled, running over his skin. Ash held up his arm so the wind would catch the scent.

"Oh, Ash," Charlotte whispered. "What are you doing?"

"They'll come for this," Ash said quietly. "It's the only sure thing. Be ready."

Charlotte tightened her grip on Pocky. Her eyes flew up and down the metal mounds, waiting for movement. Her ears strained for the sounds of their approach.

Ash held his cane in his left hand and his sword in his right. His eyes were moving as rapidly as Charlotte's, but she saw the rat first.

"There." Her gaze fixed on a scrap pile less than a meter away.

The rat stared at them. Its large black eyes were hungry. The rats were always hungry.

It rose onto its hind legs, exposing its belly—the only

spot on the creature that hadn't been girded with iron plates. Two more rats appeared beside the first, their noses twitching.

"They've gotten bigger," Ash observed.

"They're always getting bigger," Charlotte said, shuddering at the implication. On the last run the rats had rivaled cats in size. These were more comparable to collies.

"Withdraw," Ash whispered. "But move slowly. We need to pull them away from Jack."

Side by side, Charlotte and her brother began to back out of the Heap. The rats were half a dozen in number now, and new bodies covered in gray fur and black iron appeared with each passing moment, waiting, watching the two humans inch away.

"When we reach the tree line, start firing," Ash said.

Charlotte felt the soft give of grass beneath her boots instead of metal. Another minute and they would be in the trees, almost to the ship.

All at once, the rats began to move. A swarm of bodies poured over the scrap hills, surging toward them.

In her peripheral vision, Charlotte glimpsed the tangle of leaves and branches. She relaxed her shoulders and fired. Pocky didn't disappoint.

While the innovation of armoring the Heap's rats with iron plates made bullets' effectiveness dicey, the Polar Oppositional Carbine took advantage of the rats' unique composition. Each of Pocky's barrels sent a magnetic pulse—one positive, one negative—at its target. Hitting opposite sides of the rat's armor, the newly charged plating did what opposite magnetic poles do. They attracted.

The quickest elimination of a target required a dead-on shot. And Charlotte had a knack for pivoting, sidestepping, and crouching to make sure each pull of Pocky's trigger had a devastating result.

Charlotte whistled as the rat she'd hit exploded in a fountain of blood and gore, its iron sides crumpling inward, crushing the beast. She aimed again, and again. Rats continued to implode.

As she fired off shot after shot, body swaying with the rhythm of Pocky's recoil, Charlotte waited for a break in the wave of rats. It wasn't coming.

Beside her, Ash cursed. "We're going to have to run for it."

She didn't dare take her eyes off the rats, but she shouted over Pocky's blasts, "Why aren't they backing off?"

Usually if she took down enough rats, the rest would retreat, seeking easier prey.

"It's my blood," Ash said through clenched teeth. "They're mad for it."

"Wonderful." Charlotte watched another rat crumple into a heap of crimson and iron.

"Now!" Ash grabbed her arm.

Her throat tightened at turning her back on the horde of blood-crazed animals, but she fled with Ash. Even as they ran, she could hear the rats chasing them, their clawed feet crackling as they surged through the underbrush.

Charlotte could hear the bubbling of the riverbank, and a moment later, the *Pisces*'s scales flashed sunlight into her eyes. She gave a whoop of relief, but beside her Ash cried out in pain and stumbled.

Throwing her arms around his waist so he wouldn't fall, Charlotte saw the intrepid rat that had outpaced its fellows. Its teeth dug into Ash's calf. Ash balanced against Charlotte and struck with his sword. Two halves of the rat's bisected corpse rolled to the ground.

"Come on!" Charlotte pulled her brother toward the river.

Ash's jaw clenched as he limped at her side. "Run ahead. I'll catch you."

"No!"

Charlotte pushed him in front of her. She whirled around, not bothering to take aim but sending a barrage of fire into the furry mass at their heels. A few rats imploded, but most squeaked when the shots wounded them.

"Charlotte!"

She glanced over her shoulder to see Ash wading into the river. Firing off a few last haphazard shots, Charlotte turned and made a break for the *Pisces*.

The rats were so close. She could hear them, but what frightened her more was the expression on Ash's face. He wasn't going to make it to the ship.

From the river, a roar erupted, accompanied by a fount of steam. The blisteringly hot jet of water arced over Charlotte, tracing a line behind her. Rats screeched their agony as the water cannon blasted them back.

Ash gave a shout of relief when Charlotte reached him. She helped him climb up the slippery metal scales. The water cannon continued to propel boiling water at the horde of ravenous rats.

After they threw themselves inside, Ash collapsed on the metal grating while Charlotte closed the hatch and sealed them in the ship. She darted toward the bridge, grabbing the voice tube.

"We're in, Scoff. Nice shooting!"

"My pleasure," Scoff's voice piped. "Horrid things, aren't they? And getting awfully big."

Charlotte returned to Ash. He'd already cut away his shirtsleeve, using the cloth to bind up the torn flesh of his calf.

"How bad is it?" Charlotte asked.

"A few bites." Ash grimaced. "Hardly a meal worth being cut in half for."

"Meg will take care of you." Charlotte helped him to his feet, and he leaned on her as she led him to the bridge.

Scoff appeared behind them. He pulled a bottle out of his pocket, forcing it into Ash's hand.

When Ash immediately tried to give it back, Scoff laughed. "No fear, Ash. It's not one of mine. That's Meg's tonic. Drink it quick before those rat bites put poison in your blood."

"Thanks," Ash said and knocked back the tonic in one swallow, shuddering after he did so. "Yours might not be as predictable, Scoff, but they definitely taste better."

"Of course they do. I care about how they taste." Scoff grinned. "Meg only cares about how they work."

His smile began to fade. "Where's Jack?"

When Ash didn't answer quickly enough, Scoff began to shake. "He's not—"

"No," Ash said. "He had something else to take care of. That's the reason the rats were coming after us. We couldn't let them hunt Jack."

Scoff looked relieved, but then he frowned. "What did he have to do? Is he still out there?"

Ash shook his head. "He'll meet us back at the Catacombs."

"We're not waiting for him?" Charlotte asked, horrified. They couldn't presume Jack was okay on his own in the Heap. It was too much of a risk for anyone.

"Jack can take care of himself." Ash signaled Scoff toward the controls. "It's time for us to go home."

While Scoff guided them beneath the river's surface, Charlotte strapped herself into her chair. Feeling Ash's gaze on her, she turned to look at her brother.

"He'll be fine," Ash said.

Charlotte nodded, but she didn't think the knot in her belly would untie itself until she saw Jack for herself.

7.

THE RESTLESS BOUNCING of Ash's knee for the duration of the trip home channeled into his leaping from the chair and out the hatch as soon as the sub was docked.

"What's that all about?" Scoff asked as he climbed after Charlotte.

"I don't know," Charlotte answered. When her head poked out of the hatch, she saw that despite his limp, Ash was already halfway up the spiral staircase.

Birch was waiting for them at the end of the dock. "How'd she go?" He offered his hand as Charlotte stepped from the gangway.

Scoff skipped the gangway, jumping directly from the *Pisces*'s scales onto the dock. "Perfect."

"Glad to hear it," Birch said. "I saw that Ash was bleeding. Was there trouble?"

"Rats," Charlotte told him.

"And Pocky didn't take care of them?" Birch asked. "I'm disappointed."

"Pocky did her best," Charlotte said. "But when they got a whiff of Ash's blood, the gun wasn't enough."

Birch nodded. "It's a shame he was hurt. I've been trying to tell Ash no one should go into the Heap with skin exposed. Too easy to get cut. When rats think there might be human flesh to savor, they're difficult to stop."

Charlotte gave Birch a long look before saying, "Ash cut himself on purpose."

"He did what?" Birch gaped at her.

Scoff stumbled back and almost fell off the dock. "That's why I had to use the cannon? I thought you'd just riled them up."

"Well, we had," Charlotte told them. "But it was the blood that did the riling."

Birch paced the width of the dock. "So very reckless. Why on earth—"

"For Jack," Charlotte cut in. "To give him time."

Jack's name pulled Birch up abruptly. He looked at Scoff and Charlotte and then up at the stairs Ash had rushed to climb.

"Where is Jack?"

"He didn't come back with us," Scoff said. "I still don't know why."

"I don't know either," Charlotte added. "Did you know anything about a separate mission for Jack on this run?" she asked Birch.

"I knew nothing of the kind." Birch frowned. "And I'd never suggest sending someone into the Heap alone. What was Ash thinking?"

Charlotte took Birch's hand, pulling him to the staircase. "Let's find out."

"Wait just a minute," Birch said, hauling her back. "I need to check out my beauty first. Make sure everything is as it should be after her voyage."

"You can tune up the ship later," Charlotte said. "Ash and Jack are up to something, and I need you to back me up."

"Back you up how?" Birch stopped tugging Charlotte backward.

"You know Ash won't listen if it's just me," Charlotte told him. "He'll tell you if you ask."

"You want me to play the pawn when you're controlling the board?" Birch laughed.

Scoff pushed past them, running to the stairs.

"Where are you going?" Charlotte called after him.

"To get Pip," he shouted. "She won't want to miss this."

"Oh, dear." Birch sighed, but he followed Charlotte up the winding staircase. When they reached the tunnels, he asked, "Do you even know where Ash went?"

"No," Charlotte said. "But I can guess."

Jack had said he'd meet them back at the Catacombs. There was only one other entrance by which he could return.

When they arrived at the platform and found it empty, Charlotte kicked the railing in frustration. Jack wasn't here yet. The more time that passed before he returned, the less likely he'd ever come back.

"Why is he in the wheelhouse?" Birch asked, frowning. "There aren't scheduled arrivals today."

Charlotte peered at the wheelhouse, and sure enough, Ash was inside, looking harried. At least her brother was as anxious awaiting Jack's appearance as she was.

"This is an unscheduled arrival," she muttered to Birch. She stepped behind the tinker and pushed him toward the box. "Go on, then."

"You're not coming?"

"I'm just going to stay back a bit." She tried to muster a reassuring smile, but Birch snorted at her before he went to the operator's box and stepped inside.

Ash, who'd been bent over the controls, started at the unexpected company. Watching as their mouths moved in a conversation silent to her, Charlotte inched toward the wheelhouse. She stopped when Birch began to gesture wildly. Ash watched him solemnly, nodding every so often.

Birch abruptly burst from the wheelhouse, storming away.

"What happened?" Charlotte asked as he brushed by her, heading for the tunnels.

"Can't talk," he blurted out. "Too much to do. Preparations."

He bumped into Scoff, who was coming out of the passageway, but didn't stop then either.

Scoff had Pip with him, and to Charlotte's surprise, Grave had accompanied them too.

"What did you do to Birch?" Scoff asked Charlotte.

"I didn't do anything to him." She pointed at the wheelhouse and found that Ash was glaring at her through the glass barrier. "He went to talk to Ash and then he just ran off."

"That's odd," Pip said. "Birch never gets mad at anybody." She glanced at Scoff. "Unless they steal his tools."

"I was borrowing them," Scoff said. "And it was only once."

"What's this all about anyway?" Pip asked her. "Scoff said there was going to be a spectacular surprise."

Scoff's brow crinkled. "I said we didn't know what was going on."

"Which means we'll be surprised," Pip told him. "And I'm hoping for spectacular."

Charlotte was hoping to find out what had happened to Jack, but was bothered even more that she continued to be excluded from whatever scheme her brother had hatched. Now Birch knew something secret as well, and that irked Charlotte more than an itch she couldn't quite scratch.

"You're safe, then?" Grave's quiet question caught her off guard.

"I'm sorry?" She looked at him, noting that he was as pale as he'd been the previous day. He did look more at ease, though.

Grave glanced at Pip. "She told me that you were out scavenging. And that scavenging is horribly dangerous."

"Pip." Charlotte put her hands on her hips. "That is not exactly the type of introduction to our home that Grave needs."

Pip twirled her pigtails in her hands. "Of course he does. And it *is* dangerous."

Charlotte smiled gently at Grave. "There are always risks when we cross into New York. But we have to do it, and we're fine."

"Are there really man-eating rats?" Grave asked in a hushed voice.

Charlotte glared at Pip again.

"It's not my fault the Empire feeds prisoners to the rats so they'll want to hunt trespassers." Pip shrugged.

"Why are you spending time with Pip anyway?" an exasperated Charlotte asked Grave. "Where's Meg?"

Pip stuck her tongue out at Charlotte. "I'm more fun!"

"Where's Meg?" Charlotte asked again.

"She's teaching the small children." Pip sounded bored. "You should know that. And she asked me to keep Grave company." She elbowed Grave, and he winced. "Come on, Grave. Tell her I'm good company."

"It's been interesting," Grave told Charlotte.

"No one appreciates me." Pip pouted. "Except Birch."

"I think you're brilliant company, Pip," Scoff told her.

"You're only saying that because I'll drink your tonics." She patted her green hair before she turned her attention back to Charlotte. "So when is the surprise happening? Are we just going to wait here?"

As if in answer to Pip's question, the lift's iron chain began to move. With creaks and groans, the elevator began to rise.

Charlotte rushed to the railing. When the basket appeared, Jack was leaning against one side, looking very pleased with himself. Seeing Charlotte on the other side of the gate, he laughed.

"Miss me that much?"

"Where were you?" Charlotte pushed aside the relief she felt now that Jack was here and obviously unhurt.

He didn't answer as he opened the door. She kept her hands on the platform gate.

"I'm not letting you through until you tell me what's going on."

"Get out of the way, Charlotte." Ash limped up beside her.

She started to protest, but when she saw that he was still bleeding from his arm and leg, she stepped back.

Ash opened the gate, and Jack hopped out of the basket. The two boys looked at each other silently until Jack gave a slight nod. Ash bowed his head, taking a long breath.

Then he suddenly grabbed Jack and lifted him up in a bear hug.

"Easy there, mate," Jack said. "You look like you belong in the infirmary."

Ash laughed and set Jack down. "I'll be fine."

Jack pointed at Ash's poorly bandaged leg. "Did the rats do that?"

Ash nodded, and Jack glanced at Charlotte. "Pocky didn't come through?"

Before she could answer, Ash said, "Charlotte did all she could. There were just too many."

Jack smiled grimly. "I owe you."

"I think you've already made it up to me," Ash said.

"Let's get you patched up, friend." Jack levered Ash against him and the two of them started for the tunnels.

Charlotte stared after them, boiling with outrage. She thought she would go mad from not knowing what they were up to.

"That wasn't a spectacular surprise," Pip complained. "That was just Jack."

"But Ash was bleeding," Scoff offered. "That's something."

"I suppose so," Pip mused with a glance at Charlotte. "He's a daring fellow, your brother."

"Ugh." Charlotte stamped her foot. "I hate him."

"That's not a very nice thing to say," Pip told her. "Especially when the rats tried to eat him."

Charlotte ignored her, stewing in her own frustration.

"Come on, then." Scoff waved for them to follow him off the platform. "We still need to offload and sort through the loot."

Sulking, Charlotte shuffled her way along the passage. She wished she could go to her room and wait for Ash to find her and apologize like he should. He wouldn't, of course. She'd wait, and he'd come and scold her for acting like a child.

Grave fell into step beside her.

"It sounds terrifying," he said. "You must be very brave."

She straightened up, surprised by his words. "I don't think I'm that brave. I'd rather be out on a run than cooped up here."

Grave glanced around the tunnel, eyes lingering on the soft blue light cast by the fungi. "I don't mind it here. I feel safe."

"It is safe," Charlotte said. "But it can get a bit dull. Going out makes me feel alive. In here it's as though the world outside doesn't exist. And I don't like that—though keeping away from the world is exactly the point of this place."

"Why is that?" Grave asked. "The world sounds bad. Yesterday that thing chased me. Today I learned there are rats bred to kill and eat people. Who would do that?"

Charlotte laughed. "Britannia. The Empire."

"Are they monsters?" he whispered.

"No, they're people like us. Only they make the rules," she said. "They just act like monsters when someone tries to go against them."

"And you're hiding from them?"

"We are." Charlotte nodded. "Because we come from families who don't want to live the way the Empire says they should. They've been fighting since the Revolution failed—at least those who weren't captured have been."

Grave asked, "Where are your families?"

"The Resistance has pockets all over," Charlotte said. "I'm not exactly sure where my parents are. They move a lot, and they don't contact us that often. It's safer that way."

"Do you miss your mother and father?"

She was surprised by the sudden lump in her throat. "Always."

He nodded. "Will you see them again?"

"Yes," she told him. "We only stay here when we're too young to help with the Resistance. Ash turns eighteen soon, so he'll go."

"How old are you?"

"Sixteen," she said with a sigh. "But I'd like to go when Ash does."

"You're very brave," he said. "You want to go fight an empire."

Charlotte fell silent. Talk of the Resistance and her supposed bravery made being angry with Ash seem silly.

She looked at Grave. "Do you remember anything today?"

He shook his head. "I don't know my name. Or if I have parents. I don't know why I was in the woods."

Charlotte took his hand. "We'll figure it out."

8.

IRCH SHOUTED INSTRUCTIONS as they rifled through the sacks. Sorting loot never failed to require both tenacity and endurance. Charlotte forced herself to be patient as she murmured instructions to Grave, explaining how to differentiate scrap metal from potentially working parts.

A whoop brought all of their heads up and sent Moses spiraling from Birch's shoulder into the air.

Doing a little jig, Birch held up a small object.

"I think this will prove a good run indeed!"

"What's that?" Grave whispered.

"A mouse," Charlotte answered. "That's what saved our lives yesterday."

Grave spared her a glance. "You had one of those in your pocket?"

She nodded. "It's a magnet mouse. They're explosive devices. Once they're wound, they'll chase the most metallic object in the vicinity. And for us that's usually Rotpots."

"The thing that was chasing us?" he asked.

"Yes," Charlotte said. "We call them Rotpots, but they're really called Imperial Labor Gatherers."

"Labor Gatherers?"

As she spoke, Charlotte's skin crawled. "Life in the lower levels of the coastal cities is hard—and that's a kind way of putting it. Sometimes the workers try to escape. The Gatherers are sent out to catch runaways and return them to the Empire."

Grave continued his methodic sorting of parts—for it being his first time, he caught on quickly. "Does anyone think the Empire is good?"

"The Brits." she laughed coldly. "It's working out beautifully for them."

"They don't have to work in the cities?" He picked up a brass gear, turning it over slowly in his hand.

Charlotte cast a sidelong glance at him. "You really don't know?"

His shoulders hunched in embarrassment. "I'm sorry. I'll stop asking questions."

"No," she said. "It's just strange . . . and you must feel so lost."

He didn't look at her, but nodded.

"The resistance began in 1774," she told him. "The Declaration of Independence was signed in 1776—Patriots who wanted independence for the colonies pitted against Loyalists who supported the British. The Patriots were sure that France would aid them, maybe the Spanish and Dutch as well. But American diplomats failed to convince any other countries to fight with us. Britain was there at every turn with a counteroffer. They made Canada into Indian territory to appease their native allies. They gave Florida back to Spain and promised to leave the southern Mississippi corridor and the French Caribbean untouched. Without naval assistance from the French, the Patriots couldn't hold the ports. The British navy was too powerful. The colonists surrendered in 1781."

"What happened to the Patriots?" Grave asked.

"All signers of the Declaration were hung as traitors to the Empire," she said somberly. "Boston—where much of the Patriot support was concentrated—was razed. It's a prison now. Whenever members of the Resistance are captured, they're sent to Boston and are never heard from again."

Charlotte's hands paused from their methodical sorting. "British policy toward the colonies after the war was called 'benevolent reform.' The colonies were divided into three provinces: Amherst, from New Hampshire to New York; Cornwallis, from Pennsylvania to Virginia; and Arnold, the Carolinas and Georgia."

"Why did they change the names?" Grave asked.

"The provinces are named after British war heroes," she said. "But the names weren't all they changed. The 'benevolent reforms' were meant to teach the Patriots a lesson."

"How?" He was staring at her now, eyes wide.

"They claimed that the Revolution took place because the colonists had grown selfish and corrupt," she said. "To prevent future dissent, the policy was put in place that all Patriots owed the Empire twenty years of indentured labor. It didn't stop there. Any children born to Patriots were subject to fifteen years. And their children to ten. And so on."

"They had to work for the Empire." Grave resumed sorting. "But eventually it would stop."

Charlotte laughed. "So they said. But once the Resistance formed and continued to fight in the borderlands along the Mississippi, the Empire changed the policy. Now it stands that as long as there is a Resistance, each child born to an American is indentured for twenty years."

"But are they free after the twenty years?" he asked. When she frowned at him, he said, "Not that it sounds fair, but at least that's something."

"No one survives the twenty years," she told him. "Unless they manage to curry favor with the right authorities and somehow regain Imperial Citizenship. That's rare. The Empire needs laborers, especially since they abolished slavery."

"What?" Grave asked, surprised. "Isn't the term of indenture like slavery?"

"In practice, yes," Charlotte said. "But until 1807, slavery of Africans was tied to their mother's status. Anyone born to a slave became a slave. The Empire declared chattel slavery to be immoral because it wasn't punishment for a crime, whereas the postwar indentures were. *Pietas super omnia.*"

He scratched his head, brow knit in confusion.

"It's Latin." She smiled thinly. "Loyalty above all—the policy of the Brits."

He was still frowning, and Charlotte said, "Please don't misunderstand. Slavery was appalling. A horror born of man's cruelest tendencies. The Empire claimed benevolence by bringing about its end. But they forfeited that role by replacing slavery with punitive indentures. And the indenture system is much more beneficial to them, since they don't need as many people to work the fields anymore."

"Why is that?"

"Mr. Whitney's Harvestman," Charlotte said. "One of the Empire's innovations. It looks a little like a Rotpot, but instead of a cage, it has a storage compartment and more arms. It can harvest five times as fast as a man and works for any crop—cotton, tobacco, indigo. It's all picked by Harvestmen now, and each machine only needs one operator where the fields used to be full of slaves."

Grave was quiet, sorting parts but not asking further questions. Charlotte returned to her task as well, mood soured by the conversation.

"Do you really think the Resistance has a chance?"

Grave's question was so quiet that Charlotte almost didn't hear it.

"Maybe." She shrugged. "Since the French and Spanish have started helping, it's more likely."

He dropped a cog. "But why would they help now? You said they wouldn't help in the Revolution."

"There were more wars after the Revolution," she said. "Wars in Europe. France and Britain had tinkers creating more machines. Huge war machines. Napoleon sent up the first fleet of airships, but Britain's built their own fleet. Each time, one side or the other unleashed some fearsome new invention that wreaked destruction across Europe. When Spain began building a Doomsday machine, they negotiated peace."

"A Doomsday machine?"

"They claim it's a device that can break apart the earth itself," Charlotte said. "Spain threatened that if their borders were violated, they would use the machine to sever the Iberian peninsula from Europe and let it float away from the continent."

"Can they do that?" Grave gasped.

"They say so," she told him. "No one has ever actually used a Doomsday device. Rumors have it that they're building one in Florida too."

They both looked up when Birch gave a joyful shout.

"Whatcha got?" Pip asked the tinker.

"A heap of parts to build us dozens of mice! I've already put two together," he told her, lifting his hand. In his grasp was a second fully assembled magnet mouse. "Let's test out this one's motion, shall we?"

He turned the key several times and set the mouse on the ground. It whirred to life and zoomed across the floor. As everyone watched, it raced toward Grave.

"What the—" Birch gaped as the mouse bumped into Grave's foot and climbed onto his ankle.

Pip screamed. Grave began to flail, beating at the critter that had whirred up his leg and now latched on to his chest. Moses swooped around Grave, nearly crashing into the boy with each dive.

Birch tugged off his goggles, which retracted from their telescoped position when he tossed them on the workbench, and his eyes bulged.

"Keep calm, Pip! I haven't armed them yet."

Birch dashed to Grave, grasping the mouse and tugging hard. The magnetic creature wouldn't budge. "Holy Hephaestus . . ."

Grave began to shout. "Get it off! Get it off!"

"I'm trying," Birch cried. "Hold still, man."

The mouse still clung to Grave's chest as if it had been welded to his flesh. Despite Birch's assurances, Pip was still screaming.

Ash appeared in the mouth of the tunnel that led to the infirmary with Jack at his side. His leg freshly bandaged, Ash was using his cane to aid his steps.

"What in Athene's name is going on out here?"

He looked at Birch trying to pry the mouse off of Grave,

and his face went chalky. Beside him, Jack drew a sharp breath. Ash gave him a pointed stare and handed Jack his cane.

Jack strode across the room, shoving Birch aside. Moses flew to the tinker, landing on top of his head and clinging to his mad thatch of hair.

"What are you?" Jack hissed into Grave's face.

Grave stared at him, shaking and speechless.

Jack shook his head. "Sorry, mate."

He brought Ash's cane up in a swift arc. It cracked into Grave's temple, and though the force of the blow made Charlotte cry out, Grave stood still, unfazed. He watched as Jack took a step back. When he swung the cane again, Grave grabbed the handle and jerked it out of Jack's hand. He didn't attack but simply gazed at the long ebony cane in his hand. All eyes in the room were locked on him, some filled with fear, others disbelief.

"What are you?" Jack asked again.

Grave sighed and dropped the cane. "I swear to you, I don't know."

In the center of his chest, the mouse still whirred and chirped, unwilling to release its target.

9.

"PLEASE DON'T PUT him in a cage." Charlotte tugged on the sleeve of Ash's waistcoat.

Ash didn't look at her, continuing down the hall with rigid steps, his spine stiff as he did his best to hide the slight limp in his gait.

Walking before Ash was Grave, flanked by Jack and Birch. Jack held Grave's right arm in a firm grip, guiding his prisoner through the narrow corridor. Though Grave had done nothing that Charlotte considered hostile, Jack had unholstered his revolver, which he carried in a deceptively casual manner. Charlotte knew that if Grave so much as twitched in a way Jack didn't like, Jack would put a bullet in Grave's head before any of them had a chance to blink. Then it occurred to Charlotte that a bullet might have as little effect on Grave as Ash's cane. The thought made her skin prickle.

Birch walked apart from Jack and Grave. The tinker's gaze roved over Grave's form, apprehensive but equally curious. Dipping down one minute and then straining to his tiptoes the next to observe Grave from as many different angles as he could manage, Birch looked not unlike an exotic bird in the throes of its mating dance.

"Something metal is inside," Birch commented to no one in particular. "How can that be?"

"Promise me you won't let Birch cut him open." Charlotte leaned closer to her brother. "He hasn't done anything to threaten us. If he were here to cause harm, wouldn't he have already done so?"

"Charlotte." Ash stopped mid-stride. He turned, grasping Charlotte's arms and speaking in a low, dangerous voice as he stared hard into her eyes. "We know nothing about this boy—or whatever he is. Not all weapons are guns or blades; the most dangerous are subtle, hidden."

"You think he's a spy." Charlotte didn't break Ash's gaze. While she couldn't deny the potential dangers that Ash was suggesting, her instincts shouted down any pragmatic thoughts about who Grave might be. Charlotte simply *knew* he wasn't their enemy.

Recognizing the stubborn lift of his sister's chin, Ash sighed and released her arms. When he closed his eyes, Charlotte winced. Her brother looked so tired, so much older than his seventeen years. She didn't want to cause him more strain, but she was unwilling to condemn Grave before she understood who the boy was.

"Ash, I'm just worried—"

He cut her off. "Charlotte, have I ever acted rashly since I took charge of the Catacombs? Have I given you cause to doubt my choices?"

"No, but—"

"Then trust me to act wisely now," Ashley interrupted again. "I have to consider what's in the best interest of everyone who lives here. I don't know whether Grave is a spy, or a weapon, or a fool boy with an impossibly thick, or rather unbreakable, skull. But until I'm certain of who he is, he will be locked up . . . but not cut open. We're not monsters here. Not like our enemies out there."

Charlotte knew she was beaten, but she blurted out, "I'll stay with him. Sit by his cage to make sure he knows that he has a friend here."

"As long as you get your work done, Lottie, you can do whatever you please with your free time." With those words, Ashley turned to continue down the corridor, leaving Charlotte to taste the stale desperation in her lame outburst. What did it matter if she kept Grave company? Ash had declared her stray a serious threat to them, and that was that.

Trying to pretend it wasn't a childish thing to do, Charlotte huffed at her brother's back and spun on her heel. She took off in the opposite direction, unwilling to watch as

Jack and Ash muscled Grave into a cage while Birch took notes. Still hoping for a sympathetic ear, Charlotte went in search of Pip and Scoff.

Pip wasn't in Birch's workshop where she'd been standing, white-faced, after the incident with Grave and the mouse, so Charlotte headed for Scoff's laboratory. As soon as he was old enough to leave the children's quarters, Scoff had announced his plans to build a live-in laboratory. Given the volatility of Scoff's experiments, it had been concluded that the best—nay, only—place for the laboratory was adjacent to the river, where there was an endless supply of water to extinguish inevitable flames. Charlotte thought Ash really should have insisted that Birch move his workshop down to the river's edge as well.

"Are you sure this will work?" Charlotte heard Pip query.

Scoff was tugging at his wild lilac hair as Charlotte entered the laboratory. "It should work—"

He stopped talking when he caught sight of Charlotte. If she hadn't known how dangerous Scoff's lair could be, Charlotte would have considered it the most beautiful part of the Catacombs. The spacious cavern was bursting with shelves and tables, which in turn were crammed with beakers, bottles, vases, bowls, tubes, and measuring tools. The menagerie of objects was mostly glass, with a few metal and wooden pieces scattered throughout. Few of the containers were empty, and Charlotte could identify only a handful of their contents. The variety of powders, liquids, dried herbs, and preserved oddities filled the laboratory with a kaleidoscope of colors.

Jumping off the stool on which she'd been perched, Pip greeted Charlotte with a warm smile. "Hi, there!"

"Charlotte," Scoff said more warily, "can I help you?"

"I'm just seeking asylum from my brother's boorishness," Charlotte told them.

Pip bobbed her head and giggled. "Ash can be a bit bossy, huh?"

"He is the boss," Scoff chided. "I don't think 'bossy' can be used as an insult when you're supposed to be in charge."

Charlotte let that slide, wanting to get her mind off Ash and knowing that Scoff would never miss an opportunity to expound on his latest discoveries. "What's new in the laboratory?"

"Scoff's a genius!" Pip replied, and Scoff went red behind the ears.

"A genius, eh?" Charlotte said.

Nodding a little too enthusiastically, Pip said to Scoff, "Go on, tell her."

With a flourish, Scoff produced a stoppered bottle full of a dark, viscous substance. "It's a formula I've been working on for an event just such as this."

"Such as what?" Charlotte raised an eyebrow. She couldn't think of any precedent that would make Scoff anticipate Grave's arrival.

Scoff lowered his voice to a conspiratorial whisper. "The capture of an enemy."

"Grave is not an enemy!" Charlotte hadn't meant to shout, but she had, and Scoff went pale.

Pip wedged herself between Charlotte and Scoff.

With her hands on her hips, Charlotte said, "Tell me what's in that bottle."

"I call it the Elixir of Intentions." Scoff held up the mixture as if to admire its color, but Charlotte found nothing appealing to look at. The slimy concoction reminded her of congealing blood.

When Charlotte failed to appear impressed, Scoff added, "When Grave drinks this, he'll be compelled to tell us the truth of his identity."

"Have you tested it?" Charlotte asked.

Scoff let out an exasperated breath. "I haven't had anyone to test it on!"

"Are you sure it won't hurt him?" Charlotte looked meaningfully at Pip's green locks.

Pip grinned and tugged at her pigtails. "This didn't hurt at all . . . I suppose it itched for a day or two."

Charlotte ignored Pip, who'd wrinkled her nose and was now scratching at her scalp, instead saying to Scoff, "And how can he be compelled to tell the truth when he remembers nothing?"

"He could be lying." Scoff sounded hurt, but Charlotte was too frustrated to care.

"Has everyone gone mad?" Charlotte stomped her foot. "He's just a boy. He's like us. Grave needs our help, not cages and poisons."

Scoff cradled the glass bottle against his chest. "It's not poison."

"I'm sure it wouldn't kill him," Pip said to Scoff. Her smile was reassuring at first but then faded. "Would it?"

Charlotte turned away from them just in time to hear the clang of a bell echo through the Catacombs. "Ugh."

"Ooh! Dinner!" Pip exclaimed as Charlotte exited the laboratory.

Charlotte cursed under her breath and grabbed her skirts so she could move more quickly. Hurrying up the stairs and dashing to the mess hall, Charlotte tore off part of a round loaf of brown bread and grabbed some cloth-wrapped hard cheese from the larder before retreating to her room. She was too miffed to eat in a room crowded with jostling children and the constant buzz of conversation, and she wanted to be sure Ash knew. And Jack too, for that matter. As she ducked out of the mess hall, Charlotte wondered if she shouldn't force herself to share a table with her brother just to be sure that Scoff didn't persuade Ash to try out that elixir on Grave. She quickly pushed the thought away, telling herself that even if Ash gave in to Scoff's assurances, Meg would never allow Scoff to experiment on Grave. At least there was one person in the Catacombs Charlotte could trust to act with some sense.

As she sat on the edge of her bed, Charlotte barely tasted the hunks of bread and cheese as she chewed and swallowed. She was already contemplating her next move. Ash might view Grave as a threat, but Charlotte could still show the boy some kindness. She'd visit him while the others were at dinner, reassure him that all would be well soon enough. Satisfied with her new plan, Charlotte returned to the winding corridors. She was careful to choose a route that would not take her past the mess hall.

Her mood buoyed by this new course of action, Charlotte stepped lightly through the passageway. Nearly smug with satisfaction, Charlotte pulled up with a start when she suddenly heard voices just around the bend in the hall before her. She quickly backtracked until she reached a side passage. Ducking around the corner, Charlotte pressed herself up against the wall and listened.

Meg's gentle tone reached Charlotte's ears. "When he's alone, I sometimes hear him talking to himself."

"What does he say?" Charlotte tensed when she recognized Ash's voice.

"He whispers of clocks," Meg answered.

"Clocks?" Ash said. "What do you mean clocks?"

Meg uttered a low laugh. "It really is odd. 'Ticktock, ticktock. Never, never stop.'"

"That's what he says?"

She made a soft, affirmative noise. "It's almost like a song. There's something about him, Ashley . . . I don't think he's overtly dangerous, but he unnerves me in a way I can't explain."

"Of course he unnerves you. He's a nutter," Ashley said sharply. "Lottie never should have brought him here. What was she thinking!"

"She was trying to save him from the Rotpots," Meg answered. "What would you think of your sister if she'd seen him running for his life and not done anything?"

Charlotte heard Ash grunt in reply, and Meg laughed again. "Someday you'll have to let her grow up."

"Athene have mercy, not you too," Ash moaned.

"Me too?" Meg asked.

"Nothing," Ash replied quickly. "Just something Jack said earlier . . . Speaking of Jack, I should—"

Meg picked up where Ash's voice trailed off. "You should go. I'll oversee dinner."

"Thanks, Meg."

"Hurry back."

There was a long pause and Charlotte held her breath, worried it would give her away. Finally, Ash spoke again. He sounded nervous.

"Um, yes. Well. I'll be off, then."

"Don't forget to tell me that you're safely returned. No matter how late it is," Meg said quietly.

"Of course," Ash said and cleared his throat. "Always."

Charlotte heard the scuff of Ash's boots as he passed her hiding spot and continued down the corridor. A moment later, Meg's soft footfalls moved off in the opposite direction.

Where was Ash going?

The swell of self-righteousness that had carried Charlotte toward an imprisoned Grave lost out to her curiosity.

Ignoring a twinge of guilt, she snuck back into the corridor after Ashley.

Following her brother proved to be more of a challenge than Charlotte had anticipated. She was forced to stay out of sight to avoid discovery, yet at the same time keep close enough behind Ash so that she didn't lose him in the labyrinth of tunnels. It was also difficult not to be distracted by the route he was taking. The corridor had begun to slope upward. The path wasn't unfamiliar to Charlotte; she knew it to be one of the tunnels that wound its way to the surface, but the few exits like this one were for emergency use only. All arrivals and departures from the Catacombs were strictly regulated by use of the wheelhouse.

"Ho, there!"

Charlotte pulled up sharply and held her breath at the sound of Jack's voice.

"Evening, Jack." Ash's reply carried along the dark passage.

"Took you long enough," Jack said. "Any trouble getting away?"

"No," Ash told him. "I was just talking things over with Meg."

"Ah." Charlotte could hear the grin suffusing Jack's tone. "If I'd known *that* was it, I wouldn't have complained. You should take all the time you need with Meg. Hephaestus knows you could use it."

"Shut your trap, Jack."

The scuff of boots signaled that the boys were moving again. Now that they were talking, Charlotte could move more freely. Their voices covered the sounds of her pursuit and made it much easier for her to track them, though she found she couldn't follow their conversation and still creep silently along behind them. Since Jack seemed keen on continuing to hound Ash about Meg, Charlotte decided it didn't much matter what they were saying.

As they climbed through the caverns, the boys suddenly veered into a side passage where no phosphorescent mushrooms had been cultivated, causing their path to be swallowed up by darkness, and Charlotte became more and more perplexed. Neither Ash nor Jack carried a lantern, which meant they were feeling their way along the stone walls just as Charlotte was. She thought she knew where they were, but if she was right, their location didn't make any sense. The natural formations of the Catacombs afforded them a safe, secret habitation, but it wasn't without its drawbacks. Such as that several tunnels came to an end in unhelpful or, worse, dangerous places. And one of those dead-end corridors was precisely where Ash and Jack were headed.

If Charlotte had guessed correctly about the passage they were in, it would only be another few minutes until they arrived at a wide rock shelf that led nowhere. The opening in the hillside was partially covered by a jutting slab of rock precariously overhanging the shelf, above which was a steep face made slick by rivulets of water that coursed over its surface. Only an intrepid squirrel would dare to climb it. At its far edge, opposite the narrow entrance to the Catacombs, the cave's gaping maw opened onto a sheer cliff that dropped into the gorge below. Neither up nor down provided a means of escape; thus, this passage was one that remained unused.

Until now.

Very slowly, the moon's cool silver light trickled down the path from above, offering Charlotte a reprieve from the darkness. She watched Ash and Jack's tall silhouettes crest the steep corridor ahead and then disappear from view, leaving Charlotte to gaze at the bright orb of the full moon that hung in the night sky.

Afraid the light would give her away, Charlotte dropped to her hands and knees and crawled the remaining distance up the path. Her fingers curled over the lip of the corridor, which dropped down abruptly onto the rock shelf. Charlotte gasped and clapped her hand over her mouth, silently cursing herself for letting her surprise get the best of her.

Neither Jack nor Ash turned at the sound, but for good reason. They were enraptured by the giant object that filled the shelf from end to end. If Ash hadn't taken the time to teach his little sister about the Imperial Air Force, Charlotte's gasp would likely have been a scream, because nothing less than a monstrous war machine crowded the space before her.

The bulbous cockpit of the Dragonfly offered its pilot clear views of the sky, while the machine guns under its wings could target enemies at multiple angles. Built for speed and maneuverability, only the most skilled airmen were assigned to Dragonfly combat squadrons, which, like the insects that inspired the aircraft's design, were meant to function as agile and deadly aerial hunters.

"Couldn't have been easy to pilot her in." Ash eyed the Dragonfly's wingspan.

Jack laughed drily. "That's the beauty of a Dragonfly. She can move in ways that most fliers can't."

Ash took a few steps back from the aircraft, trying to get a better view of the whole machine. "And she's completely intact? No defects?"

"I told you she's perfect," Jack replied. "Don't you trust me?"

"Do you really want me to answer that?" Ash said with a chuckle. "I can't believe you actually pulled this off." He hesitated before asking, "Are you sure you're ready to go back?"

Jack turned away from Ashley and looked directly into the shadows where Charlotte lay hidden, her belly pressed to the cold stone and her chin tucked against the lip of the path. "Why don't you come over and take a closer look, Charlotte?"

10.

FOR A MOMENT, Charlotte considered running. If she made it back to her room, she'd at least have the benefit of a little more time to come up with an excuse for spying on her brother before he caught up with her. But running implied guilt, and Charlotte was determined to justify her actions.

What right did Ash and Jack have to keep a secret like this, anyway? A Dragonfly? In the Catacombs? Charlotte also stung from Ashley's implied distrust of his sister; hadn't she done enough to prove her worth to him?

Charlotte stood up and brushed the dirt from her clothes. Trying to appear unruffled despite Ashley's glower, she walked slowly down the rock slope to the floor of the cavern. She lifted her chin as she faced her brother.

Ash's features were drawn, his lips thin with rage. Charlotte braced herself, waiting for him to berate her, but Ashley startled her by turning on Jack.

"How long did you know she was there?"

The fury in Ash's question startled Jack as well. He staggered back a step, spluttering, "I, uh, well, I—"

"How long?"

Jack coughed. "I heard her behind us when we turned into the last passage."

"And you decided not to say anything?" Ash glared at him.

Straightening his shoulders, Jack stared right back at Ash. "You were going to have to tell her soon enough. You're a stubborn lout for dragging your feet about it. This way was easier."

Charlotte watched her brother's face go white as his fists clenched.

Jack gave Ash a measured look and said, "We can have a good tussle if you want, or you can just accept that I'm right."

The indecision etched on Ash's features prompted Charlotte to ask, "What do you have to tell me?"

"Stay out of this, Lottie," Ash snapped without sparing her a glance.

"No!" Charlotte stepped into her brother's line of sight. "This is about the homingbird, isn't it? And why Jack was missing when we left the Heap. Tell me what's going on! Or are you forgetting that Pocky and I kept you from being a feast for rats while Jack went to fetch this big secret of yours?"

Ash scowled at her, but spoke to Jack. "Are you sure you're ready for her to know the truth?"

Behind her, Charlotte heard Jack sigh. "I always knew it was coming."

The strain in Jack's voice pulled Charlotte around to look at him. Her throat closed when she saw the tightness around his eyes.

"Try not to hate me," Jack said. "It had to be this way. I didn't want to lie to you."

Lie to me? Charlotte's skin felt cold.

Ash buried his hands in his hair and paced beneath the Dragonfly's wings. As she heard her brother muttering angrily under his breath, Charlotte began to wish she hadn't followed the boys after all.

"I didn't come from the Foundry." Jack's voice grounded Charlotte in the present. Despite her sudden fear, Charlotte looked at Jack and nodded for him to continue.

Jack drew a long breath, his next words coming out in a huff. "I'm from the Floating City."

Laughter bubbled up Charlotte's throat. The bright sound died when Jack didn't crack a smile. He waited until she regarded him solemnly.

"You're serious?" she asked.

"I'm afraid so," Jack answered.

Charlotte no longer felt anxious. She didn't feel anything. Numbness curled around her limbs, stopping her breath. She wobbled, and Jack reached out to steady her, but Charlotte jumped back as if his hand were a striking snake.

Then Ash was beside her, his arm slipping around her shoulders.

"Easy, Lottie," he murmured. "Let Jack tell his story. Trust me—it's going to change everything for us. For the better."

Jack cast a grateful look at Charlotte's brother, then fixed his eyes upon Charlotte once more.

"I left the city so I could find you." As the words left Jack's mouth, he paused, frowning, and then said, "I mean all of you. This place. There were rumors that the children of the Resistance had a hideout north on the river. I hoped to make contact, and I was lucky to run into Ash. Well . . . lucky once I convinced him not to shoot me."

Ash laughed gruffly. "What's lucky is that you're a fast talker."

"That too." Jack grinned. "Things in New York are going badly, very badly. There are those of us who want to make a change before it's too late."

Charlotte shrugged herself away from Ash's arm. Now that she'd recovered from her shock, a hard rage settled in her bones. Why should she believe the words of anyone who came from the Floating City? They were all enemies, murderers. Nothing more.

"Why would you leave a home where you have everything?" Charlotte spat at Jack. "Who are you?"

Jack offered her a thin smile. "Everything isn't all you'd imagine it to be."

"Ugh." Charlotte didn't want to look at him. His perpetual arrogance and bravado made perfect sense to her now. Jack didn't just pretend to think he was superior to the rest of them. He believed it—that was how citizens of the Floating City justified their rule.

"Charlotte." Ash moved to stand beside Jack. "Stop judging him and listen."

Charlotte tried and failed to rein in her emotions. Jack's admission had gutted her in a way she couldn't explain.

Making an effort to mask her discontent, she said, "I'm listening."

"My father is an important man in the Empire," Jack continued. "And I was groomed to follow in his footsteps by serving in the Air Force."

Charlotte looked at the Dragonfly. "You piloted one of those?"

"I'm cleared to fly half a dozen Imperial aircraft." Jack's eyes shone in a way Charlotte had never seen. "But the Dragonfly has always been my favorite. My brother's too."

"Your brother?" Without meaning to, Charlotte took a step toward Jack, her anger tempered by fascination.

Jack nodded, smiling slightly. "Three years older. His name is Coe."

Charlotte glanced at the Dragonfly. "He's the one who sent the homingbird."

Nodding again, Jack said, "Yes. He sent the homing-bird to let us know when and where he'd ditch the Dragon-fly in the Heap so we could retrieve it."

Charlotte went quiet, impressed and a little frightened. No wonder Ash had been willing to bleed himself to draw the rats away from Jack. And yet . . . astounding as the feat was, Charlotte couldn't fathom what possible use the Dragonfly would be. Unlike *Pisces,* which stayed hidden in the dark waters of the river, the Dragonfly's bright metal plating would make it easy to spot in the sky. But Ash and Jack wouldn't have taken the risk of bringing it to the Cat-acombs unless it had immense value to their cause.

Charlotte gasped. "You're going back to New York?"

"We," Jack replied, not taking his eyes off Ash. "*We* are going to New York."

"Dammit, Jack," Ash muttered, but didn't offer further argument.

Charlotte gazed at her brother, cold clamping down on her chest. Ashley was going to the Floating City, the site of everything they strove to hide from.

Turning to Charlotte, Jack said, "We've gathered al-most enough support within the military and aristocracy to act, but we want to secure an alliance with the Resis-tance. We'll need them when the time comes."

"Are you telling me that you're planning to stage a coup?" Charlotte gaped at Jack.

"The body of the Empire is strong," Jack told her. "But it's ruled by a sick and twisted head. Corruption and decadence run rampant in the upper echelons of Imperial society. If we don't act soon, the Empire will go the way of Rome. It will be bloody and ugly, and this continent will be ruined while its conquerors fight for scraps."

"Won't a coup be just as bloody and ugly?" Charlotte asked.

"Not if we execute it correctly," Jack replied. "But that's why enlisting the aid of the Resistance is so important. There will be fighting, but if we can both surprise and overwhelm the old guard of the Empire, we may be able to contain the violence and keep it from throwing the entire country into chaos."

Ash spoke up. His voice carried a fervor of hope Charlotte hadn't heard before. "A coup would mean a clean slate. No more punitive labor for descendants of the revolutionaries."

Charlotte tried to catch some of Ash's enthusiasm, but she was still thrown by the notion that anyone who benefited from the Empire would be willing to turn against it.

"What about those who are fighting now?" Charlotte queried.

"Full pardons," Jack answered. "So long as they fight on our side when they're called upon."

"That's why I have to go, Lottie. Jack has arranged for me to meet with Lazarus as an official envoy of the Resistance. I'll see for myself if it's worth joining our cause with theirs."

"Lazarus?" Charlotte asked. "Who's Lazarus?"

"That's the code name for the leader of the rebellion that's taking place within the Empire," Jack told her. "His true identity is the movement's most closely guarded secret, but it's rumored that he's one of the highest-ranking officers in the Imperial Armed Forces."

Charlotte's head was spinning from all the information being hurled at her. "But how can you trust this Lazarus if you don't know who he really is? What if the rumors are lies?"

"They can't be," Jack answered, shaking his head. "He wouldn't have been able to gather the following he now has if he weren't a person of great influence within the Empire. People would be too afraid to follow a nobody."

Charlotte flinched. *He means nobodies like us, like the Resistance our parents have been fighting for all our lives,* she thought. Charlotte found herself a bit resentful of Jack's presumption that she'd be enthusiastic about these revelations.

"And you think we should join this rebellion?" Charlotte said to Ash. "Have you contacted Mother or Father?"

Ash shook his head too quickly for Charlotte's liking. "It's an opportunity like nothing the Resistance has been offered before, but it's not worth distracting them from the war until I've made sure Lazarus would be a true ally and asset to the cause. If he's all Jack claims, it could mean access to Imperial warships and artillery, which might convince the French to give us outright support when we move against the Empire."

Hiding her uneasiness, Charlotte said, "If this meeting goes well, and you decide the Resistance should ally with this Lazarus, what happens then?"

Ash and Jack exchanged a look that made Charlotte's hands balls into fists.

"Then I go to the front lines and rendezvous with the Resistance commanders," Ash said quietly. "To negotiate an alliance."

Charlotte bowed her head, trying to organize her jumbled thoughts. This was all happening too fast.

"It's nearly time for me to join the battlefront anyway," Ash continued. "You knew that was coming."

"Fine," Charlotte said. "But if you're going to New York, then so am I."

"Lottie." Ashley began to laugh—until he saw the determination in Charlotte's eyes. "No."

"You need me," Charlotte pressed. "I'm always at your side when we go into battle. I've saved you more than once."

"I don't deny that," Ash said. "But this is different."

"No," Charlotte replied. "It's a different sort of battle, but it's still a battle, and I'm fighting this war as much as you are."

Jack shifted his gun belt on his hips. "This isn't a place you can fight, Charlotte. Women in the city aren't like you."

"I don't care," Charlotte said, ignoring how silly that pronouncement sounded. "I'll find a way to help."

"Yes, you will." Meg's voice startled all of them.

She'd entered the cave unnoticed while they'd been arguing.

Ashley went to meet her, reaching for her hands but then quickly pulling them away with a glance over his shoulder toward Jack and Charlotte. "What are you doing here?"

"Charlotte's not the only one who knows how to sneak through the Catacombs," Meg told him with a teasing smile. "You should know that better than anyone, Ashley."

Though it was dim in the cavern, Charlotte thought she noticed a blush painting her brother's cheek.

"I've been thinking about this." Meg gave a meaningful look at the Dragonfly. "And about Grave."

"What about Grave?" Jack asked.

"He can't stay here," Meg replied. "I don't know why, but I know it's not safe. If I can take him to the city, there are people I believe can help me to understand why the boy troubles me so."

Disappointment fell heavy on Charlotte's shoulders. She'd assumed Meg had taken her side when it came to Grave. "But you've been so kind to him."

"And I'll continue to be," Meg said. "But I can't ignore my instincts about him. Until I understand who . . . or what he is, I won't risk this place and the people I love."

Ash raked his fingers through his hair, giving Meg an uneasy look. "I don't disagree that Grave presents an unusual problem. We don't know who he is, but Meg—you know that this mission is important. We can't take the extra risk of bringing him along."

"I'm telling you that you must." The steel in Meg's voice made Charlotte straighten up in surprise. She'd never heard Meg talk to Ash, or anyone, that way.

Jack and Ash looked as startled as Charlotte felt. Jack recovered first. With an apologetic but uncomfortable clearing of his throat, he said, "I don't think there's a way for us to conduct our business and keep an eye on Grave."

Ash quickly nodded in agreement.

"You won't have to," Meg said, calm but unyielding. "Charlotte and I will deal with Grave while you see to your secret meetings."

Charlotte's eyes widened, and she clapped her hand over her mouth to cover her smile when Meg spared her a tiny, conspiratorial smile. Charlotte couldn't help but marvel at Meg's brilliance. Of the Catacombs' inhabitants, Meg was the one person Ashley couldn't say no to.

Tugging at his collar, Ash went mute and threw a pleading glance at Jack.

Jack's shoulders hunched up as he faced Meg. "I don't think you have a realistic grasp of this situation. How do you propose we should take you and Charlotte into the city?"

"Leave that to me," Meg told Jack. "Though I will need you to acquire some papers for me. I assume you'll have no trouble doing that, given that you must be forging your own."

Jack replied with a grudging nod. "What kind of papers do you want for Charlotte?"

Ignoring Jack's glower, Meg answered, "As I'm sure you know, the social season is about to begin in New York."

Charlotte's brow furrowed. "What's that?"

"It's when the young women from the Empire's best families are presented to society," Meg said. "You're the right age to make your debut. It will give us the perfect cover under which to move freely through the Floating City."

"Why would they have to be presented?" Charlotte asked.

"It's a formality," Jack said. "More silly trappings of an overindulgent system that fattens its rich while starving its poor."

Ash grunted, making a sour face at Meg.

"Don't be so somber, Ash," Meg quipped. "Charlotte, the girls are presented so everyone knows they're looking for husbands. It's basically the starting line for a great race of matchmaking."

"Oh." Charlotte frowned, then she blushed. "*Oh.*" She looked at her brother in alarm.

"I'm not going to let Meg marry you off," Ash sighed. "This is a ruse, Lottie. A good one, I'll admit, but I don't like it. Not at all." He finally directed his frustration toward Meg. "My sister is not some society peacock. I don't want her anywhere near this."

"It doesn't matter what you want," Meg replied. "She is the best person for this role, and she can handle herself if things go badly." Lowering her voice, Meg continued, "Ashley, I would never ask this if it weren't important."

Ash held her gaze and then nodded.

A sound crawled out of Jack's throat that was something of a sigh mixed with a groan. "I guess I have some homingbirds to send."

Meg turned to give him a beatific smile. "Yes, my dear, you do."

"Escorting a debutante will make moving through the city much easier," Jack said to Ash, with a sour face. "As much as I hate to admit it."

Finding herself flushed with excitement, Charlotte wrapped her arms around her waist. "When are we going?"

"Ash and I were planning to leave in a few days. We have the aircraft, and if I can get the papers to establish your lineage for partaking in the season, I don't see why we shouldn't stay on that schedule." Jack pointed at the Dragonfly. "She'll get us transport to the dirigible traveling to the Floating City." He swiveled around so that his finger pointed at Charlotte. "You give us access to the city itself."

"I truly can give you access to the city?" Charlotte lifted her brows.

"Well, not you, you." Jack tugged at his shirt collar. "But the fine lady Meg has proposed we make you out to be will enjoy all the privileges of New York society."

Despite her suddenly dry throat, Charlotte managed a tart response. "Are you suggesting I'm not a lady?"

Ash laughed, and Charlotte glared at him.

"Trust me," Jack told her. "You should thank Athene you're not the type of lady I'm talking about. Once Meg starts teaching you all the rules and etiquette, I think you'll be cursing the moment she came up with this cockamamie scheme. I'd say your best bet would be to adopt a shy and docile persona. Then again, I realize that's probably asking too much."

Before Charlotte had a chance to return Jack's insult, Meg interjected, "Don't worry, Charlotte, you'll never be alone. Ash will be there too."

Charlotte threw an impish smile at her brother. "As a fine gentleman?"

"Not quite," Meg told her. "He'll be posing as your manservant."

"I beg your pardon?" Ash exclaimed, sending Charlotte into a fit of giggles.

When Meg nodded, Jack put his hands up. "I'm afraid she's right, old chap. A fine lady needs to be attended. You fit the bill."

"But you don't?" Ash retorted.

"Can you pilot the Dragonfly?" Jack shrugged. "If you can and for some reason haven't told me yet, she's all yours. I'll be happy to wait on Charlotte hand and foot while you play the military officer and escort Charlotte around town.

Oh, wait. You don't have connections in the city who've created a paper trail that explains your absence and will also accommodate your return."

"Don't push me, Jack."

Jack smiled without sympathy. "Sorry, mate."

Ash spewed out more curses than Charlotte ever imagined her brother knew. Meg gave him a disapproving look but kept silent.

"Shameful, Ashley." Jack snickered. "A gentleman would never use that sort of language."

Ash picked out a few more choice words with which he addressed Jack.

Charlotte slipped her arm through Ash's. "Don't worry, dear brother. I shall be a kind and generous mistress."

"You'd better be," Ash growled. "Keep in mind that our visit to the city is temporary, and when we get back here, I'm still your elder brother."

"How could I ever forget?" She batted her eyelashes at him.

With a sharp laugh, Ash squeezed her arm. "Let's get back to the others. Now that the cat's out of the bag, we can move forward with the plan."

"We don't have any time to waste," Jack said, already heading toward the opening to the Catacombs. "Coe is waiting for me to return the homingbird, which signals that we're on our way. And he'll help facilitate Charlotte's entry into the city."

Still holding Ashley's arm, Charlotte walked with her brother toward the corridor. She glanced back at the Dragonfly. Even in the moonlight, its surface gleamed. In the sunlight, it would be dazzling. And she would fly in it.

She doubted she'd get a wink of sleep until they were on their way to the Floating City.

11.

CAN'T BELIEVE YOU'LL walk the platforms of the Floating City." Pip sat cross-legged on Charlotte's bed. "You should take one of Birch's Wing-O-Matics and jump off the edge! Wouldn't that be fun?"

"Birch hasn't tested the Wing-O-Matics, and besides, I'm supposed to be blending in. I think people would notice if I jumped off a platform with wings strapped on my back."

Pip scrunched up her nose in disappointment. "You could do it at night . . ."

Ignoring that remark, Charlotte said, "What I can't believe is that this is what Imperial ladies wear every day." She turned quickly, and the light silk of her gown floated along her calves as if it were made of air. "Aren't society women supposed to be modest?"

The leather corset Charlotte was accustomed to wearing cinched her shirt and skirt to her waist, and doubled as light armor. For as long as she'd lived in the Catacombs, Charlotte had begun each day by layering her clothing and weapon belts strategically. Her skirts, though cumbersome, had pockets to stash mice and tools in. She always kept a dagger strapped to her boot.

In this new dress, which Jack had produced without explanation, along with a trunk full of the latest metropolitan fashions, Charlotte felt almost naked. The light blue bodice clung to her breasts, and the gown's high waist only served to further accentuate how well the dress fit Charlotte's curves. The skirt, while made of flowing material, skimmed close to her hips and legs. Silk slippers had replaced her sturdy boots.

"You look lovely," Meg assured Charlotte, seeing the distress on the younger girl's face.

Charlotte frowned at Meg and spun in a circle for inspection. "Are you sure you can't see through the silks?"

"Women of Imperial society try to emulate the goddess Athene," Meg said quickly. "Their dresses follow the style of the ancient Greeks."

Noting with some distress that Meg hadn't actually answered her question, Charlotte resigned herself to feeling exposed.

"I know it's quite warm still." Meg rummaged through

the trunk. "But you'll want something for travel. Here we are."

"Ooh! Ooh!" Pip clapped her hands, her green pigtails bobbing as she nodded in approval at the cropped jacket of midnight blue silk that Meg held up.

"Thank Athene," Charlotte breathed, snatching the jacket from Meg's hand and slipping it on. The delicate jacket was hardly as durable as Charlotte's usual clothing, but at least it wasn't as transparent as the gown.

Among the trio of young women, Pip was the only one still wearing her normal clothes: a dark leather skirt and a cotton chemise nipped in by a leather halter vest. Meg's dress had changed to reflect her adopted station for the mission. Meg's preferred wardrobe consisted of full muslin skirts dyed in bright colors and soft, white cotton shirts cinched by corsets she embroidered herself. But this morning she wore a simple high-waisted dress in the muted shade of a rainy sky, and a watery blue grosgrain ribbon circled the dress just beneath her bosom. It was a costume—just like Charlotte's.

When Jack explained that Meg would accompany Charlotte to the Floating City as her maidservant, Charlotte had immediately been uneasy with the arrangement. Not only was Meg two years older than Charlotte, but Meg played the part of kind caretaker, in counterpart to Ash's gruffer leadership style. It was Meg to whom Charlotte went when she needed advice or to blow off steam about her brother. As much as Charlotte was grateful to have Meg's company in the Floating City, the thought of anyone regarding Meg as a servant, and therefore a lesser being, left a bitter taste in her mouth.

Meg regarded Charlotte wistfully, then said, "We should go. They'll be waiting for you. Pip, help me with the trunk."

"I can help you—" Charlotte began.

"No, you can't," Meg cut her off, taking one of the trunk's handles. She gestured for Pip to lift the other side. "And you must remember that, Lottie. As a lady of society, you do not do anything for yourself. You have servants for that. If you act otherwise, it will cast suspicion on your story."

Though her stomach twisted with disgust, Charlotte forced a nod. She and Jack had almost come to blows several times over the past two days as he'd led her through the ridiculous maze that was life as an aristocratic lady in the Floating City. Their near fisticuffs were the result of Charlotte constantly interrupting Jack, suspicious that he was making up the behaviors and rules she found so ludicrous. Finally, Meg had to join their lessons and chaperone. Whenever Charlotte objected to something Jack told her to do, Meg was there to reassure Charlotte that Jack was not in fact winding her up for his own amusement. Even though Charlotte trusted Meg to keep Jack in line, the bizarre customs of the Floating City left Charlotte more than a little bewildered. Her initial sense of triumph at gaining a role in the mission had faded, and she approached her departure from the Catacombs with more trepidation than excitement.

Meg offered Charlotte an encouraging smile. "Good. Now lead the way to the Dragonfly and keep your gown lifted. You don't want it completely soiled at the hem when you arrive in the city."

As Charlotte picked her way through the Catacombs, Pip's voice bubbled into the air, full of speculation about what sights and adventures awaited them in the Floating City. Pip seemed remarkably optimistic about the mission, whereas Charlotte felt like they were flying straight into the mouth of a hungry lion. But Pip wasn't the only one who'd taken the revelation of Jack's true identity as something marvelous and wonderful when they'd joined the others at dinner two nights past.

Scoff had immediately peppered Jack with questions about whether the Imperial Armed Forces mandated a regimen of tonics. Birch wanted to know if Jack could start smuggling better parts to the Catacombs than what came from the scavenging runs to the Heap. While her friends flocked around Jack, seeking knowledge like baby birds begging for food, Charlotte had snuck away to sit with Grave. Since the strange boy had taken to his cage without complaint, Ash had relented and agreed to keep Grave in a locked room rather than behind iron bars. They'd learned nothing more about his origins or why he could be bludgeoned in the head to no effect.

Scoff had tried to convince Meg that his Elixir of

Intentions was their only option, but fortunately Meg put her foot down. And after she caught Scoff sneaking a few drops of his concoction into a cup of water intended for Grave, Meg banished him from the captive boy's presence.

The Dragonfly's arrival and the imminent journey into New York kept most of Charlotte's companions occupied with preparations, and their attentions drawn away from the mystery of Grave. Meg took the strange boy's well-being as her responsibility, in addition to preparing him for the part he'd play during their excursion to the city. Though now that Charlotte knew a bit about Meg's wariness of Grave, she wondered if Meg wasn't hovering around him as a guard rather than a friend.

When Charlotte crested the rise of the seldom-used path that would take her to the Dragonfly, she saw Grave standing beside her brother, giving assistance with the ship's preparation for departure. Grave's lean frame and absurdly pale skin were unmistakable, but his hair had changed color from translucent blond to pitch-black. Noticing their arrival, Ash ran up to them, taking hold of Meg's side of the trunk.

"Didn't you offer to help?" Ash scolded Charlotte.

Meg clucked her tongue. "Of course she did, Ash. I told her she shouldn't offer help when I'm to be her maidservant. She needs to act the part. No exceptions."

"Of course," Ash said, giving Meg an abashed glance. "Sorry, Meg."

Charlotte looked at her brother expectantly, but Ash

didn't bother apologizing to her. With a little huff of annoyance, Charlotte trotted ahead of the trunk bearers to join Grave near the Dragonfly's gangplank.

"What happened to your hair?" Charlotte blurted out, but Grave didn't appear bothered by her lack of tact.

A little smile graced his mouth. "Scoff gave me an elixir."

Temper boiling up, Charlotte asked, "The Elixir of Intentions? I thought Meg had banished him from experimenting on you."

"Experimenting?" Grave's eyes widened. "No. It was just to change my hair."

Recognizing a scent, Charlotte leaned closer to Grave and sniffed. Licorice.

"Are you sure that's all it was?"

He nodded, and Charlotte tamped down her anger, determined to take him at his word.

"It's beautiful, isn't it?" Grave said, looking up at the aircraft.

"Yes," Charlotte replied, admiring the hammered sheets of copper and bronze that decorated the Dragonfly's body. Spying the machine guns that protruded from the craft's underbelly, she added, "And frightening."

Grave sighed, and Charlotte was sorry she'd said something to upset him. "I'm glad Ash came to his senses."

Grave's brow furrowed.

"You aren't locked up," Charlotte supplied. "And we'll figure out who you are once we're in the city."

Another sigh. "Maybe I should be locked up. What if we find out who I am, and I'm something we don't want me to be?"

Fumbling for words, Charlotte was saved from the awkward pause by Ash's arrival.

"Grave, let's get this trunk into the cargo hold," Ash said.

Pip prepared to hand off her side to Grave, but he spread his arms along its length and pulled it away from both of them.

"Holy Hephaestus!" Pip jumped up, banging her head on the underside of one of the wings. "Ouch!"

"I'm sure Scoff has a tonic for that." Jack laughed as he came down the gangplank. "Though it might mean giving up your green hair."

He halted when he reached Grave. "You're not finding that big box a little too heavy?"

"Erm . . . no?" Grave answered.

"Righto." Jack's wary gaze slid to Ash, but he told Grave, "Better take it on up, then."

Jack jumped off the side of the plank so that Grave could carry the trunk into the aircraft.

"Brilliant plan, mate," Jack remarked in a wry tone to Ash. "No doubts about it at all. Though I sure hope he doesn't accidentally punch a hole in the Dragonfly's side while I'm piloting her."

"He'll be fine," Ash replied curtly. "I see you finally got dressed."

"I do what I have to do."

Jack's "dress" was precisely the reason Charlotte couldn't stop staring at him.

He'd traded his brown buckled and dagger-laden boots for knee-high black boots that were polished to a sheen. Close-fitting gray breeches hugged his thighs, hips, and waist. The open-collared shirt and suspenders Jack usually wore had been replaced by a stiff scarlet military coat closed by two rows of shining brass buttons and crossed by a gleaming white sash that fell from his shoulder to his hip. Charlotte couldn't find any signs of Jack's preferred weapons. Instead a light sword hung at his waist, and opposite the sword, the bright silver handle of a pistol, crafted to resemble a lion's head, peeked out of its holster. Charlotte frowned, knowing Jack liked his weapons innovative and practical. This gun and sword looked like pieces of art, not arms.

Feeling her gaze, Jack looked at Charlotte. When he met her eyes, he winced and she caught a self-mocking cast in his expression. Her cheeks reddened at being caught staring, but Jack went pale as he took in her carefully pinned hair and silk gown. Casting his gaze downward, Jack scuffed his heel on the ground.

"Looks like you're ready for the trip."

"You too," Charlotte said.

He nodded in reply, but wouldn't look up at her.

Did she appear utterly foolish to him dressed like this? It would have been unsurprising, and possibly reassuring, for Jack to tease her about her costume, but his silence was like a slap in the face.

Jack shifted his weight and said to Ash, "You're set on this plan? You really think it's safe to take him with us? We could still call it off. The two of us can get into the city to meet Lazarus easily enough."

Charlotte caught Jack's quick glance in her direction. He didn't want her on this trip, and seeing her gussied up in this costume was making him realize what folly their plan was.

Ash said, "The plan is set. We're not changing anything."

Jack spun on his heel and ducked back into the Dragonfly.

"He doesn't think I can pull this off." Charlotte picked at her filmy skirt. "I can't say I blame him."

"Don't be a ninny." Ash gave her a withering look. "Jack knows you'll be fine. He's just . . . distracted by other things. It's put him on edge."

"What other things?" Charlotte frowned.

"It doesn't matter," Ash replied, glancing up the gangplank after Jack.

"Do you think it will be enough that Grave's hair is black?" Charlotte asked. "In case anyone is looking for him."

Ash shrugged. "It'll do."

Knowing she should bite her tongue, Charlotte couldn't help adding, "You do realize this means you're leaving Birch and Scoff in charge of the Catacombs."

"Of course I realize that," Ash replied curtly.

Charlotte gave her brother a long look. "And you aren't worried that half of the caverns will be blown apart while we're gone? Or that we'll return to find the children have purple skin and hair that looks and smells like cherries?"

"Don't push me, Charlotte," Ash said. "Just get on the ship."

With a huff, Charlotte stomped up the gangplank. She paused once she was on the ship. The gangplank delivered her to a narrow holding bay that linked the cockpit and the cabin. Charlotte turned left and poked her head into the flight deck. Jack was at the helm, surrounded by brass gears, cranks, and levers. Mimicking a dragonfly's eyes, the front of the ship was thick curving glass framed with brass that offered the pilot a panoramic view.

"I wanted to say thanks before we go . . . for all you taught me about city society," Charlotte said, hoping to quell any doubts Jack was having about her part in the mission.

"I'm busy, Charlotte." Jack didn't turn around. "Go to the cabin and strap yourself in."

He began flipping switches. The Dragonfly shuddered as its engine came to life. Charlotte glared at the back of Jack's head, willing him to turn around, but he didn't. Making a noise of disgust, Charlotte whirled and nearly collided with Ash.

"Charlotte, why aren't you in the cabin?" Her brother frowned. "We're about to take off."

Charlotte didn't answer, but shoved past Ashley. The gangplank clanged loudly as it folded in on itself, retracting into the ship. Meg and Grave were in the cabin, already seated with leather harnesses crisscrossing their chests to secure them in their seats. Too angry to be bothered with conversation, Charlotte took a seat near the gun wells tucked into the front of the cabin. Unlike the passenger chairs, which were stationary, the gunner's station had swiveling seats to permit the weapon's operator to track targets over a broad range. Charlotte's perch afforded much better views of the terrain through its spherical glass lookout than Meg and Grave would have through the tiny portholes that ran the length of the Dragonfly. Buckling herself into the harness, she eased her foul mood by gazing out at the machine guns. Jack might resent her being there, but Charlotte assuaged her bruised pride by imagining how easily she could man the gun and protect them should the need arise.

Above the gun well, the Dragonfly's wings began to stir. The forewing and hindwing on each side of the ship beat in ever-swifter counterstrokes, and soon the craft was hovering in the cavern. Through the glass, Charlotte saw Pip at the entrance to the Catacombs, jumping up and down as she waved her good-byes.

The Dragonfly turned smoothly, and suddenly the ground fell away. Charlotte gasped when they cleared the cavern and she was staring down into the gorge below. Her stomach dropped as the ship lifted, soaring into the sky at what felt like an impossible speed.

Charlotte heard Meg calling her name, but she kept her chair turned away from the back of the cabin. The Dragonfly rose up and up; the forest and river blurred into a mess of greens and blues far below and then disappeared as they cleared the clouds. Charlotte had to shield her eyes from the dazzling sunlight that poured over her, but her heart was fit to burst from exhilaration. She wished she were with Jack in the cockpit so she could see him maneuver the aircraft and understand how the ship could move so nimbly. More than that, she wanted to see what Jack was like at the helm. Was he anxious as a pilot, having fled from the military a year before? Or had he longed to fly again? Since she'd learned about Jack's past, they'd all been so caught up in preparations for this journey that she hadn't been able to speak with him at all. And she had so many questions about the life he'd kept hidden. To see him pilot the Dragonfly would be a window into the past that so fascinated her.

Charlotte wanted to study Jack's face, to know if she'd find joy or fear in his expression. Her fingers curled around the arms of the gunner's chair as she thought of not only watching Jack, but sitting close to him as he controlled the aircraft. Her daydream evolved of its own accord, and she imagined reaching out to rest her hand over Jack's to feel the way he guided the ship.

Startled by the sudden turn in her thoughts, Charlotte quickly shook her head to clear the unbidden vision. Her cheeks were heated and her breath short, but Charlotte assured herself that it was nothing and refocused on the swiftly passing clouds and endless expanse of sky.

12.

AN HOUR LATER, lulled by the tranquility of the cloud line, Charlotte began to drift off. Before sleep could steal her from consciousness, Ash's voice barked through the cabin.

"We're approaching HMCS *Hector*. Prepare to dock in a quarter of an hour."

Charlotte tried to jump up, but had forgotten that she was harnessed into her chair. When the leather straps restrained her, she dropped hard onto the seat and banged her head.

"Shield of Athene!"

"Are you all right, Lottie?" Meg called.

Rubbing the back of her head, Charlotte swiveled around. "I'm fine, Meg."

137

"You needn't worry about standing until we've docked," Meg told her. "There are bound to be a few bumps during our arrival."

Charlotte nodded, but when she turned back to the window, she was frowning. How did Meg know what docking at one of the Empire's dirigibles was like? Had Jack told her? Had she experienced it before? Were all of her companions keeping secrets?

Resenting that facts seemed to be constantly hidden from her, Charlotte leaned forward as much as the harness would allow, hoping to catch a glimpse of HMCS *Hector*. At first her view remained only a vast sea of clouds, but then something loomed at the edge of her vision. Charlotte strained against the leather straps, but she could see only a brass propeller slicing through the air.

Cursing under her breath, Charlotte unbuckled the harness and freed herself from the chair.

"Charlotte, sit down!" Meg shouted.

Charlotte ignored the command and made her way from the cabin to the cockpit. She wanted to see the airship before they docked, bumps be damned. Bracing herself in the flight deck's entryway, Charlotte gasped at the view from the Dragonfly's helm.

His Majesty's Colonial Ship *Hector* blotted out half the sky. Smoke and flame belched from towering columns into four balloons as large and black as thunderclouds. Suspended from the balloons was a long, slender craft featuring two decks—it appeared that the upper deck had been designed for military purposes, considering the massive guns that jutted from the sides of the ship, while the lower deck accommodated the needs of civilians, as it featured viewing portholes.

The figure protruding from the ship's bow was a roaring lion's head. Charlotte glanced at Jack's waist, confirming what she'd thought. The silver lion on the handle of his pistol was identical to that on the ship.

From the copilot's chair, Ash snapped, "Damn it all, Charlotte! Why aren't you in your seat?"

Keeping a firm hold on the metal frame of the cockpit's entry, Charlotte drew herself up. "I wanted to see the airship before we docked. I'll be fine."

"You've seen it," Ash said coldly. "Now go back to the cabin."

"No."

"By Athene, I will drag you there." Ash unbuckled his harness.

"You will not," Charlotte snapped.

Ash started to rise, but Jack threw his arm out, knocking Ash back into his chair.

"Quiet, both of you." Jack didn't take his eyes off the dirigible. "I have to dock this ship, and you brawling won't make it any easier."

"Jack, she shouldn't be up here," Ash said.

"I don't care where she is as long as she stops distracting me," Jack answered. "That goes for you too. Besides, I'm a good pilot. If Charlotte has any grace at all, she'll be fine."

"I have plenty of grace," Charlotte snapped, though she gripped the entryway tighter. There was no way in hell she would let herself fall after that remark.

Ash threw a withering look at Jack, who paid him no notice. Jack began tapping a thin brass lever rhythmically, and Charlotte's gaze flicked out to the corresponding flash of lights in the sky. A minute later, an answering barrage of bright flashes shot toward them from the dirigible.

"We're cleared to dock," Jack told them. "Last chance to ditch."

"Just fly the damn ship," Ash growled.

"Aye, aye, sir," Jack replied, adding, "Though technically I outrank you—so you should be calling me sir."

Ash raised his hand as if to cuff Jack on the back of the head.

"No attacking the pilot, Ash!" Charlotte glared at her brother.

Ash shrugged. "I'm menacing the pilot, not attacking. Though he deserves it."

"Of course he does," Charlotte said. "But the rest of us don't deserve to crash because Jack can be an ass."

"I'm just trying to help you stay in character, dear man," Jack objected, but he kept his eyes on the looming dirigible and his grip firm on the controls.

Dismissing Jack's outburst, Charlotte leaned forward, observing the rapidly approaching airship. Jack guided the Dragonfly toward the larger ship's underbelly, where large glass and brass columns protruded. Charlotte thought the design gave the dirigible a rather obscene resemblance to a bloated cow and its udder. The HMCS *Hector* lacked the grace and sleekness of the Dragonfly. Though buoyant, the craft looked as if it would only lumber through the sky, its bulk plowing a path across the clouds.

Their ship was closing in on the udder-like protrusions.

"You're up, Ash," Jack said without a glance at Ashley. "Remember what I told you?"

"Despite your doubts, I'll stay in character."

Ash unbuckled his harness and ducked out of the cockpit. Charlotte started toward Ash's vacated chair, but hearing the rustle of her skirts, Jack shook his head.

"Sorry, Charlotte. Ladies don't sit in the cockpit, and in another minute, you'll be spotted by the *Hector*'s crew. Step back and stay out of sight."

Charlotte felt the urge to cuff Jack like Ashley had, but instead she retreated to the holding bay and began to mutter about Jack's character flaws under her breath. She was still compiling her list when the Dragonfly slowed until it was hovering. A rush of wind from the rear of the craft lifted Charlotte's dress hem to her knees as the roar of the dirigible's engines poured into their ship. When she reached down to cover her legs, the Dragonfly lurched and then shuddered, and Charlotte was sent sprawling onto the cargo bay floor.

The steady hum of the aircraft stilled, and Jack appeared in the cockpit entryway to find Charlotte on her hands and knees, cursing up a storm.

"Plenty of grace?" Jack grinned at her.

Refusing his outstretched hand, Charlotte stood up, grateful that she hadn't scraped her knees in the fall. She doubted bloodstains on one's skirts were part of current fashion in the city.

With a sigh, Jack let his hand drop to his side while Charlotte smoothed out the delicate fabric of her dress. When she looked at him again, he offered his arm.

"In the city, you'll be expected to take a gentleman's arm if offered, Charlotte," Jack said, heading off her objection.

Charlotte sniffed. "You're hardly a gentleman."

"Usually I'd agree." Jack's laugh was cold. "But in New York, I am a gentleman. And no matter what you actually think of me, while we're here, you have to play along."

His voice was laced with resentment that drained any impudence from Charlotte, and she slipped her arm through Jack's. He led her into the cabin. Meg and Grave were unbuckling themselves from their seats.

"Go get the luggage," Jack told the pair, but kept guiding Charlotte toward the rear of the craft.

At the point where the cabin tapered toward the Dragonfly's tail, Ashley had opened a portal in the roof. Now he watched an extension of the glass and brass column that Charlotte had seen on the dirigible telescope its way into the Dragonfly. The tube's segments stretched all the way to the floor of the aircraft. Other than the brass fittings, the column was transparent and hollow, except for what appeared to be a brass capsule hovering just inside the tube. It was also large; wide enough for Charlotte to stand beneath with her arms outstretched. The last segment of the column featured a brass wheel about the size of a man's fist. Another blast of air swirled around Charlotte's ankles, and a moment later, a length of slender brass-plated tubing snaked its way down the column. Ashley grabbed the end of the tube and screwed it into a soundbox on the Dragonfly's wall.

Removing Charlotte's hand from his forearm, Jack approached the tube. He gave the wheel a half-turn and one panel of the tube hissed open, revealing an oval door in the side of the capsule.

"Nice work," he said to Ashley, who merely nodded.

Jack glanced back at Charlotte. "Come on, Charlotte. Etiquette demands that the most esteemed passengers board first."

Charlotte joined Jack and her brother beside the telescoped column.

Peering at the glass tube and its resident, person-sized capsule, she said with a frown, "What is this?"

"Just step into the capsule," Jack answered. "You'll get where you need to go."

The way he seemed to be barely containing laughter did little to encourage Charlotte.

A tinny voice piped from the soundbox. "Please embark."

Jack opened the door and shoved Charlotte into the capsule, which afforded her enough room to stand up straight, but that was all. "Don't keep 'em waiting."

Before she could turn to scold him for his ungallant behavior, Jack smiled wickedly, slammed the door shut, and turned the brass wheel.

Charlotte heard a whoosh of air and then yelped in surprise as suction from above jerked the capsule up the glass tube. After a short but violent journey, the door sprung open and Charlotte popped out of the entry valve into the arms of three waiting butlers, who quickly ushered the startled young woman to a settee upholstered in emerald velvet.

"Will you require smelling salts, Miss Marshall?" one of the butlers asked. The men were dressed in uniforms that struck Charlotte as a cross between military and domestic service: knee-high, glossy leather boots, a formfitting jacket with bright brass buttons left open at the throat to reveal a scarlet silk kerchief, and white kid gloves.

Embarrassed that she'd been caught off guard, Charlotte tried to compose herself, but just as quickly remembered that she was playing the part of a pampered heiress. She placed her hand at her throat and took deep breaths, all the while feeling the rapid pace of her pulse beneath her fingers.

"Thank you, but I believe I'll recover without them."

Thus assured, the trio of uniformed men hurried away.

• •

"Oooo-ohhhh!"

The cry drew Charlotte's gaze to the left side of the room, where a stout woman shot up through the floor from another tube. Apparently she was familiar with the arrival process, because she thrust her arms out the moment the capsule door opened as if expecting to be caught. Her generous figure had been stuffed into a frock of stiff violet silk, and the butlers staggered back when she fell against them.

There were four valves, one in each corner of the room, while the central space was crowded with velvet settees and overstuffed silk pillows. The butlers shuttled the woman, who moaned all the while, to Charlotte's side.

"Salts, Lady Ott?" a butler inquired as the large woman swooned. There was a dry note in his voice that made Charlotte suspect Lady Ott was a regular passenger and that the butler thought her distress an affectation.

Lady Ott kept her eyes shut and shook her head. "Just faerie fans, good man. Be quick about it."

The butler snapped his fingers, and one of his peers hurried away, only to return a moment later bearing a gilt box. He placed the box at Lady Ott's feet and set about turning the minuscule crank that protruded from one side of the mysterious container. When the butler released the crank and stepped back, the box's golden lid sprung open. A tinkling melody typical of a music box filled the air, but so did whirring and clicking noises.

Charlotte managed to stifle her gasp as four mechanical

faeries emerged from the box, their gold mesh wings holding them aloft before Lady Ott's face while slender golden chains tethered the tiny creatures to the box. Charlotte went still, enthralled by the faeries, as Lady Ott sighed and leaned toward their beating wings.

Her astonishment waning, Charlotte's eyes narrowed. The four little mechanical beasts couldn't be creating any real sort of wind—their wings were much too small to generate serious air flow—clearly these faerie fans were more spectacle than practical.

Charlotte clucked her tongue in disapproval, giving Lady Ott occasion to notice there was another person, besides the butlers, in the arrival bay.

After taking a few minutes to scrutinize Charlotte's appearance, and apparently liking what she saw, Lady Ott smiled and said, "Horrid, isn't it, my dear? These men and their contraptions. They simply don't understand how important it is for a woman to arrive with unmussed hair and smooth skirts."

The plump woman continued to bask in the light breeze created by the faerie fans. "What sort of transport did you take to the *Hector*?"

"A Dragonfly." Charlotte's cheeks went cold with dread. She may have been trussed up like a noble lady of the Floating City, but now she'd have to act the part as well, and her tongue wanted only to tie itself into a knot.

Casting a curious sidelong glance at Charlotte, Lady

Ott said, "A military craft. Much too cramped for my taste, made for war rather than comfort. My husband and I came in a Scarab. Even so, I was more than ready to be off that small craft and onto the *Hector*, as is proper for ladies. Glories of the Empire, they call these airships. I've found it to be true. I'll travel no other way. The seafaring versions just aren't the same. Don't you agree?"

Charlotte didn't know if she agreed, but she nodded.

Fortunately, Lady Ott was happy to keep talking.

"It can't be helped," the plump woman continued. "We can't keep to our country halls during the social season, now, can we?"

"No?" Charlotte supplied, with some hesitation.

Taking Charlotte's uncertain tone as a jest, Lady Ott tittered with laughter, making her ample but constrained bosom quiver like jelly. Charlotte was a bit nervous that the woman's stays would snap if put under too much stress.

"Of course we can't," Lady Ott agreed. "But I haven't seen you at any of the balls or tourneys, my dear. Surely you haven't been neglecting your social duties?"

Trapped by the question, Charlotte could only think to say, "Perhaps I have been. I'm afraid this is my first visit to the Floating City. I'm from the islands, and until now I haven't been away from my father's plantation estate."

Lady Ott pursed her lips, and Charlotte worried she'd said something wrong, but suddenly the older woman's face lit up.

"By Athene's grace, you're being presented, aren't you?" Lady Ott beamed. "Such a demure young lady to keep quiet about it. Ah, how well I remember my own debut into New York society. What house has sponsored you?"

Charlotte forced her mouth into a demure smile and nodded with as much shyness as she could manage. Before she could reply, however, a voice answered.

"The House of Winter."

Charlotte startled; her silk skirts nearly made her slip from the settee. As she half turned to look at Jack, he placed his hand on her shoulder, steadying her. Jack must have emerged from the arrival valve while Charlotte was distracted by Lady Ott and her faerie fans.

Lady Ott gasped. "You can't mean Admiral Winter's estate?"

"The same," Jack answered, a bit stiffly.

The noblewoman's gaze returned to Charlotte. "Wherever have they been hiding you? What a coup this is! All of New York will be aflutter when they hear of this."

It was clear Lady Ott was thrilled that she would be the source of such juicy gossip. Charlotte lowered her eyes as if reluctant to answer, but in truth it was the best way to avoid having to carry on a conversation with this ridiculous woman.

Jack spoke again. "Miss Marshall is the heiress to her father's plantation in the Bermudas."

Maintaining her meek pose, Charlotte nodded at Jack's statement. When procuring papers to give Charlotte an appropriate background, Jack had assured her and Ash that New York society had long since lost interest in the goings-on in the Empire's "quaint" island holdings, so that while her fictional identity supplied the necessary status to join the elite of the Floating City, no one would be surprised they'd never heard of a Lady Charlotte Marshall from Bermuda.

"Well, well, well." Lady Ott flicked her hand dismissively at the hovering faeries, and a butler instantly swooped in to collect the box. "The young men will be clamoring for your attention, my dear. And more than a few tongues will wag in the galleries, I've no doubt."

Charlotte shivered at the thought of anyone taking note of her presence in the city. Had Jack and Ash thought this plan through? She'd been assured that pretending to belong in society would keep her hidden. Hiding in plain sight, Jack had said. Maybe that meant something other than Charlotte thought.

Another whoosh of air announced Ashley's appearance on the arrival deck. The butlers acknowledged his embarkation but, seeing his porter's garb, made no move to assist him. When Meg and Grave appeared in sequence a few minutes later bearing luggage, the butlers didn't even bother to greet them.

"My, my, my," Lady Ott was saying. Charlotte turned to see the stout woman gazing at Jack admiringly. "Flight Lieutenant Winter! What a pleasure this is. You've been missed in the city."

Jack's smile was little more than a grimace. "You're too kind."

Lady Ott's overbright smile didn't waver. "But of course you're so young, you would be disappointed to be pulled away from the excitement of battle for these social niceties."

Jack replied with a polite nod. He turned to Charlotte and offered his hand. "My lady, you'll be wanting to refresh yourself after our voyage, I'm sure?"

Charlotte took Jack's hand, knowing she gripped his fingers a little too hard when she stood.

"Of course, of course." Lady Ott smiled at them. "But I insist you join me for dinner. I'll have the invitation sent to your cabins."

"You honor us." Jack smiled, tugging Charlotte away from Lady Ott.

Motioning for Ash, Meg, and Grave to follow them with the luggage, Jack led Charlotte away from the arrival lounge and toward a small staircase. One of the butlers awaited them at the landing and opened a door to let them pass.

Charlotte leaned in to Jack. "We're not really having dinner with that woman, are we?"

"I'm afraid we are," Jack whispered. "Her husband is Roger Ott—one of the most prominent financiers of the city and a friend of the Resistance. Besides, Lady Ott will be full of news that might prove useful. He will as well;

Lord Ott is known to trade on the black market as well as in more seemly forms of commerce."

"And I suppose I'll have to answer all her questions," Charlotte murmured.

"Play the game right, and she'll give you more answers than you have to offer her. Just keep up that shy-girl pose you've been assuming," Jack replied. "I can do most of the talking, if you like. Actually, I'm fairly certain Lady Ott will talk enough for all of us."

13.

WHAT DO YOU mean I have to change my dress?" Charlotte protested, but Meg had already turned her around, pulled her jacket off, and begun to unbutton her gown.

"You're wearing traveling clothes. They're meant for daytime only," Meg explained. "You can't be seen in the same gown at dinner. Now lift your arms."

Charlotte complied, but was aghast at the impracticality of changing clothes for the sake of a meal.

"How many times a day do I have to change?" she asked as Meg lifted the dress over Charlotte's head.

"It depends on each day's particular activities— No, don't put your arms down yet," Meg admonished. "We'll have to put you in a finer petticoat as well."

Charlotte's brow crinkled as Meg pulled the petticoat off. Even that plain undergarment was finer than any piece of clothing Charlotte had ever owned, and yet it wouldn't be fine enough for dinner aboard this ship. She shivered, uneasy in her own skin.

"Shhh, Lottie." Meg came around to stand in front of Charlotte and gave her shoulders a little squeeze. "I know it's cold in the stateroom, but we'll have you dressed again in a moment."

Charlotte offered her a limp smile.

Meg pursed her lips, assessing Charlotte's pale face and dark hair. "I think the lavender."

After helping Charlotte into a petticoat with a hem finished in lace and a neckline that Charlotte found disconcertingly low, Meg went to the wardrobe and selected a silk gown in the blue-purple shade of its floral namesake. Despite her protests about changing, Charlotte's breath caught at the sight of the fine silk. She lifted her arms without prompting when Meg approached and let out a tiny sigh of pleasure as the silk slid over her skin.

That pleasant sensation flagged in the face of Charlotte's sudden surprise.

"Is part of the gown missing?" Charlotte asked Meg in alarm. "Or is my petticoat perhaps too large?"

Meg was already buttoning up the dress. "What do you mean?"

"Meg, look." The back of Charlotte's neck began to burn. "You can see everything!"

"Oh, Lottie." Meg tried to cover her giggle. "It's just the fashion."

"The fashion?" Charlotte kept gaping at her exposed bosom.

The traveling gown and spencer she'd worn aboard the Dragonfly had clung to her figure, but fabric had covered her from throat to wrist. The lavender gown Charlotte had just donned was obviously designed to expose that region of her body. Its neck swooped low and wide, baring her shoulders. Its tight, high waist hoisted her breasts up, forcing pale, curving flesh to strain against the silk bodice.

To make matters worse, the gown was accented with silver lace that featured crystal beading. The embellishments ran all along the low bodice and, while exquisite, caught the light whenever Charlotte moved, which could only draw more attention to how much of her skin was showing.

"I can't go to dinner in this."

"Of course you can," Meg replied, handing her a pair of long white gloves. "You look beautiful. I'll fetch the seed-pearl and gold comb for your hair."

"Meg, I can't!" The hot blush that first attacked Charlotte had surrendered to an icy horror. "What will Ash say . . . oh, Athene, what will Jack say?"

Meg had pinned Charlotte's curls up, and now she finished the style by securing the pearl and gold comb toward the back of Charlotte's head. "Jack will not say anything because this is not the Catacombs and he knows he can't play the rake. And as for Ash . . . well, he won't be there, so don't worry about him."

"Where will Ash be?" Charlotte asked, only slightly appeased.

"He'll be with Grave and me," Meg answered. "In the maid and valet dining room."

That's probably for the best, Charlotte thought. She suspected that no matter how sumptuous a feast was set before her this evening, the food would only leave a sour taste behind. So far Charlotte hated everything about this ship. She despised having to simper and pretend shyness rather than speaking her mind. She loathed the way that she was expected to do nothing for herself, but instead required Meg to do something as simple as dress her, while Ash and Grave toted her baggage through the ship to her opulent stateroom and then they slunk away to share an adjacent tiny double bunk. In their current roles, they couldn't even eat a meal with her.

Charlotte had long known the history of the failed War for Independence. She'd learned about the subsequent years in which the Empire hunted down Patriots and shipped them off to internment, and inevitable death, at the Crucible, Boston's notorious prison. She'd heard of the horrible Hanging Tree there, but she'd also heard that by the time the Crucible's prisoners were sent to their executions, they welcomed death.

Most of all, she knew the war and the Empire had taken her parents away. Her mother and father continued the fight, risking their lives each day, while she and Ash hid in the ground waiting for the day they would take up arms for the cause as well. Charlotte had never believed that she could hate the Empire more than she already did, but pretending to be a part of it made her despise it even more.

As if she'd read Charlotte's thoughts, Meg laid a gentle hand against the younger girl's cheek. "It will be all right, Lottie. You're a fighter. Even if that dress doesn't feel like armor, it doesn't change the mettle that's in your blood and bones."

Swallowing her outrage, Charlotte nodded.

Meg turned away when a sharp rap came at the door. "That'll be Jack."

Charlotte fidgeted, wanting to put her hand to her throat so her gloved arm would cover at least some bare skin, but she couldn't spend all of dinner clutching at her neck. She forced herself to face the door and stand still.

"Meg," Charlotte heard Jack say, "Ash took Grave to the servants' dining room. They'll expect you there."

"Of course," Meg said, then she stepped aside to let Jack in.

He stopped just inside the doorway and stared at Charlotte. She braced herself, standing with her spine stiffer than an iron rod as she waited for him to speak. They weren't in the company of strangers yet, so Jack had no call to leave her be.

It was all she could do to not run and snatch a pelisse from the wardrobe to cover herself.

Jack kept staring. A funny expression took hold of his face. His jaw began to twitch.

Is he trying not to laugh? Charlotte's hands fisted in her white gloves.

Jack looked at the floor, drawing a deep breath. Stepping close to her, Jack reached out and took her right fist in both his hands and raised it to his lips.

"My lady."

Charlotte remained stone-still, staring at him in disbelief. *Was that all he had to say?*

When Meg politely cleared her throat, Charlotte stammered, "Lieutenant Winter."

Jack grimaced at the title, but offered Charlotte his arm. "Shall we join the Lord and Lady Ott for dinner?"

"If we must," Charlotte replied, taking his elbow.

Meg curtsied as they left the stateroom, and Charlotte groaned inwardly. It seemed that no one was bothered by all this role-playing the way she was. Admittedly, she hadn't seen her brother since he left the arrival lounge, trying not to glower while he hefted Charlotte's belongings from the ship. Surely Ash was as uncomfortable as she was, and probably furious to boot—he was accustomed to giving orders, and here he would have to defer to almost everyone. Charlotte found that notion both comforting and unsettling.

As Jack escorted Charlotte through the ship, she accepted begrudgingly that the *Hector*'s gilded halls awed her. Metals of every hue had been beaten, bent, molded, and married to gemstones, creating tapestry-like panels that covered the walls. It appeared that the designers of HMCS *Hector* thought it a crime to leave any surface without ornamentation.

They passed from the staterooms onto a landing, where began a great winding staircase carved of ebony. Jack remained uncharacteristically silent as they descended the steps. She observed that he hadn't been forced to change his dress for dinner, though the shirt beneath his officer's coat was crisp enough that Charlotte suspected it was new since their voyage. Guiding her through the halls, Jack walked too stiffly, as if the uniform he wore had begun to transform him from the scoundrel she'd known into a tin soldier.

Charlotte wished he would say something, anything, to put her at ease. Her nerves were holding her own tongue captive, and she supposed that Jack might be suffering the same malady.

In contrast to their silence, the dining room was abuzz with conversation. Jack paused at the edge of the great room; Charlotte assumed he was searching for the Otts' table.

Finding them might be a challenge, thought Charlotte.

The formal dining hall lay in the *Hector*'s belly. Its floors matched the polished ebony of the staircase they'd just descended. A dozen or more tables, dressed in crisp white linen, awaited dinner guests. Above the tables, lighting had been cleverly masked as entertainment. A circus in miniature played out over the diners' heads. Shimmering globes outlined the silhouette of a great tent, beneath which mechanical actors performed their roles.

"There they are," Jack announced as Charlotte watched a tiny man ride a tiny unicycle along a tiny tightrope.

The location of the Otts' table bespoke their social status. Lady Ott was seated at the head of the dining hall, the table perched in front of one of the giant viewing portals featured in the walls. The next table over was the largest in the room. There, a uniformed man with a solemn face and heavy black beard was intoning to a group of like-bearded gentlemen who hung on his every word. Given the man's dress and his supplicants, Charlotte guessed him to be the captain.

Lady Ott stretched out a hand in welcome as Charlotte and Jack approached.

"Miss Marshall, you are radiant! Wherever did you come by silks in that hue?" Lady Ott said, patting the seat of the chair next to her. "Sit beside me, dove."

If Charlotte had thought her lavender gown to be scandalous, Lady Ott's sapphire blue dress was downright obscene. Every time the woman moved, Charlotte feared that Lady Ott's ample bosom would explode out of its bodice, which made it rather difficult not to stare while awaiting that inevitable disaster.

Jack pulled the chair out for Charlotte and tucked her close to the table after she sat, which made her feel rather like a child being settled into bed. She was grateful, however, when he sat on the other side of her.

"My husband is just having a word with the ship's captain," Lady Ott told them. "He should join us momentarily."

No sooner had she finished speaking than a man loomed at their table. Jack stood up immediately, and Charlotte thought to rise, but Jack's firm hand pressed down on her shoulder, forcing her to stay seated.

"My Lord Ott." Jack inclined his head in respect.

Lord Ott looked like a boulder with arms, legs, and a head, but not much of a neck.

"I don't believe I've had the pleasure, young master," Lord Ott replied.

Lady Ott turned in her chair to address her husband. "I chanced upon this lovely pair in the arrival lounge, my dear."

"Chanced upon?" Lord Ott guffawed, and Charlotte decided he was more like a bear than a boulder. A bear that could crush her with an embrace or smother her with his shaggy gray and silver beard. "More like ambushed, I'd wager."

"Oh, you!" Lady Ott giggled when her husband pinched her plump cheek.

Jack smiled tolerantly before saying, "I have the pleasure of knowing you by reputation. I'm Jack Winter, flight lieutenant of Her Imperial Majesty's Air Brigade, Fourth Squadron."

Lord Ott's bushy eyebrows lifted. "Winter, eh? The wing commander?"

"I'm afraid not, my lord," Jack answered, and Charlotte heard a bit of iron in his reply.

"But still Admiral Winter's boy?" Lord Ott queried.

Jack nodded.

"Well then, you'd better start building yourself up, lad," Lord Ott told Jack. "That brother of yours is the toast of New York. Time that we start hearing stories of your exploits."

"Commodore Winter does the family proud," Jack said stiffly. "I doubt he can be eclipsed."

"Ah, but the fun's all in trying, my boy!" Lord Ott boomed. "Keep your brother looking over his shoulder, that's what I say!"

Charlotte tensed when Lord Ott's bright gaze settled on her. "And who do we have here?"

Lady Ott tittered in her chair, but Jack spoke first. "I have the pleasure of bringing Lady Charlotte Marshall to the Floating City for her first season."

"So the hunt begins. No doubt all the hounds will be chasing after this one." Lord Ott snatched Charlotte's hand out of her lap and kissed it noisily. At first she was taken aback, but the smile he offered her when he released her hand was genuinely warm and bursting with mirth. Charlotte found herself smiling back at the big man.

"I remember how great a hunt I had to catch this one,"

Lord Ott told them as he took the chair at the round table on the other side of his wife. "Ah, the pursuits of youth. Let's drink to that!"

Charlotte further warmed to the rotund man when he gave his wife an adoring look before waggling his eyebrows at her jiggling bosom. Jack covered his burst of laughter with a cough, but the besotted pair paid him no mind.

Lord Ott beckoned to a waiter, and soon each of the golden goblets at their table was brimming with ruby wine.

"To young love!" Lord Ott bellowed, so loudly that a few heads turned to gaze in his direction. When the other passengers noted who the proclaimant was, however, they smiled and nodded in approval—Lord Ott appeared to be quite popular among his fellows.

Charlotte, Jack, and Lady Ott raised their glasses. "To young love."

When Charlotte spoke the words, she glanced at Jack. He was looking right back at her. She quickly averted her gaze, as the wine spurred heat through her veins. Surely it was the wine.

Despite her bare shoulders, Charlotte's skin felt hot. Too hot. She wished she could take her gloves off, but Meg had reminded her that gloves remained on until dinner was served. Thus, she was relieved the waiter returned bearing silver chafing dishes and lifted the lid to reveal mussels steamed in a white wine broth.

Charlotte stripped off her gloves with as much decorum as she could muster. The shellfish were tender, and Charlotte savored the delicate flavors of the broth.

"So, Lieutenant Winter," Lord Ott addressed Jack, "how did you come by such precious cargo? I'd think one of your station would be flying missions for the Empire, not escorting her virgins. Though how one would win such an assignment is valuable intelligence indeed!"

"Roger!" Lady Ott gasped. Red-faced, she turned to Charlotte. "You must pardon my husband, Miss Marshall."

Charlotte was trying too hard not to choke on a mussel to reply.

Even Jack appeared flustered. "Uh . . . my lord, I don't—"

"A thousand pardons, ladies." Chortling, Lord Ott blew a kiss to his wife. "And, Lieutenant Winter, you must forgive me for not being able to resist teasing your ward. My real intention was to inquire about your service."

Jack managed to regain his composure. "Ah, yes. My most recent assignment was training new combat pilots in the Empire's Caribbean holdings."

"Mmmm." Lord Ott nodded, folding his hands around his keg of a belly. "I've heard there's a renewed fear that the French will strike at the islands rather than along the Mississippi."

"It's hard to know what rumors have substance when it comes to France's intentions," Jack replied.

"And the Resistance, of course?" Lord Ott continued. "No telling what those rascals are up to."

"No good, to be sure," Jack said, taking a sip of wine.

Ott smiled before he said, "If a storm's to come, may the wind be with us."

Jack stiffened, but he tipped his goblet toward Lord Ott. "May the wind be with us."

As servants appeared to whisk away porcelain dishes, Lady Ott clucked her tongue. "The men will no doubt spend the entirety of dinner discussing this dreadful war. We need not bother; let's talk of pleasant things. Tell me, Miss Marshall, have you had any suitors?"

Two thoughts jumped into Charlotte's head. The first: she didn't find talk of the war at all dreadful. She was rather desperate to hear it. The second: she had no idea how to answer Lady Ott's question.

The waiter placed a steaming bowl of cream-based fish soup before Charlotte as she tried to come up with an answer.

"No need to confess, my dear," Lady Ott said, taking Charlotte's delayed response as reluctance. "I've no doubt that a bevy of gentlemen have pressed for your hand. However, I must commend your father's patience. No need to pass you off to an islander before you've taken your turn about the city."

Charlotte decided that nodding was her best course.

Lady Ott rewarded her with a beatific smile. "What would you prefer? Would you like to be a plantation mistress? Or have you longed to join the esteemed ladies who stroll the golden streets of the Colonial Platform?"

What strange choices Charlotte had in the fictional life of Lady Charlotte Marshall. Did the sum of her existence lie solely in whom she married? Charlotte had never imagined either possibility that Lady Ott had presented. One life on an island with a fortune tied to sugarcane harvests. Another in the colony's greatest metropolis. But both were tied to the identity of her imaginary husband—who he was seemed to matter a great deal more than anything about Lady Charlotte Marshall.

Without meaning to, Charlotte found herself glancing at Jack. He was deep in conversation with Lord Ott. Charlotte turned back when she heard Lady Ott draw a sharp breath.

"I'd advise against it, sweetling," Lady Ott said, shaking her head. "No matter how dashing, an officer will always be away, and you'll find yourself quite lonely. My husband travels the world for commerce, but he always takes me along on these mercantile adventures."

She nodded in Jack's direction. "That one won't show you the world. A wife is not taken to war."

Charlotte felt blood draining from her cheeks. Had she linked husbands and Jack in the same thought?

Watching the younger woman's face pale, Lady Ott patted Charlotte's hand. "Oh, dear, dear. I didn't mean to upset you. Of course it's only natural to become attached to the young officer who has escorted you from your father's estate to the city. But believe me, Miss Marshall, when you make your debut, you'll find the young men will be clamoring to catch your eye. As my husband would say, you shouldn't make a purchase until you've surveyed all the merchandise."

Managing a nod and a weak smile, Charlotte turned her attention to her soup. Though delicious, the heavy cream settled poorly in her stomach. After a few spoonfuls, Charlotte pushed her plate away. A waiter appeared instantly to remove her bowl.

"A delicate appetite, eh?" Lord Ott broke off his conversation with Jack to address Charlotte.

Jack snorted, but quickly faked a sneeze. Charlotte pursed her lips, but didn't give him the dagger-glare she wanted to. They both knew that Charlotte's appetite was anything but delicate. She always came back from scouting trips and scavenging runs absolutely ravenous. But the strange surroundings of the ship and excessive richness of the food were tempering her hunger.

"Perhaps the next course will be more to your liking," Lord Ott offered as new dishes were placed before them. Steaming slices of roast pork, a generous pour of gravy, and spiced baked apples had been heaped upon the plates. Charlotte doubted she'd manage more than a bite or two.

Charlotte leaned over to Jack. "How many courses are there?"

"Four," Jack replied. "Five if you count the cheese and fruit course that comes after dessert."

"*After* dessert?" Charlotte rested her hand on her stomach. How could anyone eat like this on a regular basis?

A bell toned throughout the dining room. All around them applause broke out and diners rose from their chairs.

"What's happening?" Charlotte asked.

"They've sighted New York." Lord Ott stood and came to Charlotte, offering his hand.

"You don't mind, lad?" he asked Jack.

"No, my lord," Jack replied. "I've no doubt you're a better man to introduce Miss Marshall to the city than I. And I'll take advantage of my chance to speak with your lovely wife."

Lady Ott giggled and accepted Jack's arm.

They left the table and walked the short distance to gaze out the giant viewing portal. Though the ship was still well away from the city, even at a distance New York rose up against the dark of sea and sky like a great heap of gold and jewels hoarded in the shadows of some dragon's lair.

"Athene's helm," Charlotte breathed, forgetting herself.

Lady Ott gasped and covered her mouth. Jack cast a reprimanding glance at Charlotte, but Lord Ott guffawed.

"Never mind my wife, Miss Marshall." Lord Ott smiled generously at Charlotte, then smirked at Jack. "They make them saucier in the islands, don't they, lad."

"Indeed, sir." Jack nodded solemnly, and Charlotte decided she was going to have to keep a running list of affronts to yell at him for when they were alone.

"The Floating City of New York." Lord Ott moved his hand across the portal as if opening a curtain. "The wonder of the Empire. Jewel of the colonies. A marvel of art and engineering, its Great Wheels of Fortune connect five floating platforms. Each platform hovers at a different height, and of course, the closer one lives to the heavens, the higher one's station on this good earth. New York is the only city in the world that floats thus, gazing down on the world just as the Empire watches over its citizens."

"It's extraordinary," Charlotte said, though she didn't know if she was captivated or frightened by the sight.

"You think it's stunning from here, my lady," Lord Ott said. "But I'd wager you shall nigh faint at New York's glory when you walk the gilded streets of the Colonial Platform and marvel at the wonders of the Arts Platform."

"I hope I will not faint, my lord," Charlotte replied. "Lest I miss any of the brilliance of the Floating City."

"That's a good girl." Lord Ott winked at her. Leaning closer, he whispered, "And if you can sneak away from your watchful soldier, you must visit the Tinkers' Faire. Once they find you a husband, he'll doubtless forbid you from frequenting that motley place. But I say innocence is overrated, and you'd have a damn good time in the Commons. Have your fun before you're put on display in some colonial mansion."

His words perplexed Charlotte, but it seemed like he expected her to blush, so she tried to make her laughter sound scandalized and she lowered her eyelashes.

"We should return to the table," Lady Ott announced. "Our meats grow cold while we dally. We'll dock at the city soon enough."

Lord Ott began to lead Charlotte back to her seat, but she pulled away. "Pardon me, Lord and Lady Ott, but I'm afraid the excitement of seeing New York has affected me. I must return to my stateroom and lie down."

Charlotte had been worried her departure would cause a fuss, but her dining companions took the news calmly.

"Of course, dear." Lady Ott patted Charlotte's cheek. "These travels are always trying to one's constitution. And it being your first, you must be simply overwhelmed."

Charlotte nodded, though she couldn't believe how silly these Imperial ladies must be that they could plead faintness so easily.

"I'll see you back to your rooms." Jack moved toward Charlotte, but she stepped away.

"No, thank you." Charlotte waved him off. "I can find my own way. Please enjoy the rest of dinner."

Those words made Lord Ott's eyebrows lift, but Charlotte turned her back on them before anyone could make further comment. She forced herself to depart at a steady pace until she was out of the dining room and up the stair. But when she reached the upper hall and found it empty, she ran.

14.

WHEN CHARLOTTE REACHED her stateroom, she discovered she wasn't alone. Ashley sat in a stiff-backed chair alongside a writing table. It was obvious he'd been waiting for her.

"Enjoy your dinner?" Ash asked.

"It was a bit much for me," Charlotte admitted. "Do people in the city really eat five courses every night?"

Ash smirked. "The ones living on the top platforms do. Excess is the benchmark of Imperial success. But those at the bottom of the city are pretty much scavenging like we are." He looked expectantly at the open door behind Charlotte. "Where's Jack?"

"Still at dinner," Charlotte said. "He's chatting up some bigwig merchant."

"Fair enough." Ash shrugged. "Close the door, Charlotte."

She complied and then looked at her brother expectantly. Ash withdrew a slender object from his jacket.

"I should have given you this before we left the Catacombs," Ash told her. "But I got distracted. Here."

Charlotte took the object from him. Silver glinted at the end Charlotte grasped, and the rest of the piece was sheathed in leather. Guessing what it was, Charlotte drew the blade free. It was barely longer than her palm.

"You want me to take up needlework?" Charlotte teased.

Ash offered a flat smile. "It might not be Pocky, but if you stab a man in the eye with that, it will kill him quickly enough."

"And messily enough," Charlotte added.

"You'll be able to hide it easily under your skirt," Ash said. "There's a small loop on the sheath. Tie the blade to your calf with a leather cord."

Charlotte set the stiletto aside and sat on the chaise longue. "How are the others?"

"Grave is odd as ever, but at least he knows enough to keep quiet," Ash said. His voice softened. "And Meg is . . . Meg. I should get back to them. It's unseemly for servants to loiter in their masters' staterooms."

"All these rules make my head ache." Charlotte dropped back against the chaise, throwing her arm over her eyes.

Ash laughed quietly. "Just be thankful you don't have

to haul that trunk around. I could swear Jack filled it with bricks and not dresses."

Charlotte heard the door open, then Ash asked, "Do you want me to have Meg bring you a tonic?"

"No," she answered, without moving her arm off her closed eyes. "I just need to sit quietly, and I'll be fine."

The door clicked shut, and Charlotte discovered that her last words to Ash had been a lie, at least in part. Though Charlotte's headache departed after a bit of sitting in the silence of her room, a new restlessness seized her. She took a few turns around the lavishly appointed stateroom. She considered reading one of the books that lined the built-in shelves, but they all appeared to be stories of the Empire's glory, and Charlotte felt she'd had her fill of that tonight.

Despite the spacious accommodations, as Charlotte paced the stateroom, she felt oddly confined. The weight of satin and velvet upholstery, the heaviness of carved ebony paneled walls, began to press in on her. She needed to get out of that room and drink in fresh air. Charlotte fled and wandered the ship's halls until she found a staircase that she followed up until she reached the *Hector*'s promenade deck.

A canopy attempted to shield the deck from the massive balloons that held the ship aloft, but the thin veil did little to muffle the roar whenever new bursts of burning air shot up into the balloons. Charlotte walked to the edge of the deck, where the high iron railing curved up and in, reaching well over her head, doubtless to keep a sudden gust of wind from pushing a hapless passenger over the side of the ship.

The sky had turned to ink above, and stars speckled the heavens. She walked along the rail, much preferring the wind in her hair and the open space of the promenade to the interior of the ship.

"Enjoying an evening stroll, miss?"

Charlotte pivoted to find a uniformed man approaching. She stiffened until he was close enough that shadows no longer hid his face.

"Jack." She laughed nervously. "I still hardly recognize you in that getup."

"That makes two of us," he said.

Running her palms over the silk of her skirts, Charlotte said, "I suppose I look ridiculous."

"Not at all," Jack replied. "The current fashions suit you. If I didn't know better, I'd assume you were one of the girls I grew up with."

"What were they like . . . the girls you knew?" Charlotte's skin prickled as she asked the question. She wasn't certain she wanted to know the answer.

Jack shook his head. "Not worth talking about. There's something I want to show you."

He crooked his elbow toward her.

Charlotte frowned at the gesture. "What are you doing?"

"Offering you my arm. I thought you'd be used to that by now."

"But we're alone," Charlotte countered.

When Charlotte continued to frown at Jack, he snickered. "It's expected. Besides, Ash shouldn't have let you wander above deck alone. Young ladies of good breeding don't go without an escort. Meg should be with you. Or Ash."

"I don't think Ash is taking to his role." Charlotte laughed.

Jack smiled at her. "No doubt. Now take my arm, and we'll have a proper turn about the foredeck . . . and then some."

"And then some?"

"You'll see," Jack replied, then wagged his elbow at her.

Charlotte slipped her arm through Jack's. He brought his elbow back to his side, drawing her close beside him. The wool of his jacket scratched her skin, but Charlotte didn't mind. She noticed how she could feel the warmth of his body through the fabric, a sharp contrast to the rapidly cooling night air.

Jack guided Charlotte up the deck to the fore of the ship. He stopped in front of a metal hutch that reminded her a bit of the Catacombs' wheelhouse. Jack rapped on the hutch door, and a man whose clothing marked him a member of the ship's crew stepped out. Taking in Jack's uniform, the crewman straightened up and saluted.

"May I be of assistance, sir?"

"I hope you may," Jack said. He stepped forward and said something in tones too low for Charlotte to hear.

The crewman glanced at Charlotte, smirked, and told Jack, "Of course, sir. Go on up."

Jack took Charlotte's hand and led her into the hutch. Its resemblance to the wheelhouse was even more striking on the inside. Charlotte recognized the engineering of a line and pulley system, but while the baskets in the Catacombs departed and arrived outside the control room, this hutch contained a small basket that was only half enclosed.

Charlotte glanced back toward the door. The crewman leered at her, and she quickly turned away.

"What in Athene's name did you say to him?" she asked Jack.

Jack stepped into the basket and helped Charlotte in after. "Something that would get us in here."

The metal weave that edged the basket rose only to her knees, and the round platform upon which they stood was barely large enough to accommodate two people. Jack reached to a crank on the hutch wall and gave it half a dozen rapid turns.

"You'll want to hold on to me," Jack said as the basket lurched upward.

Charlotte had little choice but to do as he said. She wrapped her arms around Jack, hanging on tight as the line dragged the basket away from the deck and up into the sky. The wind tore strands of hair free of Meg's carefully placed pins to whip Charlotte's cheeks.

Up and up and up they went, slowing only when they'd reached the height of the great balloons.

"Here we are," Jack announced.

Charlotte blinked away the tears that the wind had pulled from her eyes during their rapid ascent. The basket swayed as Jack tethered it to the brass rail that ringed the lookout station.

"Welcome to the crow's nest," Jack told Charlotte. "The finest spot on a bloat float like the *Hector*."

Charlotte laughed as she stepped onto the crow's nest. She was grateful for its stability in comparison to the constant swaying of the transport basket.

"A bloat float?" she repeated.

"You think a beast of a ship like this has any maneuverability?" Jack answered. "There's a reason cows don't have wings. It's common knowledge at the air academy that this is the assignment for pilots who don't show promise enough to merit a combat rank. I'd sooner serve a sentence in Boston than captain one of these."

"Don't say that," Charlotte said with a shudder. "Nothing is worse than Boston."

"I'm sorry," Jack replied quickly. "Of course you're right."

He took her hand and led her to the opposite side of the lookout. From their new vantage point, the Floating City glittered, its mélange of colors and lights beckoning. But the city's allure couldn't compete with the sky that spread above them with its infinite stars.

Casting a sidelong glance at Jack, Charlotte saw that

his eyes were fixed on the sky, and she joined him in quiet stargazing. Her fingers were still laced in his. She wondered if he could feel the way her pulse stuttered at her wrist.

After a long silence, Jack squeezed her hand. "No matter what contraption the tinkers are touting as their latest breakthrough, it's the stars that guide us. They always will. At the academy you have to memorize star charts before you ever board an aircraft."

Charlotte heard the longing in Jack's voice. She lifted her free hand, moving her fingers through the air as if the constellations were a delicate pattern of lace she could touch. The open sky beckoned to her. She wished she were weightless and floating ever up into the softly gleaming expanse.

"I could stay up here forever," she breathed. "How did you leave this? This endless sky. Your own ship. All traded for our life in the Catacombs, buried under rock and water. A life where we almost never see the stars."

"Because it isn't the stars that give orders," he said quietly. "If they did, then maybe I would have stayed."

They turned toward each other in the same moment. Charlotte went very still, not knowing what to do. Her blood thrummed with each heartbeat.

Jack reached out, snatching a loose tendril of Charlotte's dark hair from the wind's grasp. He tucked the stray lock behind her ear. His thumb grazed her cheek and lingered there.

"Jack," Charlotte whispered. She had nothing else to say, but she'd wanted to speak his name while he was close. While he was touching her.

Jack broke their gaze. "We should head back down. The night watch will be coming up soon."

Disappointment rattled through Charlotte's bones, but she nodded as Jack led her to the basket. She was relieved to see that he would control their descent with a hand-brake, and she hoped that meant the trip down wouldn't be at the breakneck pace of the ascent.

"You should hold on." Jack's voice was hoarse, and Charlotte felt his body tense when she slipped her arms around him. She was desperate to know what he was thinking. Did Jack suddenly not want to be alone with her? But hadn't he been the one to seek her out and bring her to this place, so isolated and beautiful? Charlotte's mind swam with questions, and her rapid pulse refused to abate.

Jack released the lever very slowly and they began to drift away from the crow's nest toward the deck. His face was turned from her so she looked at him in profile, but she could see his frustration in the way his jaw twitched. His fingers closed on the brake, slowing them even more. Slowing the basket until they stopped completely.

"Jack," Charlotte murmured his name once more, but this time followed it with a question. "What are you doing?"

"I don't know." He looked at her and drew a slow breath. His gaze moved from her eyes to her lips and stayed there.

Her heart jumped as she asked, "Do you want to kiss me?"

His fist clamped down hard on the brake and they came to a stop, hanging in space between the ship's deck and the crow's nest.

"I shouldn't kiss you," he said, still looking at her mouth.

She smiled slightly. "Because of Ash?"

"That's one reason," he replied with a half smile that quickly vanished. "But not the most important one. There are others."

What other reasons? Charlotte searched Jack's face for an answer, but found none.

Suspended in the cool night air, they began to spin as if they were dancing without moving their feet. She didn't want to leave this moment. She wanted to float in the sky in Jack's arms as long as she could. The swell of feeling threw Charlotte off balance. This was Jack. Jack, who could rarely be anything other than annoying. Jack, whom she'd sworn not to speak to for at least a month last year, but who had then made her so angry she'd had to yell at him. Who teased her at any opportunity. But with utter clarity, Charlotte became aware in that moment how much she adored all those things about him.

What had provoked this sudden turn of her heart? Charlotte wanted to believe she wasn't a ninny enough to swoon at Jack's dapper uniform, nor pine after him because of his secret past.

A voice deep inside her whispered that the turn should be viewed as neither surprising nor sudden; that Charlotte knew well enough that her scorn for Jack had long served as a shield against much more dangerous sentiments. Jack challenged her, treated her as a worthy opponent in wit and war. He made her blood boil, but it was with a heat she longed for in ways she was only beginning to comprehend.

Though she was already holding on to Jack, she pulled herself closer still. "I didn't ask if you should. I asked if you wanted to."

The arm Jack held her with tightened and she was fitted against his body. She could feel his warmth pushing away the brisk wind.

"I want to, Charlotte."

Jack is going to kiss me, Charlotte thought. She was uncomfortably aware of how very much she wanted him to. More than she could stand. Charlotte closed her eyes and lifted her chin.

The only kiss came from the cool wind that touched her lips. The handbrake squeaked and then the wind was rushing over them as they sailed down, down, down to the deck far below.

Charlotte's eyes flew open as they hit the deck hard. She would have fallen, but Jack still held her tight against him.

"Everything all right, sir?" The crewman was standing in the hutch's doorway.

Charlotte turned her back on Jack and pushed her way past the crewman. Not caring if she drew attention to herself, Charlotte ran down the deck. She heard Jack calling her name, but she didn't slow.

She'd almost reached the staircase that would let her escape the deck when Jack caught her arm. He wheeled her around.

"Charlotte, don't do this," he hissed at her. "Calm down."

"Calm down?" It was all Charlotte could do not to screech. "What was that? Why did you take me up there?"

Jack wouldn't meet her gaze. "Because I wanted to show you something I love. Because . . . I want you."

Charlotte moved close to him. Her arms encircled his neck, and she would have fastened her mouth to his, but Jack grasped her forearms and firmly dislodged himself from her embrace.

"Stop," Jack told her. "I can't kiss you."

Humiliation seized her limbs, and she began to tremble. "Why?"

"Because I care for you, but I'm not who you think I am." He leaned in as if to place a chaste kiss on her forehead, but Charlotte shoved him back.

"*You* stop," she snapped. "If this is your game, I don't want to play."

He gazed at her, face pale as the starlight, and slowly nodded. "It might be best if that's how you see it."

Charlotte turned away from him so he couldn't see the tears that pricked her eyes.

"Let me take you back to your quarters," Jack said.

When Charlotte didn't answer, he added, "I have to . . . for appearances' sake."

Lifting her chin, Charlotte took his arm. But she didn't speak another word to him that night.

15.

GIVEN THAT JACK was Charlotte's escort, she found it impractical to avoid him, so instead she ignored him. Speaking to him was out of the question, except to acknowledge his queries in short, clipped sentences, or even better, with one-word answers, and she preferred not looking at him. Should her eyes wander to Jack's face, Charlotte's body reacted as if she'd been punched in the gut.

Jack's behavior the previous night had left Charlotte in a tizzy. She was furious, but sad. Outraged, but deflated. Her conflicting emotions were unpleasant enough, but even worse was the simple fact that she had no idea what to do about them. Charlotte couldn't puzzle out Jack, nor could she stop herself from mulling over the scene, despite how miserable it made her. Every time she blinked, Jack's face was there, inches from hers. Her skin remembered his touch too well. Maybe she'd been wrong to want something more than verbal fencing with Jack.

As the *Hector*'s crew tossed mooring lines to waiting docksmen, Charlotte tried to set her mind to the coming day. New York was no longer a glittering object she could look down upon from afar; the morning had revealed it to be a behemoth that looked down on her and all the other puny arrivals at the airship docks.

The city dwarfed the massive dirigibles tethered to the military platform. The docks buzzed with activity. Swarms of passengers stepped onto automated staircases that had been rolled out to meet the arrivals. Brawny dockworkers shouted commands and gave directions as cargo was off-loaded from the ships. Smaller patrol aircraft zigged and zagged above them. Bells clanged as trolleys sped along the platforms, whisking travelers from the docks into the heart of the city.

Charlotte lifted her skirts, taking care that the fabric didn't snag in the staircase's moving parts. Jack stood rigidly alongside Charlotte. She glanced at him and found his expression bleak. His mood worried her. Ash had explained that while they were in the city, Jack's childhood home would serve as their residence. But judging by Jack's demeanor, this homecoming wasn't one he looked forward to.

When they reached the end of the staircase, Charlotte waited for Meg and fell into step beside her, letting Jack lead them forward but preferring to keep company with her "maid" rather than take the proffered arm of her sullen escort. Grave and Ash hauled the baggage off a ramp that adjoined the staircase, bringing up the rear of their party.

While Jack seemed to despair at their arrival in the city, Grave's expression could only be described as bewildered. Charlotte wondered if the strange boy's continued amnesia grated on Ashley's nerves. Although he'd been dressed in garb from the city, Grave gave no sign of familiarity with his surroundings.

Jack led them to join a throng of travelers awaiting the next trolley. The trolley that slowed to a stop before the small crowd boasted the same rich ornamentation of Charlotte's stateroom aboard the *Hector*. Its exterior featured carved ebony paneling accented with brass. Glass windows had been cranked halfway down to allow the fresh air of the fine morning to circulate through the car. The men and women of New York's society began to board the trolley. Before Charlotte could follow, Jack turned to Ash.

"Servants and luggage on the rear car," Jack told him. "Disembark in five stops."

Ash nodded, and Grave followed Charlotte's brother silently as they carried the luggage to a simple flatbed enclosed only by a brass railing and partially covered by a simple canvas canopy. Charlotte presumed the canopy was meant to protect the luggage in case of rain—not the servants.

Meg started after Ash, but Charlotte stopped her, saying, "Meg, wait."

Turning to Jack, Charlotte asked, "Can't my maid accompany me in the trolley?"

Meg and Jack exchanged a look, but Jack answered, "Yes. Ladies' maids are permitted in the main car."

"Come on, then." Charlotte took Meg's arm and joined the boarding line for the trolley without waiting for Jack.

Charlotte found a window seat, and Meg settled next to her. Out of the corner of her eye, Charlotte saw Jack sit on the bench directly in front of them, but she kept her face turned toward the window. The trolley bell clanged, and the car moved forward as an overhead cable drew it along the tracks. As they sped away from the docks, a chiming melody sounded above their heads. Charlotte looked up to see that the inner ring of the trolley's ceiling was decorated with automated men in uniform bearing tiny instruments. The other passengers paid no mind as miniature drums, bells, and pipes sounded "God Save the Queen."

Jack leaned back in his seat, turning his head slightly toward them. "By the time we get out of the city, I guarantee you'll hate the sound of this song."

Meg covered her giggle with her hand, but Charlotte didn't acknowledge Jack. She felt a twinge of guilt when she noticed his shoulders slump. Gazing out the window to distract herself, Charlotte watched the docks give way to neat rows of squat marble buildings fronted with Doric columns.

Unlike the docks, which had been bustling with passengers, crewmen, and workers, the Military Platform appeared to be occupied entirely by members of its name-sake. Everywhere Charlotte looked, she saw uniformed men—some hurrying from one building to the next, others in formation, chanting as they performed drills in public squares.

Though among the upper tiers of the Floating City, the Military Platform that housed the docks was not the pinnacle of the metropolis, and soon the trolley began to ascend, towed up a bridge until the tracks leveled out at the next platform. This level of the city bore no resemblance to the spare, meticulously neat Military Platform. The geometric lines of the former level were replaced by swirling sculptures of dancers, gods and goddesses of the Greek pantheon, fantastic creatures. Even the massive coliseum, in front of which the trolley stopped, was softened by flowers and vines carved into its marble face.

"It's beautiful," Charlotte murmured, gazing at the golden orb onto which a map of the world had been etched.

"The Arts Platform," Meg surprised Charlotte by saying. "I thought it would have changed, but it's just as I remember."

Charlotte turned to Meg. "I can't believe you once lived here."

Meg laughed quietly. "I'm sorry we haven't had a chance to speak of my past, Charlotte. I hope you understand that it wasn't my intention to deceive you."

"Why haven't you talked about it before now?" Charlotte said, frowning. Until a few days ago, she'd assumed that Meg had been brought from the Resistance camps, like Charlotte and Ash had. Meg was already living in the Catacombs when Charlotte and Ashley, aged five and seven, had come to join the other children.

"When my mother sent me away, she told me the past was best left behind," Meg said to Charlotte.

Questions danced on Charlotte's tongue, but she stayed quiet. Meg had spoken in low tones so that none of the other passengers would hear her over the whir of the trolley and the ceaseless tinkling of the Imperial melody. Even so, inquiring after Meg's history in public was unwise. Swallowing her curiosity, Charlotte remained silent as the trolley moved on, taking them up another bridge. When they reached the next platform, the trolley's stops became more frequent.

Each time the car halted, passengers disembarked, strolling toward wrought-iron gates that opened to manicured gardens, which in turn decorated the foreground of mansion after mansion. Though not clad exclusively in ebony like her stateroom had been, the fashion of wood bound with metal flourished here as well. The homes of New York's elite were tall, narrow, and boxy. They came in glossy shades of chestnut, mahogany, maple, and oak, accented with brass, iron, steel, and even gold.

The trolley moved on, stopped, and moved on again until only a handful of passengers remained. When the bell clanged at the next stop, Jack rose. Meg and Charlotte trailed after him. Once off the trolley, Charlotte turned to make sure Ash and Grave had disembarked with the baggage. She saw them trundling in her direction, bearing their cumbersome load.

Jack crossed the street, which Charlotte noted had cobblestones that were indeed washed with a golden hue as Lord Ott had promised. He stopped in front of an iron gate. While the fence enclosing this mansion was in the same style as the others, the house behind it was not. Jack's home had been constructed in the manner of the Military Platform's architecture. It was broad and squat, formed of pristine marble. The front of the mansion offered few hints that this place was a residence: the acanthus leaves of its Corinthian columns were gilded, and the columns themselves were inlaid with vines of jade. The building projected a cold, unwelcoming atmosphere.

"Let's get this over with," Charlotte heard Jack mutter before he opened the gate.

They were halfway up the path through the front garden, which Charlotte noted was filled with hedges sculpted into heroic figures from Greek myths, when the front door opened to reveal a man clad in a servant's uniform.

"Mr. Jack." The man smiled broadly. "Your brother told us to expect you today."

"Hello, Thompson." Jack's reply sounded warm but weary.

Thompson was an old man with only a few wisps of white hair still clinging to his scalp.

"The staff has prepared the rooms according to your

brother's instructions," Thompson continued, as his gaze settled on Charlotte. "This must be the Lady Charlotte Marshall?"

"Yes," Jack answered for Charlotte.

Thompson teetered forward into an awkward bow. "My lady, the House of Winter is honored by your presence."

Charlotte managed to thank him, though she choked a little on the words, finding his deference unsettling.

"With your permission, my lady," Thompson said, "I'll show your servants to their quarters and instruct them on the rules of the household. Mr. Jack can take you into the parlor for refreshment, which I'm sure you're needing after your long journey."

Before Charlotte could reply, Jack asked Thompson, "My mother?"

"In the courtyard, Mr. Jack," Thompson replied. Charlotte found it strange that his tone was suddenly grieved.

Jack nodded, his voice curt. "I should see her. Please have the refreshments brought to us there."

"As it pleases you, sir." Thompson stepped back to give them entry.

"I'll put Miss Marshall's servants in your charge and see her to the courtyard," Jack told him, hooking an arm around Charlotte's elbow.

Charlotte wanted to protest Jack's steering her around like a ship, but she couldn't make a scene in front of Thompson.

Thompson creaked into a bow again. Jack met Ash's steady gaze and gave a brief nod. Without another word, Ashley, Grave, and Meg followed Thompson into the house and up a grand staircase, leaving Charlotte alone with Jack. She started to pull away from him, ready to chastise him for presuming this type of intimacy with her. Suddenly Jack was holding her hand, squeezing it tight. "Charlotte, about my mother . . ."

"What is it?" Charlotte looked at him, startled by the strain gripping his jaw. The bleakness of his expression stopped her from chiding him as she'd intended.

Just as suddenly, Jack bowed his head and released her hand. "Nothing."

Without another word, Jack led her from the foyer, through a parlor and a study, and then pushed open glass doors to reveal a courtyard in the middle of the house. A balcony ringed the green space, and a fountain bubbled at its heart.

Marble benches faced the fountain, where nymphs and fauns danced. Between the benches was a chaise longue, upholstered in ruby jacquard, its presence jarring in comparison to the tranquility of the courtyard.

A woman was sprawled on the chaise. She wore a rumpled silk dressing gown. At some point, her hair had been expertly piled atop her head, but now the gray-streaked brunette locks were in disarray. One arm hung limply off the side of the chaise, her fingertips nearly touching a tray on the ground that held an empty sherry glass. Her other arm clutched a silk pillow to her chest.

"Give me a moment," Jack said, leaving Charlotte at the edge of the lawn.

He walked to the woman, leaned down, and gave her shoulder a gentle shake. "Mother."

This was Jack's mother? Charlotte didn't know where to safely place her gaze. It seemed rude to stare, but ostensibly Charlotte was in the garden to meet this woman.

"Leave me, Thompson," Lady Winter sighed. "I'm having the loveliest dream. So lovely."

Jack shook her again. "Mother, it's me. It's Jack . . . I've come home."

Lady Winter opened one heavy-lidded eye. "What?"

"Mother." Jack's voice sounded like it was about to break.

Charlotte's chest tightened as she watched the strained exchange between mother and son. She didn't know what she'd expected Jack's family to be like, but she never would have imagined the scene now unfolding before her.

Blinking into the sunlight, Lady Winter pushed herself upright on the chaise. "Jack? My little Jack?"

Jack smiled weakly. "Hopefully not so little anymore."

"Oh, Jack!" Lady Winter threw her arms around her son. "Oh, my dear, how I've missed you."

"And I you, Mother," Jack replied. He pulled back, and she beamed at him, rocking a little on the chaise. Despite

Lady Winter's recognition of her son, something about the woman still seemed off to Charlotte.

Jack asked, "Didn't Coe tell you I was coming?"

"Oh, I'm sure he did," Lady Winter answered with a dismissive wave. "But you know how forgetful I can be. Thompson will have taken care of everything of course. He always does."

"Yes, he does." Jack beckoned to Charlotte, who approached with more than a little trepidation.

Lady Winter caught the movement and squinted in Charlotte's direction. "Have you brought Eleanor to see me? Come here, dear child! Don't be shy."

Charlotte glanced sharply at Jack. *Who is Eleanor?*

Jack shook his head, saying quickly, "It's not Eleanor. Do you recall Coe also telling you we would have a guest?"

"A guest?" Lady Winter's eyes were wide and glassy. "But we never have guests."

"Miss Marshall has come to us from the islands— you'll remember how I've been stationed there," Jack told his mother. "She is an heiress to a sugar plantation, and this is to be her first season."

Lady Winter barely glanced at Charlotte before flopping back onto the chaise with a sigh. "I always wanted to see the islands. Your father said he'd take me one day."

"Father said a lot of things," Jack muttered.

A woman of similar age to Thompson, wearing a simple gray dress and white smock, appeared bearing a tray.

"Where would you like to take your tea, Mr. Jack?"

"Hello, Mrs. Blake." Jack passed a hand over his face as he greeted her. "I trust you're well."

"Nothing to complain about," Mrs. Blake answered. "How nice it is to see you home."

Jack nodded. "We'll take our tea here. You can put the service on the bench."

Mrs. Blake prepared to pour the tea, but Jack said, "Don't worry over that. I can serve the tea."

"As you like, Mr. Jack."

"Mother, do you still take two sugars?" Jack asked.

"Bah, no tea," Lady Winter replied. "Mary, bring me another glass, if you will."

"Yes, Lady Winter," said Mrs. Blake, gathering up the tray beside the chaise.

"Mother." Jack let the sugar spoon go, and it clattered onto the bench. "Take some tea."

Mrs. Blake hesitated, glancing nervously from son to mother.

"I don't want tea." Lady Winter propped herself up on one elbow and glared at Mrs. Blake. "What are you gaping at, you old mare? Another glass, I said."

Mrs. Blake curtsied and hurried off.

"Mother"—Jack snarled the word—"don't speak to Mrs. Blake that way."

"Don't speak to your mother that way!" Lady Winter spat. Her lip began to tremble, and before Charlotte knew what had happened, Jack's mother was weeping.

With a sigh, Jack knelt beside Lady Winter. "It's all right. Don't cry."

"You don't know how hard it is," Lady Winter gasped between her sobs. "I'm so lonely."

"When was Father last home?" Jack asked.

"It's been sixteen months this time. He was supposed to come for the summer," Lady Winter told him, "but he sent a letter. It arrived a few days ago."

"And he's not coming," Jack finished.

Lady Winter began to cry again, and Mrs. Blake reappeared with a glass of sherry.

"Here it is." Mrs. Blake placed the delicate glass into Lady Winter's hand.

"Oh, thank you, Mary." She turned her tearstained face up to look at Mrs. Blake. "You must forgive my ill temper. I forget myself."

"No harm done, my lady. You've tired yourself, that's all." Mrs. Blake gave Jack a meaningful look. "Perhaps you'd prefer to have your tea in the parlor?"

"Yes." Jack stood and watched his mother drain her glass in two swallows.

Mrs. Blake collected the tea service and exited the courtyard. Charlotte wondered if she should follow, but her attention was snared by a strange, high-pitched cry. She turned to see a marvelous bird calling toward the sky.

Charlotte couldn't help but stare. The peacock was vibrant; its cobalt chest and jade neck were unlike any of the small forest birds she knew. Their advantage was camouflage, whereas this creature lived to be seen. Taking notice of her gaze, the peacock preened and fanned out its enormous tail. As the feathers spread, a strange clicking noise reached Charlotte's ears. Her admiration coiled into revulsion. The bird's tail had been reinforced with metal framework, and the many eyes of its feathers did not simply boast gemlike tones, but had been embellished with real jewels. Emeralds and sapphires flashed in the sunlight as the peacock strutted past her.

"Stunning, isn't he?" Lady Winter said, noting Charlotte's gaze. "And very difficult to obtain. My husband, the admiral, had it shipped to me from India. The trick is that the metal grafted onto the feathers must be hollow so the bird doesn't tip over."

"I've never seen anything like it," Charlotte managed, utterly horrified by the bird. Rebuilding a creature to save its life, as Birch had in the case of Moses, was one thing. This bejeweled peacock struck Charlotte as grotesque in its excess.

Lady Winter gave a snort as she lay against the chaise, saying, "Of course you haven't."

"Mother, you've just apologized to Mrs. Blake," Jack chided. "Have a care or you'll have to beg Char—Miss Marshall's pardon as well."

"Mmm-hmmmm." Lady Winter's eyes were closed. A minute later she was snoring.

Jack gazed down at his mother for another moment before shaking his head and turning away. He walked back to the interior doors, leaving Charlotte to trail after him awkwardly. She followed him all the way to the parlor, where Mrs. Blake had left the tea service.

Pouring two cups of tea, Jack added milk and sugar to one cup before handing it to Charlotte with a saucer. He put one spoonful of sugar into his cup. Charlotte sat in a high-backed chair. Jack remained standing, his gaze fixed on Charlotte.

"Well?" he asked.

Charlotte sipped her tea. "Well, what?"

"You don't have anything to say?" Jack's voice was brittle.

"It's not my place," Charlotte told him.

Jack laughed, and tea sloshed over the rim of his cup. "Not your place. By Hephaestus, Charlotte, you already *sound* like you belong here."

He was baiting Charlotte, but she knew that her words weren't what had provoked his anger.

"I just meant that I don't know your mother," Charlotte said, frowning. "And I wouldn't presume to pass judgment."

"By all means, judge freely," Jack snapped. "Judge everything you see in this house, this city."

"Jack." Charlotte spoke his name softly. She hadn't forgotten how angry she was about the previous night, but she couldn't ignore his pain now.

When she didn't speak again, Jack put his teacup aside, dropped onto a leather sofa and buried his face in his hands.

After a while, Charlotte heard Jack's voice, still muffled by his hands. "She wasn't always like this."

Charlotte rose and went to sit beside him. She wanted to ask if Lady Winter was ill, but feared that if it turned out that Jack's mother was simply an intolerable snob, her question would only make Jack feel worse. So Charlotte did the other thing that came to mind. She gently pulled Jack's hands away from his face and held them in her own.

"I didn't want to come back here." Jack clung to her fingers, but he stared at the floor when he spoke. "I never wanted to come back."

16.

MUCH LATER, AFTER Mrs. Blake had retrieved Charlotte from the parlor and had the other housemaids draw Charlotte what proved to be a rather marvelous bath, Meg shooed Mrs. Blake's girls away with the pronouncement that only she would be needed to assist Charlotte in dressing for the evening. Charlotte had presumed they would be dining with Lady Winter, but Meg informed her that they would be going out.

"Is Lady Winter unhappy that we're here?" Charlotte asked Meg.

"I doubt Lady Winter remembers that we arrived today," Meg said as she buttoned Charlotte's gown.

"She's ill, isn't she?" Charlotte met Meg's gaze in the mirror.

Meg nodded. "Admiral Winter is rarely at home, and over the years, Lady Winter has developed a nervous constitution and is given to bouts of melancholia."

Nerves and sadness? Charlotte couldn't put together how that diagnosis could explain Lady Winter's strange behavior—excepting the fit of weeping.

Noting Charlotte's furrowed brow, Meg added, "She treats her maladies with liberal doses of laudanum. Jack told Ashley that his mother has been unable to tolerate even a day without several glasses of laudanum-laced sherry for several years now."

"Oh," Charlotte said, twisting her fingers as Meg fetched a jacket to pair with Charlotte's gown. "Why does Admiral Winter stay away from home for so long? Doesn't he care that it makes his wife so miserable?"

"It seems he married for duty, not love," Meg answered. "He prefers to spend his life serving the Empire in the company of his fellow officers and has little interest in overseeing his household."

"But he has two children," Charlotte protested.

Meg helped Charlotte into a spencer of pale green silk. "And he cared enough to ensure that his sons attended the best military academies and received officer commissions befitting their stations when they finished school. That was as far as Admiral Winter's penchant for fatherhood extended."

Jack must despise his father, Charlotte thought. *But of course he does. Why else would he betray the very thing his father loves to a fault, to the demise of his own family?*

Shrugging away those somber thoughts, Charlotte asked Meg, "Where are we going tonight?"

"To see about Grave," Meg answered.

A jolt of anticipation coursed through Charlotte. A clandestine expedition into the city, no matter the danger, held much more appeal than staying within this house full of sorrowful phantoms.

After Charlotte was sufficiently dressed and coiffed, she and Meg descended the mansion's grand staircase to meet Ash, Grave, and Jack in the foyer. Jack still wore military dress, but had donned a fresh uniform. Ash and Grave had similarly exchanged their rumpled travel clothes for crisp, starched servants' garb.

Jack didn't bother with formal greetings, instead saying, "We'll take the trolley to the Market Platform and board the Great Wheel there. It will be a good hour before we reach the Commons."

"Isn't there a faster way to reach the ground?" Ash complained.

"Not without drawing attention to ourselves," Jack answered, heading for the door. "You have to remember that residents of the Floating City are meant to be unfettered by the harried life of a worker. That's a key marker of the difference between living up here instead of in the Hive or at the Foundry. The elevators at the back of the platforms were designed strictly for official use or emergencies."

Ash pointed at Jack's uniform. "You look official enough."

"But the rest of you don't," Jack replied. "It's expected enough for Charlotte to have an officer escorting her to the city, but ladies and their servants don't go up and down the elevators."

Gazing up at the wheel, Ash pressed, "This is really how people come and go from the platform?"

"You're assuming people come and go frequently." Jack spared Ash a thin smile. "Most residents of the Floating City prefer not to leave the upper echelons of New York except by dirigible when they're traveling to their country houses."

"What about people from the Commons who want to come up?" Charlotte asked.

"Another service the Great Wheel provides," Jack told her. "By Imperial law, any citizen is free to enter the Floating City. But getting to the platforms is hardly free. Most workers can't afford to pay the fare. It's a fine system the city officials have concocted to keep the rabble out."

Ash was still grumbling under his breath when they boarded the trolley. Sliding into a seat beside the window, Charlotte expected Meg to join her, but it was Jack who sat with her on the trolley bench. Without saying anything, Jack slipped his hand over hers, threading their fingers and keeping their hands low, out of their companions' view. Charlotte threw a questioning glance at Jack, but his eyes were ahead as the trolley whisked them away from the House of Winter.

As the cable car collected more passengers, the mood in the trolley grew festive. They sped along tracks, passing the Arts and Military platforms, but Charlotte barely noticed her surroundings. She was far too distracted by the feeling of Jack's hand holding hers. She finally looked up when a cheer sounded through the now-crowded trolley.

The car slowed as it approached an enormous wheel. From frame to axle to spokes, the entirety of the wheel was lit. Turning perpetually, it glittered in gold and bronze, its glass-enclosed carriages hanging like baubles around its circumference.

When the trolley stopped, its passengers emptied out, streaming toward the line to board the Wheel. Though the line was long, they progressed steadily forward with the constant movement of the Wheel. Charlotte watched women draped in silks and velvet come and go from the carriages, accompanied by men dressed in tailcoats and top hats, their faces graced with neatly trimmed sideburns. Their laughter and gaiety suffused the evening air and left Charlotte feeling confused.

"Why do they need carriages when the trolley services all the platforms?" Charlotte asked Jack.

"While it's deemed acceptable to ride the trolley, it's much more fashionable to travel by private means," Jack replied. "The carriages are just another way for the city's elite to display their wealth."

Didn't they know they were at war? Charlotte stood in line beside these Imperial citizens, who would cast glances at her and presume she was one of their own, and the sweet twilight air developed a bitter flavor. How many years had she lived in hiding, surviving only by wit and will, and waiting for the day when she would take up arms against the military behemoth behind which the Floating City hid?

Charlotte doubted a single one of these giggling girls around her would know what to do in a fight. She looked at Ashley and noticed that although her brother's expression was calm, his fists were clenched. That he shared her distaste for this spectacle took the edge off Charlotte's mood.

Reaching the front of the line, Jack paid their fare. They were shuttled into one of the carriages with half a dozen other passengers, and the long descent began. After a few minutes, Charlotte wanted to echo Ash's frustration with this method of travel. The wheel turned at an interminably slow pace. A butler—apparently one was assigned to each carriage—offered flutes of champagne to the other finely dressed passengers and Jack and Charlotte (though not to Ash, Meg, or Grave), and the sound of clinking glass and toasts soon filled the air. Raising her glass for show whenever a stranger called out another foolish "huzzah!" Charlotte sipped at the bubbling wine and waited for the ride to be over.

Nearly three-quarters of an hour passed before the carriage leveled out and they were ushered out the door so that ascending passengers could take their places. When she stepped from the carriage, Charlotte's senses were assaulted by sound and light. The tumbling of water that powered the Great Wheel roared in her ears, and behind that explosion of sound came a cacophony of organ pipes, chimes, and blaring brass.

Not to be outdone by the audacious noise that welcomed her to the Commons, bright lights flared all around her. Iron rods, twice as tall as the tallest man among them, topped with spinning pinwheels shot out streams of sparks that met sizzling ends in the pools below the waterfalls. The pinwheels lined the path from the carriage, down a long staircase that ended in a broad pedestrian thoroughfare.

Nearly all Charlotte's fellow passengers laughed and jostled each other as they hurried eastward. Peering after them, she saw the pennants and jewel tones of the tents and pavilions that crowded the Tinkers' Faire. Only two passengers—both men, Charlotte noted—ducked their heads and turned westward onto the pathway.

Since she was already holding on to Jack's arm, Charlotte tugged him closer and, indicating the direction with a slight lift of her chin, asked, "What's that way?"

"The Iron Forest," Jack answered. "It began as a goodwill effort to give a cultural lift to the Commons. The forest was crafted from scrap metals, and it was meant to emulate the union between nature and machine, art and industry—the beloved aims of our divine patrons, Athene and Hephaestus."

"And now?" Charlotte looked down the westerly path. The two men she'd seen traverse that way had disappeared, their figures engulfed by shadow, though they could hardly have gotten far from the arrival platform.

"The crown financed the creation of the Iron Forest, but didn't offer any means to maintain it—handing over its upkeep to the colonial governor. Given that the forest was intended for the benefit of the Commons, the governor saw no need to pay for a 'frivolous' spectacle that wasn't enjoyed by his peers in the Floating City. It's a haven for cutpurses, assassins, and other sordid types. The city is like a piece of fruit. Up there, on the platforms, it appears to be ripe, juicy, and perfect, but down here you'll discover its true, rotten core."

"But the Tinkers' Faire?" Charlotte cast her glance at the carnivalesque silks and banners that shone brightly even after dusk. "Why isn't it sullied like the Iron Forest? It doesn't look like a rotten core to me."

Even now Jack was steering her to the east, after the bulk of the other passengers.

"Don't be fooled. The fair is sullied. It's just painted over in thousands of bright colors to hide the dirt. Many denizens of the Floating City love to spend their coins on the delights and scandals of the Tinkers' Faire. It provides entertainment and is constantly changing, whereas the Iron Forest was built and left to founder. Plus, the tinkers themselves fund the upkeep of their market. They have no need of backing from the Empire."

A blush heated Charlotte's neck, creeping toward her cheeks. "Delights and scandals?"

Jack raised an eyebrow at her. "I can trust you to avoid any mischief, can't I, Charlotte?"

"I don't know. Since you're supposed to be my escort, isn't that your responsibility?" Charlotte laughed, flashing him an impish smile.

Her heart fluttered when Jack bent close, his lips brushing her ear. "Then I shan't take my eyes off you. Nor let you go." Jack turned his hand so he could reach around her wrist. He slipped his fingers into the gap between her the sleeve of her spencer and gloves, stroking her skin. The shudder that rushed through Charlotte's limbs almost made her lose her footing.

Charlotte let herself begin to melt against Jack, feeling his breath warm her temple, wondering at the sensation evoked by his caresses on such a small patch of bare skin. *I can't kiss you.*

But in the next moment, Charlotte recalled other words, spoken by Lady Winter: *Have you brought Eleanor to see me?*

Jerking up roughly, Charlotte freed her wrist from Jack's light grasp. "I wouldn't want to distract you from more pressing matters. I can take care of myself. You needn't worry about me getting into trouble."

It was one thing to permit Jack to hold her hand for

comfort after witnessing his mother's sorry state, but now he was taking liberties she couldn't tolerate.

Charlotte tried to pull her arm completely away from him, but Jack restrained her. "I'm still your escort, Charlotte," he said.

"And I'll pretend I'm honored to be the charge of such a fine gentleman," Charlotte shot back.

"Charlotte." Jack's voice was pained, but Charlotte wouldn't look at him again.

Another memory intruded on her thoughts. *I'm not who you think I am.*

Her chest felt tight. How could she soften toward someone who said such things? What did she truly know about Jack? The only thing Charlotte was certain of was that she had no idea what he wanted from her.

They fell into silence, Jack sulking and Charlotte angry, as they entered the fair. Crammed with tents, booths, and wandering performers, the Tinkers' Faire was mad with activity. Spectators crammed the paths, jostling each other to enter this tent or gape at that fire-eater.

Meg pushed her way in front of Jack and Charlotte, casting her gaze about freely as if simply taking in the sights, although it was clear that she was leading them somewhere in particular. The crowd became more dense as they passed into the heart of the fair. Here the small booths of food purveyors gave way to opulent pavilions. Barkers cried out to the fairgoers; incredibly, their voices carried over the din of noise.

"Man or great ape? Who is the strongest? Come place your bets before the fight begins!"

"Every lady's wish granted here! Tinker Godwin sees into your heart before he crafts the perfect ornamentation for you! No two pieces alike! Gentlemen—want to win your true love? Tinker Godwin guarantees your lady will adore this matchless symbol of your devotion!"

"Can you climb Jacob's Ladder? Try to best the cleverest piece of machinery at the fair!"

Though Charlotte felt drawn to the fair's distractions, she was forced to keep following Meg. The older girl ignored the calls, intent on her goal, the largest pavilion, so big it had several entrances. The pavilion was paneled in diverse shades of metallic fabric that threw back the gleam of torchlight. Meg took them around the side of the tent.

One silver tent flap was pulled up, held open by a velvet cord secured to a post. No barker shouted an invitation to them, but a strange contraption stood alongside the opening.

At first Charlotte thought the metal sculpture was a strangely rendered tree, but when they drew near the brass arms, the piece began to move. Orbs floated around the glass globe at the heart of the sculpture as it flared to life, burning bright orange. A voice crackled at them:

"Here resides Madam Jedda, mistress of the universe. Seekers of truth may enter and know what lies hidden in the stars."

Meg looked at Jack. "You and Ash stay here. Make sure no one tries to come in while we're speaking with her."

"Are you sure you'll be all right?" Ash frowned at Meg. "It's been so long."

Meg's face was drawn in a way Charlotte had never seen. "I know how long it's been. And I'll be fine."

"If you're sure—" Ash pressed.

"I'm sure." Meg cut him off and said to Jack, "I'll need some coins."

"Of course." Jack drew a handful of silver pieces from his pocket and handed them to Meg.

"Charlotte, Grave, come with me," Meg instructed them in a brusque tone. "Do not speak unless I tell you to."

Charlotte nodded, Meg's abrupt manner startling her into dumbness. Grave, in his oddly quiet manner, followed obediently when Meg passed beneath the tent flap. It took Ash giving Charlotte a slight push to send her after them.

Inside the tent, they encountered yet another elaborate entrance to Madam Jedda's domain. A half-circle wooden panel bisected the round space that was dimly lit by candles. The signs of the zodiac had been carved into the left side of the panel, while on the right, gods and goddesses stood beside their corresponding planets. At the center of the wooden wall, a woman stood; her arms were extended, protruding from the panel, with her palms facing up and open. Charlotte recognized the figure as Ariadne, witch and beloved of Athene—patron of art and craft. Ariadne's magical threads had led Theseus from doom within the labyrinth. Emissary of the goddess of wisdom, Ariadne was known to be a guardian of arcane mystery.

Meg poured Jack's silver onto one of Ariadne's palms. The coins' weight triggered a hidden panel in the statue's hand to open. Charlotte heard the coins drop and then roll down the length of the hollow arm.

After a moment, a clicking of gears sounded on the opposite side of the wooden barrier. The left panel creaked and swung open as a disembodied voice whispered, "The querent may enter."

Without hesitation, Meg strode through the open door. Charlotte and Grave hurried after her. The door gave entrance to a tunnel draped with transparent silks that they had to push aside like cobwebs as they moved forward. They emerged into a room with a tall, rectangular object, its center covered in black velvet.

When Meg approached the tall box, the folds of dark fabric parted, revealing a glass case. Behind the glass was a giant eye crafted from sapphire and onyx. The eye had been inset in a golden pyramid and was lit from behind so that it appeared to burn with an inner fire. Both eye and pyramid were surrounded by a ring from which extended seven brass arms. The hands were moving around and around. As they passed the base of the glass box, they picked up tarot cards, turning the cards to face viewers as they moved before the glass.

"Madam Jedda is a machine?" Charlotte whispered, but Meg's sharp glance silenced her.

"Choose your card," the disembodied voice ordered.

Watching as the tarot deck was revealed, card by card,

Meg waited until one of the hands turned over the image of a heart pierced by a trio of swords and quickly pulled a brass knob with the word CHOOSE etched into its surface.

"The three of hearts," the disembodied voice whispered. "The choice is made that we may know you."

Meg pulled a knob labeled ASK.

The disembodied voice sounded. "What is the question?"

Unhooking a brass tube that hung beside the ASK knob, Meg spoke into the trumpet-shaped mouthpiece.

"Can the lost child be redeemed?"

Charlotte frowned, but held her tongue. *What kind of question was that?* She supposed that Grave was sort of a lost child, but Meg's wording was much too vague in Charlotte's opinion. Besides, she remained skeptical that some fortune-telling machine could offer them assistance. They'd wasted enough time taking that stupid wheel down to the Commons; surely there was something better they could be doing now. She glanced at Grave, hoping for affirmation of her annoyance, but the pale-faced boy was staring at the mechanical eye and hands that constituted Madam Jedda with fascination.

Grave sighed with disappointment when the hands behind the glass abruptly ground to a halt and the eye dimmed.

"What happened?" Charlotte asked.

Meg hissed at her, "Be silent!"

The heavy velvet around the case rustled as if disturbed by the wind. When a figure appeared from behind the covered box, Charlotte swallowed a scream. The dim light revealed the stranger to be a woman, but she'd moved so silently Charlotte half believed she must be a specter.

"You've returned, my child." The woman's voice was that of the machine. "I warned you not to."

"I had no choice." Meg lifted her chin. "I need your help, Mother."

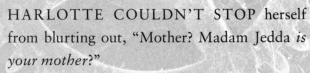

17.

CHARLOTTE COULDN'T STOP herself from blurting out, "Mother? Madam Jedda *is your mother?*"

Meg whirled around. "Hush, Charlotte!"

Jedda clucked her tongue. "Peace, child. The girl isn't one to hide her emotions. Let her be."

Meg's mother cut a tall, stately figure in the small room. Her black curls had been tamed by a woven net of gold and silver. A softly draped gown of pale green silk offset her dark skin.

"Are you so disappointed to see me?" Some of the force had gone out of Meg's voice.

Jedda shook her head, and the bells that dangled from her earlobes chimed. "How can you even ask?"

She opened her arms, and Meg rushed into them.

"I only warned you away because this city is a den of vipers," Jedda told her daughter. "You know that. Now tell me why you've come."

Meg stepped out of her mother's embrace and brushed tears from her cheeks before she gestured to Grave.

"This boy came to the Catacombs as a refugee," Meg told Jedda. "He was wearing the clothes of Hive workers, but he has no memory of who he is or whence he came."

Jedda looked at Meg sharply. "Any illness?"

"None that I could find," Meg answered.

"But why bring him to me?" Jedda frowned. "The loss of his memory is likely from trauma. It will return in time. You risk too much in coming here."

"I know the risks, Mother," Meg replied. "But there's something about him. I knew he must be brought to you."

Jedda touched Meg's cheek and smiled. "And you claimed to have none of my gift. If your blood told you to seek me out, you were surely guided by Athene's hand. What is your foundling's name?"

"He doesn't know his name," Meg answered. "But we've taken to calling him Grave."

Stretching her hand out, Jedda said, "Come here, Grave."

When Grave approached the mystic, his brow was furrowed. "You're the machine?"

"What a strange question," Jedda murmured. "I'm not the machine, dearest. I operate the machine. Machines can't channel the spirits of beyond, and without the aid of the spirits, the cards are meaningless. Will you give me your hands?"

Grave placed his hands in Jedda's open palms. She closed her eyes and went so still that Charlotte wanted to hold her breath for fear of disturbing the silence. Meg's mother frowned and shook her head.

"Something is very wrong," Jedda told Meg. "The boy is cloaked. His past unreachable. Like a spirit that does not linger but has crossed the void into the veil of the unknown."

"Someone did this to him?" Meg asked as gooseflesh prickled along Charlotte's arms.

"Perhaps," Jedda replied. "Though it's unclear if the act was one of protection or malice. And he's so cold, as if his blood is ice—are you sure he suffers no illness?"

Meg nodded. "He's not sick. In fact, he's more than healthy."

"What do you mean?" her mother asked.

"He's very . . . strong." Meg threw an uneasy glance at Charlotte, then said, "Stronger than any man should be."

Jedda's face grew troubled. "There are others who may have answers where I do not."

"Who?" Charlotte couldn't contain her curiosity.

Though Charlotte was embarrassed by her outburst, Jedda's smile was kind. "The ones who delve into Athene's mysteries and serve at her temple."

"The Sisters?" Meg cast a worried look at Grave. "Are you sure that's wise?"

"I see no other way," Jedda replied. "The Sisters can

unlock the human mind. They are the only ones who might be able to remove the veil that hides this boy's identity."

Meg bowed her head, but nodded.

"Don't be afraid," Jedda told her daughter softly. "Remember that they are servants of Athene, not the Empire."

"We should tell Ash," Meg said to Charlotte. "Can you take Grave and give me a moment with my mother?"

"Of course." Charlotte grabbed Grave's elbow, retreating into the tunnel from which they'd emerged.

"Who are the Sisters?" Grave asked her.

"I'm not sure," Charlotte answered truthfully. She knew little of the cults of Athene and Hephaestus, only that some men and women eschewed a normal life in favor of serving the Empire's patron goddess or god.

Grave's next question was barely a whisper. "Do you think they'll hurt me?"

"I don't know that anyone could hurt you, Grave. Given what we've seen you do." Charlotte wanted to laugh, but considering how serious his tone was, she supposed that would be an unkind response.

Rather than reassuring Grave, Charlotte's answer sent him into a gloomier mood.

"I wish she hadn't been there," Grave muttered. "I wanted the machine to tell me who I am."

"What?" Charlotte asked halfheartedly as they neared the pavilion's entrance.

"Machines don't make mistakes," Grave said. "Machines are perfect."

Puzzled by his strange words, Charlotte hesitated at the tent flap. "What do you mean? Why would you say that?"

Grave looked at Charlotte, blinking rapidly as if he'd just woken from a dream. "I . . . I don't know why I said that."

She had half a mind to turn around and take Grave back to Jedda. Maybe she couldn't see through whatever cloaked Grave's past, but it occurred to Charlotte that their visit may have shaken something loose from the boy's memory.

Deciding she'd best speak with Ashley first, Charlotte released Grave's arm and stepped into the night air with more than a little relief.

When they appeared outside the pavilion, Ashley didn't miss a beat. "Well?"

Annoyed that her brother hadn't bothered to so much as greet her, Charlotte snapped at him. "Did you know Meg's mother was here?"

She was rewarded by Ash's ears turning pink. "I promised her that I wouldn't say anything."

Jack gave a low whistle. "Her mother is a Tinkers' Faire mystic? That's quite a story. What were you doing with our Meg that she'd confide such things, my friend?"

"Hold your tongue, Jack." Ash's ears had gone from pink to red. Straightening his collar, he fixed a stern gaze on Charlotte. "Are you going to tell us what happened or not?"

"Madam Jedda told us—" Charlotte began, but Jack's chuckling interrupted her.

"*Madam* Jedda?"

"Jack," Ash said in a warning tone.

Charlotte ignored them. "*Meg's mother* couldn't tell us who Grave is, but she did say that—" Her words were swallowed up by the shrieking of what sounded like a thousand whistles.

Charlotte clapped her hands over her ears to stop the piercing sound. Around them the fair erupted into chaos. People burst from tents in a panic, pushing each other aside as they ran.

Jack's lips were moving, but Charlotte couldn't hear what he said. She uncovered her ears, and Jack yelled, "It's a raid!"

Before she could ask what that meant, Grave began to shout, "No! Not again!" His arms were flailing, his eyes bugged out with fear. "Not again! Not again!"

"Calm down, mate." Jack reached for the terrified boy. "We have to get out of here."

The moment Jack touched him, Grave whirled and slammed his fist into Jack's chest, sending him sprawling on the ground a good distance away. The whistles' screams were relentless, and Charlotte lost sight of Jack as the fleeing mob rushed over him.

"Jack!" Charlotte cried out. "Ash, he'll be trampled."

"Wait here," Ash told her.

"Why did you hit him?" Charlotte turned on Grave. "What's wrong with you?"

Grave didn't respond. His hands gripped his black hair, tugging hard on the roots.

"Not again. Not again. Not again."

"Grave!" Charlotte wanted to shake him, but she was afraid he'd toss her off like a rag doll.

Grave looked at her, but no recognition registered in his eyes, only confusion and fear.

Charlotte took a step toward him. "Grave, no."

But he was already running.

"Stop!" Charlotte barreled after him. Within moments, he was pushing through the sea of people fleeing the fair. Charlotte kept running, following the flashes of black hair she spotted moving amid the colorful mob. Where was he running to? Or what was he running from?

The shrill whistles were closer now. The mob surged right, and Charlotte turned to see why. Her heart clenched into a fist. If she'd been a child, she would have sworn demons were hunting her down.

They looked nothing like the carefree fairgoers. Clad in black leather, their hands were gloved in steel; the top halves of their faces were likewise masked in polished steel, their heads covered with hoods. The hulking figures snatched fleeing patrons from the crowd, tossing the captives back to their fellows. Charlotte followed the trail and saw the Rotpots looming in the distance, taller than the fair's tents. She could find neither rhyme nor reason in the way the raiders chose their victims.

Charlotte's thoughts of catching Grave dissolved as terror overwhelmed her. She was barely moving of her own volition now, but was being carried along by the tidal force of the crowd's panic. She had to get free of the mob before the raiders closed in.

She kept glancing back as she ran, checking to be sure the hooded men weren't gaining on her. What Charlotte saw when she turned made her wish she hadn't looked. The Empire's enforcers moved slowly through the panicked crowd, not only so they could take prisoners, but also to terrorize fairgoers with seemingly random violence.

A woman's face crumpled into a mash of scarlet as a steel fist plowed into her jaw. Another enforcer held a boy of no more than ten by the neck. Charlotte watched in horror as the hooded man lifted the kicking boy from the ground and slowly crushed his windpipe. Behind them, Charlotte saw the Rotpots advancing. Several of their ribbed cages were already full to bursting, but that didn't stop the enforcers from stuffing more men, women, and children into the Gatherers' hollow bellies, guaranteeing that the innermost captives would be crushed or suffocate.

Throwing elbows and shoving people aside, Charlotte fought her way to the edge of the crowd. As she was pushed forward by the throng's momentum, Charlotte reached out and grabbed the flap of a tent. Hauling herself away from the mob, she lurched free and began to run. Only when the whistles had grown softer did she slow, gasping for breath.

Jack and Ashley. She had to find them. Jack could get them out of the fair.

Charlotte turned in a circle, trying to get her bearings. She was still surrounded by tents of all colors and shapes. She spied the glittering frame of the Great Wheel in the distance and attempted to use that landmark to determine her own location.

It was useless. Charlotte hadn't paid attention to the wheel's position when she'd entered Madam Jedda's pavilion. She had no idea how far she'd chased Grave. She didn't know where she was nor how to find Jack and her brother.

As her pulse thrummed with fear, Charlotte weighed her options. The most important thing was avoiding capture. She supposed that if she was taken, she could offer up her fictional identity, play the naïve debutante, and plead innocence, but the way the entire fair had panicked at the raiders' appearance made Charlotte suspect that even upstanding citizens could run afoul of them.

Her best course, Charlotte decided, was to find a hiding place and wait for the danger to pass. How long that would be, Charlotte couldn't know, but if she was able to stay out of sight, she could find help when it was safe to come out. It was a desperate ploy, but it appeared to be her only option.

Rather than running again, Charlotte took to creeping along the edge of the tents. She clung to the places where shadows stretched. The whistles still shrieked, but they didn't seem to be coming closer. Even so, Charlotte didn't want to remain outdoors. But where to hide? Should she duck inside a tent and hope to find it empty? Would she be better off running out of the fair and into the darkness that lay beyond?

Charlotte sidled up to a broad pavilion of black and scarlet silks, pausing to weigh her options. A pair of hands shot out from a carefully concealed slit in the tent's wall. Two slender arms wrapped around Charlotte, jerking her backward into the pavilion.

"I think someone's lost," a smoky voice whispered in her ear.

Charlotte snapped her head back and was rewarded with a startled cry of pain. Freed from her assailant's grasp, Charlotte crouched and slipped the stiletto free from where it was tied to her calf.

The tent was dim, but Charlotte's blade glinted when she lifted it.

"This kitten has claws, I see," the stranger—a woman, Charlotte thought—said.

Charlotte sidestepped, holding the stiletto in front of her as her eyes adjusted to the darkness. She stumbled over something soft, perhaps a pillow, but didn't fall. The enclosure was full of a cloying scent, heavy with honeysuckle and cigar smoke.

"Come here, kitten, and put that knife away," the woman cooed. "I promise I can make you purr."

"Athene's mercy, Linnet," a new voice boomed. "Stop teasing the girl before she cuts you. I'm sure she knows how to use that little blade."

Charlotte shielded her eyes when a lantern blazed to life. The woman, whom Charlotte presumed to be Linnet, was more of a girl, possibly the same age as Charlotte, though her dress suggested otherwise. Linnet's hair was the color of molasses and poured in soft waves down her back. She wore a corset of jade satin with silver fastenings that rendered her waist minuscule and her bosom over-abundant. Her full skirt was black leather, and Charlotte's breath caught when she saw dagger hilts protruding from the tops of Linnet's suede boots. Charlotte knew how to use her blade, but she would have bet that Linnet had the greater skill.

"Augh." Linnet cast an annoyed glance at the large man behind her. "I was just playing. She's feisty! I thought we could be friends."

"You can find a playmate when we're not dealing with important business," the man replied.

Linnet's ruby-painted lips pulled back into a wicked smile. "Promise?"

The man grunted his annoyance and stepped into the full glare of the lantern light.

Charlotte gasped. "Lord Ott?"

"I see you took my advice about seeing the Tinkers' Faire, Miss Marshall," Lord Ott chortled. "Please don't blame me for this shameful display of Imperial bullying. I assure you, most nights don't take as dark a turn as this one. I happen to know that the Empire received intelligence that a meeting of the Resistance was taking place here tonight. Anywhere the Resistance is thought to find refuge, the Empire assaults without mercy or discretion for innocents caught in the cross fire."

A hard lump formed in Charlotte's throat as she remembered the woman's face turned to a pulp of blood, bone, and teeth.

"So you can tease her, but I can't?" Linnet complained.

Lord Ott cast a sidelong glance at Linnet. "When you're paying me and not vice versa, you can tease all you want."

"Watch yourself, old man, or you'll find you're prophesying." Linnet laughed. "My services fetch a high price these days."

"Don't I know it," Lord Ott groaned.

Charlotte took a moment to survey her surroundings. The room was part of a larger pavilion, but had been curtained off. The object Charlotte had tripped over was indeed a pillow, but only one of many. The room was filled with pillows and silk throws. After looking over the décor, Charlotte's gaze returned to Linnet's garb. Her cheeks burned, and she quickly looked away.

"Don't blush for me, kitten," Linnet said. "This is a sideshow, not the main event. Keeps things interesting, though." To emphasize her words, Linnet swayed her hips, revealing a deep slit in the side of her skirt through which Charlotte caught a flash of alabaster skin. She blushed again, and Linnet laughed coarsely.

Forcing her chin up, Charlotte looked directly at Lord Ott. "I thought you were a reputable businessman."

"I am a very successful businessman," Lord Ott replied. "I dabble in most enterprises. The oldest profession remains the most lucrative, while the second most profitable is closely tied to the first. My primary industry is to deal in secrets. And many a man is all too willing to give those up in a place such as this."

"Jack said you're a friend of the Resistance. Are you telling me you're a spy?" Charlotte frowned. *For whom?*

"As I said before, I am a businessman," he told her. "Information is but one of the commodities I trade in. For instance, that the Empire would order a raid on tonight's fair was particularly valuable to the rebels who avoided capture tonight."

Charlotte went very still. Was he trying to tell her he was on her side? How could she know if his words were true? Lord Ott could simply be setting a trap for her to walk into.

Lord Ott's self-congratulatory smile fell into disappointment. "Ah. Your young pilot didn't tell you, I see. Very well, then. I can't expect you to trust me without knowing who I truly am. I didn't reveal myself to you on the ship because there were too many prying eyes and perked ears straining to see and hear what they should not."

Linnet's hands were on her hips. "If Jack didn't bother to fill her in on any of the details, how do we know we can trust her?"

"Jack does trust me!" Charlotte objected, embarrassed by the sudden shrillness of her voice.

"My dear, we are all actors on the great stage of this world," Lord Ott replied. "Jack likely wanted to keep things as quiet as possible on the *Hector*. Too many eager ears and prying eyes on such a transport."

Turning to Linnet, he continued, "There's no reason to suspect Lieutenant Winter's confidence in Miss Marshall. If he's withheld certain details, he's probably just trying to ease her into the madhouse that is this city. The girl's been hiding in a cave, after all. The Resistance is a different animal here."

"I have not been hiding in a cave!" Charlotte glared at them.

Linnet sniffed in disdain. "That's not how Jack tells it."

"How do you know Jack?" Charlotte snapped, and then wished she hadn't.

Smiling slyly, Linnet answered, "Wouldn't you like to know?"

"Linnet, stop tormenting Miss Marshall," Lord Ott growled. "Must I remind you that she's here under our protection? Jack will be cross with you if you keep going at her."

"I'm more than a match for my brother," Linnet said tartly. "Let him be cross."

Charlotte's breath exploded out. "Your brother?"

It couldn't be true. Jack had said nothing of a sister, only an older brother.

"*Half* brother," Linnet answered, examining her long nails in the lantern light. "And he doesn't like to admit even half a relationship with the likes of me."

Charlotte didn't think she could handle another shock. She almost expected to wake up in her bed back at the Catacombs. This night was too full of madness to be real.

She wanted to collapse onto the pillows until her mind stopped reeling, but then she thought of what usually happened on those pillows and decided she'd best stay on her feet.

The heavy curtain that cordoned off the small room from the larger pavilion drew back, and a stranger—a man half the age of Lord Ott—stepped inside.

"She's here?" He addressed Lord Ott.

Linnet rolled her eyes. "If you'd take one more step, you'd see her for yourself."

"It's nice to see you too, Linnet." The new arrival wore a military uniform similar to Jack's, but his jacket boasted numerous decorations that the younger Winter brother's had lacked.

He leaned forward, eyed Charlotte, and said to Lord Ott, "When Jack said she was pretty, he wasn't lying."

"Athene save us," Linnet huffed.

The stranger ignored Linnet and smiled at Charlotte. "And just who are you planning on sticking with that?"

Charlotte had nearly forgotten that she was still brandishing her stiletto. Then again, she wasn't sure she had good reason to put it down.

"She's wary, this one," Lord Ott said. "Good head on

her shoulders. Come now, Miss Marshall. He's here to take you back up top."

"I don't know this man," Charlotte said firmly, and backed away without lowering her blade. "I'm not going anywhere with him."

"Weren't at home to greet your guests, eh?" Lord Ott's bushy eyebrows lifted. "That's bad form, Coe."

"Don't try to teach me etiquette, you pirate," Coe replied, grinning. "You know how busy I am. I wasn't at home today, but it couldn't be helped."

Lord Ott said to Charlotte, "Don't listen to his slander, girl. I'm just a clever businessman. Should you chance to meet a real pirate someday, you'll know this lad for a liar."

"I've met plenty of pirates," Coe told them. "The only difference between you and them is that you know how to wear a costume."

"Coe?" Charlotte's eyes narrowed. "Jack's brother."

"The same." Coe gave a short bow. "Though I'd beg you not to judge me because of my brother . . . or my sister here."

Linnet jabbed an elbow at Coe's ribs, but he jumped out of the way.

"Yes, yes." Lord Ott shoved Coe forward, and Charlotte barely got the stiletto out of the way before Coe bumped into her. "Miss Marshall, meet Air Commodore Coe Winter."

"You almost bought me a knife between my ribs, old man." Coe pivoted to glare at Lord Ott.

Lord Ott guffawed. "Maybe that'll teach you to be on time. Now, get her out of here before the raiders come to check out this pavilion."

"Are you going to stab me intentionally now, or will you be coming along without a fight?" Coe offered Charlotte his hand. "I did promise my brother *and yours* that I'd get you out of the fair safely."

Looking up at the officer, Charlotte noticed similarities between the two brothers. Coe was the taller of the two. While both boys had brown hair and sideburns, Coe's hair was dark as chocolate, whereas Jack's shone like bronze. Jack wore his hair long at the crown, but neatly clipped at the nape of his neck. Coe preferred the more traditional style—his hair would have grazed his shoulders had it not been tied back. Jack's eyes were sharp and hazel, but Coe and Linnet had blue eyes, speckled with brown like a sparrow's egg. All three siblings had the same straight, narrow nose.

"Jack and Ash are safe?" Charlotte asked Coe.

Coe laughed roughly. "In this world no one is ever safe, but if you mean did they escape the raiders' notice—then yes, they're both safe enough."

Charlotte knelt and returned her blade to its sheath. She stood up and took Coe's hand.

"Let's go."

Coe smiled at Charlotte, and her chest tightened. It was Jack's smile, the one that made her pulse quicken, even when she was furious with him. Coe started toward the gap in the tent through which Linnet had first grabbed Charlotte.

Charlotte pulled back. If Lord Ott was all he claimed to be, she could use his help.

Charlotte turned to address the large man. "There's someone else you need to find," she said.

"And who might that be?" Lord Ott asked, hooking his thumbs through his waistcoat.

"A boy," Charlotte said. "The raid frightened him, and he ran off, but he'll be in danger in the city. He's sick."

Charlotte didn't want to say anything more about Grave, hoping that Lord Ott would accept her brief explanation at face value.

"It's not our practice to go chasing after infirm runaways," Linnet scoffed, but she glanced at Lord Ott. "Right?"

"Did your brother say anything about this?" Lord Ott asked Coe, who shrugged.

"No, but the girl has no reason to lie to us."

"Very well," Lord Ott said. "And, Linnet, you're right. It's not our practice to go chasing after infirm runaways. But in this case, we'll make an exception. Go fetch him."

"Fine." Linnet sighed. "But I should change. Can you get my cloak?"

She turned to Charlotte. "What's your boy look like?"

Charlotte described Grave as best she could, which left Linnet frowning.

"No color to him? What kind of sickness does he have?"

"I'm not sure," Charlotte told her, but quickly added, "He's been with us for many days, though, and no one else has sickened."

That seemed to satisfy Linnet. "Do I bring him here?"

"What am I going to do with him?" Lord Ott replied. "Return the missing boy to his companions at Winter mansion."

"A trip to my home that never was?" Linnet smirked. "How lovely."

Coe grimaced. "I haven't ever told you to stay away."

"Your mother has said I'm not welcome there," Linnet replied. "And I'm happy to oblige."

She pushed her way past Lord Ott and out of the room.

"Are you sure she should come to the house?" Coe asked. "If my mother sees her—"

"Linnet doesn't want to see your mother any more than your mother wants to see her," Lord Ott said. "Just don't let that brother of yours give Linnet trouble."

"I'll keep Jack in line," Coe said, but he didn't look happy.

Lord Ott half turned. "I'll chat with Linnet, remind her to behave." He left the room, and Charlotte found herself looking up into Coe's blue eyes.

The smile he gave her this time was bitter. "The House of Winter—such a happy family are we."

18.

AFTER LINNET HAD swapped what she called her "reconnaissance" garb for a linen shirt paired with a leather corset and muslin skirt, she accompanied them from the pavilion into the darkness beyond the fairgrounds. Linnet bade them farewell before they slipped into the shadows, taking opposite routes.

"Don't worry, kitten," Linnet said to Charlotte. "I'll find your sick boy and get him home safely."

"You can stop calling me that," Charlotte replied, lifting her skirts to reveal her stiletto. "You know that I'm no kitten."

"You act like I've insulted you." Linnet smiled. "But like I already said, even kittens have claws."

"Take care, Linnet," Coe told his sister.

"If a storm's to come, may the wind be with us," Linnet answered.

Coe nodded. "May the wind be with us."

When Linnet was gone, Coe said, "You'll have to forgive my sister. She's used to speaking her mind."

"Don't let my clothing fool you, Commodore Winter," Charlotte answered. "Where I come from, we speak our minds too."

"You're right to chastise me." Coe laughed. "But if you don't mind my saying, you make that finery more appealing than any of the ladies on the Colonial Platform."

Glad the darkness hid her suddenly warm cheeks, Charlotte murmured, "You flatter me, Commodore."

"It's not flattery, it's the truth. And please, call me Coe."

"If that's what you prefer," Charlotte said. She felt strange walking beside Jack's older brother and found herself wanting to watch him, to observe the similarities and differences between the two siblings.

"It is what I prefer, Charlotte."

They were passing through a tangle of metal pipes and glass tubes that snaked from high above to the floor of the Commons. Some of pipes disappeared underground. Others reached all the way to the Hudson River.

Coe sniffed the air and grimaced. "I apologize for the smell. I'm trying to avoid as many of the sewage pipes as I can, but we can't steer clear of them all."

"It's fine." There was a sour stench in the air, but not one that Charlotte found intolerable.

The occasional campfire appeared amid the maze of metal and glass. Flames cast light on ramshackle hovels, and small groups of people huddled near the fires.

"Who are they?" Charlotte asked Coe, pointing toward one of the sorry-looking camps.

"Most are just scavengers or vagrants without sufficient skill to live in the Hive and who prefer life under the city to work in the Foundry," Coe answered. "Enough debris falls from the platforms for them to eke out an existence. But it's also home to a handful of the criminal sort who've managed to avoid prison. We won't likely be bothered, but you should never come here alone."

"We just sent Linnet off on her own," Charlotte protested.

"Linnet can handle herself."

So can I, Charlotte thought, but held her tongue. Instead she asked, "Doesn't it bother you?"

"What?"

"That Linnet works . . . in that place?"

Charlotte quickly looked away when Coe cast a sidelong glance at her. "Do you think it should bother me?" he asked.

"It's not my place—" Charlotte began, and then remembered Jack chiding her for using those very words earlier in the day.

Coe didn't seem to mind. "Linnet makes her own decisions and wouldn't listen to me if I did try to tell her what to do or how to live. But what you saw today isn't her real work."

"So she doesn't . . ." Charlotte grasped for an inoffensive word. "Service men?"

She wasn't sure if Coe laughed or choked, but a moment later, he answered, "Only when she gets bored, or so she says. Ott has been Linnet's guardian from the moment she was born. Linnet's mother worked in one of Lord Ott's establishments in Charleston. It was there that she caught my father's eye. According to Ott, the Admiral adored Linnet's mother and visited her often. She died in childbirth, and my father furnished Lord Ott with enough funds to look after Linnet's well-being. Ott treats Linnet like she was his own—Lady Ott was never able to have children."

A horrified noise escaped Charlotte's throat. "But if Lord Ott thinks of Linnet as a daughter, why would he let her do that kind of work?"

"Lord Ott would have been delighted to find Linnet a wealthy husband and a home in one of Charleston's finest mansions," Coe replied. "But Linnet would have none of it. Whenever Ott raises the issue, Linnet is fond of saying, 'I must be my father's daughter, for I know a spouse and house won't keep me happy.'"

"Does Admiral Winter visit Linnet?" Charlotte asked.

"Rarely," Coe told her. "But that's about how often he visits the sons from his marriage as well."

Charlotte hesitated before her next question. "Does your mother know about Linnet?"

"Yes, my mother knows," Coe said harshly. "Though she pretends she does not. My father thought it right for

Jack and me to meet Linnet when we were still children. He arranged the meeting with Ott at one of Ott's stores on the Market Platform. I understood why Linnet wasn't part of our family, but Jack was too young, and father should have known better. When we were having dinner at the house that evening, Jack asked my mother why our sister didn't live with us."

Charlotte drew a sharp breath. "What happened?"

"My mother smashed all of the china in our house and then wouldn't leave her room for a week." Coe let out a heavy sigh. "My father was furious with Jack, more than furious. He took a leather strap to him and left the poor boy bloody. I told Jack it wasn't his fault, and do you know what he said?"

"What?" Charlotte whispered.

"He said, 'I know. It's Linnet's fault.'"

"Does he still hate her?" Charlotte asked, remembering Ott's instruction that Coe keep Jack from giving his half sister trouble.

Coe sounded tired when he spoke. "I don't think he hates Linnet, but he blames our father for our mother's misery—and rightly so. Jack sees Linnet as part of our mother's suffering, so he finds it hard to show our sister kindness."

"But you don't."

"No," Coe said. "I don't."

The sudden scuffle of feet among the trees made Coe grab Charlotte's arm and draw her close. More sounds of movement were followed by the silhouettes of men looming from the dark forest.

Glancing around, Charlotte drew a sharp breath. They were surrounded.

A rasping voice called out, "Leave your coin, your weapons, and the girl, and we'll spare your life."

"I'll be leaving nothing to you, gentlemen," Coe answered. "You've made a poor choice in your quarry. Walk away, and I won't pursue you."

A chorus of guffaws and chortles boomed around them. Charlotte guessed the scoundrels were eight, maybe ten. And they were only two.

"Stay behind me," Coe murmured, drawing his sabre.

The rush came before Charlotte had a chance to answer. As she reached for her dagger, Coe tossed something into the air. A whirring sound was followed by a burst of light that temporarily made Charlotte see spots, but had the same effect on the thieves, who grunted and tried to shield their eyes. Having anticipated the blinding flash, Coe lost no time taking down the assailants.

With his pistol in his left hand, he smoothly fired off several shots. Two of the attackers dropped to the ground and didn't move again. Uncaring of their fellows' misfortune, four of the remaining men descended on Coe. Armed with crude, but vicious, spiked cudgels formed from wood and scrap metal, the brigands tried to take Coe down in a flurry of blows.

Coe shot one man full in the face, leaving little of the marauder's head sitting upon his neck. The others Coe fended off with deft strokes of his sabre. Though outnumbered, Coe's defense proved fluid and deadly compared to the wild, clumsy assault of his foes. If Charlotte hadn't known better, she would have described Coe's swordplay as relaxed, almost careless. But she could see that he simply regarded the outlaws with disdain. He knew he was the superior fighter and that the truth of it would be made plain shortly.

Watching Coe toy with his opponents, Charlotte began to back away from the brawl. She sensed the two scoundrels lunging at her just in time to whirl around and drive her stiletto into one man's throat. He fell gurgling, mouth open in surprise, causing a blood bubble to form and pop as he died. Charlotte jerked her blade free but not in time to fend off his companion, who grabbed Charlotte from behind. She held her dagger tight as he lifted her off her feet and began to carry her into the forest.

Charlotte's captor was huge, and his grip strong to the point of nearly cutting off air to her lungs. Though the latter was almost a blessing, because he smelled as if he hadn't washed in months.

Bowing her head and letting her body go limp, as though she'd fainted, Charlotte waited until she felt the man's arms relax slightly. She abruptly threw her head back, cracking the brigand's face with the back of her skull. He cried out and dropped her. Charlotte somersaulted away, but when she tried to stand, her legs caught in the clinging silk of her dress.

"By Athene," Charlotte spat as she struggled to her feet to face her assailant.

Blood streamed from the man's nose. He swiped his hand beneath his nostrils and then spat out a tooth.

"You'll regret that, missy."

"We'll see," Charlotte replied, keeping her dagger low and ready.

With a bellow, he threw himself at her, as if hoping to cow her with the noise and his size. Charlotte ducked beneath the reach of his arms and thrust her blade. The stiletto dragged through the soft flesh of his belly as his momentum carried him past Charlotte. The man grasped for her, but caught only the fabric of her dress at the shoulder. The flimsy material tore like paper. On his knees, the man held a long swath of Charlotte's gown in one hand. His other hand pressed to his middle, trying to hold in the tangle of intestines that peeked out from between his splayed fingers.

The marauder stared at Charlotte with wide, disbelieving eyes that soon went glassy, and he slumped to the ground.

Coe emerged from the shadows, rushing to her side. "Charlotte!"

His sword was bloody, but Coe appeared unharmed. He looked at her and then at the dead brigand.

"You *can* handle yourself well."

Charlotte nodded. "Are there any more?"

"No," Coe said. "Between the two of us, we dispatched them all."

His gaze moved from her face to her torso. With a cough, he quickly looked away. Charlotte glanced down and saw that her torn gown had exposed her delicate undergarments as well as a scandalous amount of bare skin.

Charlotte crossed her arms over her chest, not knowing what else to do, but Coe was already shrugging his officer's coat from his shoulders.

"Turn around," he instructed her. "I'll help you into this."

Charlotte turned her back to Coe. She let him guide her arms into the coat's sleeves. Coe's broad chest and shoulders made it so the coat engulfed Charlotte's frame, which did a marvelous job of restoring her modesty.

"Thank you," Charlotte said, feeling strangely shy as she noticed how warm the coat was from Coe's lingering body heat. She also noticed the way his hands rested on her shoulders as the coat settled upon them.

She turned to face him and met his bemused, yet curious gaze.

"I've never fought beside a woman before," he said. His tone didn't reveal whether he was pleased or disconcerted that Charlotte had changed that fact.

"Not even Linnet?" Charlotte asked.

Coe answered in all seriousness. "Linnet and I don't fight in the same circles."

Charlotte stared at him a moment and then began to laugh. Coe seemed taken aback by her response, but soon he was laughing too.

"All right, my little Athene," Coe said, catching his breath and taking Charlotte's arm. "We should get away from here."

Charlotte smiled up at him, appreciative of the compliment. It wasn't every day that one was compared to the goddess of war. Coe smiled back, and Charlotte had to look away, too conscious of the way her heart tittered. She couldn't have the same reaction to Coe that she did to Jack. How could she be as fickle as that?

They fell silent until Coe halted beside a wide metal pipe. "Here we are."

He ran his fingers along the surface of the pipe. "And the latch should be right . . . here."

Charlotte heard a click, and a panel half her height slid open to reveal an empty, hollow tube.

"I'm afraid it's going to be a tight squeeze," Coe told her. "The lift is intended only for one."

Charlotte frowned at him. "Will it bear our combined weight?" She didn't want to take the chance of plummeting back to the ground from halfway up the tube.

"Weight isn't the issue," Coe assured her. "It's just a little narrow inside, and without exception, no part of our bodies can touch the sides of the tube. Go on. I'll follow."

Crawling into the pipe, Charlotte discovered that Coe hadn't exaggerated with regard to the tube's width. When he joined her and closed the panel, there was nothing they could do but press against each other.

"Have you traveled via air compression?" Coe asked.

Charlotte looked up at him; the crown of her hair brushed his chin when she moved her head. "No."

"It's a bit jarring the first time," he said. "You should hold on to me. And don't scream. We can't risk being heard."

Charlotte wasn't certain what disturbed her more, the suggestion that the trip would frighten her enough to scream or how much Coe telling her to hold on to him reminded her of Jack and the crow's nest. She rested her hands tentatively on the sides of Coe's waist as he opened a control box and flipped a lever. A quiet whir filled the tube and the metal disk under her feet gave a slight quiver.

Without any further warning, they shot into the air. Charlotte threw her arms around Coe and bit the fabric of his shirt so she wouldn't scream. Oh, how she wanted to scream. They were flying like a bullet out the barrel of a gun, and Charlotte had no reason to believe that they wouldn't be crushed at the pipe's end. Had Coe even mentioned when or how this lift would stop?

The trip seemed to go on endlessly. Charlotte was vaguely aware that Coe was cradling her head while speaking to her in a soothing tone. She realized they were slowing when the wind no longer roared around her.

Coe's voice became clearer, and she began to make out his words.

"Charlotte, let go. You can let go now. We've arrived."

Slowly, she lifted her head. Coe was looking down at her. The amusement in his eyes reminded her of Jack, and that startled her back to her senses. She pulled away, but when she released her grip, she found that she'd been holding on so tight her fingers ached. And she was horrified to see that her teeth had left their impression on his shirt.

Hoping that Coe hadn't noticed the bite mark on his clothes, Charlotte asked him, "Where are we?" They seemed to be in a small, empty room with wooden walls and a metal floor of the same material as the base of the transport tube.

"In a closet," Coe answered. He reached out and turned a doorknob. The door swung open to reveal a clockmaker's workshop. "This is one of Lord Ott's stores. We're on the Market Platform."

Coe stepped out of the closet, and Charlotte hurried after him, eager to get away from the compression lift. Coe shut the closet door and gestured for Charlotte to follow him to the workshop's rear door.

As they walked to catch the trolley, Charlotte attempted to smooth her hair and straighten her clothes. She was grateful for the benign movement of the cable car after her harrowing trip up the pipe. The realization that she was out of danger set in, and exhaustion made Charlotte's shoulders slump.

When the trolley stopped before the Winter mansion,

Coe offered his arm. Charlotte took it gratefully and leaned against him as they walked up the path to the house.

The door swung open, revealing Thompson with a lantern in hand. "Mr. Coe, we're relieved to see you home. Word of the raid on the fair just reached us."

"You should have retired for the night, Thompson," Coe told him with a kind smile. "I'm fine."

Thompson shook his head. "There's no rest for me until the house is at peace for the night. Your brother has been terribly worried."

Coe frowned at that. "Have Jack meet me in the drawing room."

"What can I bring you, sir? A brandy?" Thompson asked.

"I'll serve myself," Coe replied. "Tell Jack I'm waiting for him and then get to bed."

Thompson looked none too pleased at the dismissal, but he assented. Turning to Charlotte, he said, "I'll rouse Mrs. Blake to draw you a bath."

Charlotte blushed, knowing how disheveled her appearance must be.

"Now, now, Thompson," Coe chided. "I've just told you to turn in. Don't go getting Mrs. Blake up at this hour."

"My maid can assist me," Charlotte offered.

"As you wish, Miss Marshall," Thompson replied, deflated. "Good night, then."

Thompson left them, and Coe took Charlotte through

the long dining hall into the drawing room. Charlotte was grateful when he led her to a velvet sofa. She was so tired she could barely hold herself upright.

"Brandy?" Coe asked, pouring himself a glass of bright amber liquid from a crystal decanter.

"No, thank you," Charlotte said. She wanted to see Jack and Ash before she slept, but that was the only reason she hadn't yet sought her bed.

Coe came to sit close to her on the sofa. He put the etched tumbler of brandy in her hand.

"Have a nip of this," he urged. "It will take the edge off your nerves. You've had quite an evening."

"That's true enough," Charlotte agreed. She sipped the brandy, which had a smooth fire, rich and spicy, when she swallowed.

A light touch on Charlotte's jaw surprised her. Coe slipped his fingers beneath her chin, turning her face toward his.

"Are you all right?" Coe asked, his blue eyes holding hers. "It was a lot to take in. The fair, Lord Ott, Linnet."

Charlotte stiffened. Coe's touch was gentle, but his face was so close to hers. Too close for someone she'd just met. Yet she found herself leaning toward him.

"I'm fine," she said. Coe's thumb stroked along her jaw, making her shiver. He wasn't Jack, and Charlotte didn't understand why Coe had such a similar effect on her. Was it only because they were brothers? Was there something in the Winter boys' blood that Charlotte found irresistible?

She was about to pull away when she heard someone enter the room.

"Charlotte!" Ash came through the door. "By Athene's mercy, you're safe."

"Yes," Charlotte replied. She would have said more, but then she saw Jack standing at the drawing room door.

Jack was staring at Charlotte and Coe, and Charlotte realized that Coe was no longer touching her face; he had taken her hand and now held it on his thigh. The color began to drain from Jack's face.

"Why is she wearing your coat?" Jack asked his brother.

He should have asked me, Charlotte thought, and answered before Coe could. "We were set upon by brigands in the Iron Forest. My dress was torn."

Charlotte withdrew her hand from Coe's grasp and rose, going to Ash and embracing him.

Ash held her tight. "I was so afraid for you," he whispered. "Were you hurt?"

"No," Charlotte said, hugging him. "And all is well now."

"Mostly well," Ash told her when he let go. "Meg returned with us, but Grave is still missing."

"Not for long." Coe rose from the sofa and joined them. Jack stood stiffly at the door. Coe smiled at his brother. "Linnet's gone to fetch him."

Jack's already bleak expression became even more strained. "Linnet?" He glanced at Charlotte. "She's seen Linnet?"

"Of course Charlotte has seen Linnet," Coe replied. "Our sister retrieves all the pirate's lost treasures. You know that."

Jack didn't reply, but his face had taken on a gray pallor.

Ash looked at Coe. "Do you really think she'll find Grave?"

"I do." Coe smiled. "Ott controls a larger network of informants than the Imperial Espionage Bureau can boast. And Linnet is Ott's right hand. She'll find your runaway and have him back here soon enough."

"Linnet is coming here?" Jack stormed across the room, giving Coe a hard shove that made Charlotte gasp. "Do you care about our mother at all?"

"Mother will never know Linnet was here," Coe said, changing his earlier tune to echo Lord Ott's assurances. "Linnet isn't sloppy enough to let our mother see her. You know that."

Jack glared at his brother, but remained silent.

Ash gently took Charlotte's arm. "You should sleep."

"We all should," Coe agreed. "There's nothing more to be done tonight."

Coe raised his tumbler and knocked back the brandy in one swallow. "I wish you a good rest."

Offering Charlotte a quick bow, Coe left the room. Ash still held Charlotte by the elbow, and she walked beside him from the drawing room. When they reached the door, Jack called out, "Charlotte, could I have a moment?"

Ash frowned at him. "She should rest, Jack. What's the matter?"

"I'll see her upstairs shortly, Ash," Jack said as he crossed the room. "You have my word."

Ash glanced from Jack to Charlotte, his brow knit together. "I don't—"

"Please, Ashley," Jack said quietly.

"Very well," Ash replied, though he was clearly taken aback. Leaning in to kiss Charlotte's cheek, Ash said, "Good night, Lottie."

"Good night." She gave Ash a tired smile, but her heart was pattering against her ribs.

When Ash left them, Jack took Charlotte's hands in his, and Charlotte was suddenly very awake. He reached up and unbuttoned the brass fastenings of Coe's coat.

"What are you doing?" Charlotte pushed his fingers away when he sought to bare her shoulder.

"I don't trust that you're not injured," Jack said. "Let me see."

"I'm not," Charlotte told him. "What gives you the right to inspect me?"

"My concern for your well-being." His voice was so gentle that Charlotte relented and allowed him to open the coat.

It took only a glimpse of Charlotte's naked, unmarred flesh for Jack to clear his throat and avert his gaze. He kept his other hand linked with hers.

"I told you," Charlotte said as heat crept into her cheeks.

"Are you sure you're all right otherwise?" Jack asked. "After the attack? I know how unsavory the Iron Forest brigands are."

Charlotte nodded. His fingers were strong and warm as they clasped hers.

Jack averted his gaze. "Linnet—"

"Seems very brave and very capable," Charlotte finished for him. He looked up at her in surprise. And Charlotte surprised herself by adding, "I liked her," and she knew it was true.

Her words didn't seem to make Jack happy, but he nodded. "I'm just relieved no harm came to you."

Charlotte laughed quietly. "So am I."

Her laughter brought a smile to his lips that made Charlotte's breath quicken.

"Shall I take you upstairs?" Jack asked. Something about the question sent warmth pooling into Charlotte's belly.

"Please," she whispered.

Jack kept her hand in his as he escorted her up the grand staircase. They stopped at her bedroom door, shrouded in darkness.

"Charlotte," Jack murmured.

She could barely make out his face, but she felt his hand against her cheek. Without thinking, Charlotte leaned her cheek into his palm, turning her face so her lips brushed the heel of his hand. She heard Jack stifle a groan.

Charlotte quickly straightened, shocked by her own

behavior. What had she done? Was she so wanton as this? She'd practically swooned into Coe's arms earlier that night, and now she was playing the seductress with Jack.

"I should say good night." Charlotte's voice cracked.

But the weight of Jack's hands rested on her waist, then moved to her lower back, drawing her forward. The silk of her gown rustled when her body pressed against his.

"Jack." Coe's voice was like the crack of a whip.

Jack swore. "Hang it all, Coe. What do you think you're doing?"

Charlotte couldn't see Coe through the darkness, but she heard his footsteps as he came down the hall.

"I could ask you the same thing," Coe said to Jack. "It's time to bid Miss Marshall good night."

"Mind your own business," Jack snarled.

Rattled by Coe's appearance, Charlotte pulled out of Jack's embrace.

"Charlotte, don't." Jack clasped her hand.

"Let her go, Jack," Coe said.

Jack squeezed Charlotte's fingers, but with reluctance said, "Good night, Charlotte. I'll see you in the morning."

All Charlotte could do was murmur, "Good night, Jack."

Coe stood like a sentinel while Jack stomped down the hall. Charlotte opened her door.

"Good night, Commodore Winter," she said quietly. Her mind was a jumble of shock and disappointment.

"Charlotte." Coe's voice made her look over her shoulder.

"What exactly has my brother told you about his life before he came to the Catacombs?"

"Very little," Charlotte answered. *Almost nothing at all*. She didn't voice that thought, given how palpable the tension was between the two brothers. And Charlotte didn't know what the source of that conflict was.

As if to himself, Coe said, "That's what I thought." Then added, "Sleep well, Charlotte."

Coe retreated into the shadows, and Charlotte closed the door.

19.

WHEN LINNET HAD not returned Grave to them by lunch the next day, Charlotte worried her way through the opulence of the Winter mansion.

"Don't fret," Coe assured her. "Linnet knows what she's doing. I'd be shocked if she hasn't already found the boy, but she'll be careful to find a way to bring him here without drawing notice. That means it may take a bit longer."

Jack had been absent from breakfast and lunch, but Coe offered no explanation. When Charlotte asked Ash about Jack's whereabouts, her brother dismissed her query with a shake of his head.

"Jack has other business in the city, Charlotte. It's not your concern."

Charlotte's other worry had been the chance of another uncomfortable exchange with Lady Winter, especially when she learned they would spend the day confined to the mansion, but Jack and Coe's mother seemed to split her time between her rooms and the garden. The lady of the manor never joined them in the dining hall, drawing room, or parlor.

Whiling away hour after hour with Meg and Ash—like his brother, Coe had excused himself to see about his affairs at the Military Platform—Charlotte's sympathy for Lady Winter increased tenfold. The house was huge and lonely. For all its elegance, the high ceilings and sweeping rooms soon grew oppressive—and unlike Lady Winter, Charlotte had company.

"Gah! This is intolerable." Ash stood up as afternoon faded to dusk. "I'll go out of my mind if I have to sit here another hour."

"Hush, Ashley," Meg said. Of their trio, Meg had remained the most serene that day. She hadn't spoken of her mother, at least not when Charlotte was present, and Charlotte was surprised Meg could be so calm just hours after that strange reunion.

"What exactly are we waiting for?" Charlotte asked. "Grave's return? Or something else?"

"Jack went out to arrange a meeting for tonight," Ash admitted.

"With whom?" Charlotte frowned.

Ash picked up a kaleidoscope that served as a table

decoration and held it up to his eye. "Lord Ott and some key figures of the rebellion from within the Empire."

Ash turned the kaleidoscope, but Charlotte saw through his overly casual posture. "Including Lazarus?" she asked.

"The meeting was supposed to take place last night." Ash put the kaleidoscope down with a sigh.

"At the fair," Charlotte concluded.

"Jack is worried that Lazarus will go into hiding for now. Last night came too close to exposing him. I don't know if he'll be there tonight," Ash said.

"But I thought Lord Ott and his associates knew about the raid," Charlotte said. "Wouldn't this Lazarus have known as well?"

"Our friends in the city learned of the raid only an hour before it took place. Most of the meeting's attendees had already arrived at the fair, including Lazarus. He and the others had to flee to avoid capture," Ash told her.

"Like us." Charlotte remembered too well the onslaught of the hooded enforcers and the Rotpots.

Ash nodded. "Coe was on his way to warn us about the raid, but you and Grave ran off before he reached us."

"Grave ran off," Charlotte corrected him. "I chased after him."

"It doesn't matter," Meg interjected, pouring a cup of tea from the service Mrs. Blake had provided. "I needed to speak with my mother, and I think her advice about Grave is sound."

Ash looked at her with a frown. "We may not have time to visit Athene's temple."

"We have to make time," Meg insisted. "Grave is important. I can feel it in my bones."

Ash seemed skeptical, but Charlotte remembered what Jedda had told her daughter: *And you claimed to have none of my gift.*

Since they'd returned to the House of Winter, Meg had withdrawn into herself, contemplative but peaceful. Charlotte wondered if Meg was likewise considering her mother's words.

A polite cough sounded at the door to the parlor.

"I'm informed that you'll be dining at the house this evening," Thompson told them. "Dinner will be served in an hour."

Charlotte sighed. "I suppose that means I should dress for the meal."

"I'll help you change." Meg rose, and the two women retired to Charlotte's bedroom.

While Charlotte brushed out her long hair, Meg opened the wardrobe. "Is there a color you'd prefer for tonight?"

"No." Charlotte couldn't bring herself to care what color her gown was. There were so many gowns. All exquisite, but all reminders of the fiction Charlotte lived while in the city.

"The amethyst is quite lovely—" Meg dropped the gown she'd just pulled from the wardrobe when Jack burst through the door.

"Charlotte, I have to speak with you." He was gasping for breath, as if he'd sprinted all the way to her room. His coat was unbuttoned, and his shirt collar was loose at his neck.

"What's wrong?" Charlotte asked. "Is it Grave?"

Jack shook his head and threw a pleading glance at Meg. Meg gave Jack a long look and then left the room without a word, shutting the door firmly behind her.

"Jack, please tell me what's happened." Charlotte was so frightened she could hardly breathe.

Closing the distance between them, Jack said, "I'm so sorry, Charlotte. I don't know what else to do."

Charlotte took a step back. The wildness in his voice made her even more fearful.

"I have to do this," Jack told her. "Just this once before tonight. I have to know for sure."

"What exactly is happening tonight?" Charlotte asked, thinking of the meeting Jack had arranged. Was there a danger Ash hadn't spoken of?

Jack didn't answer; there was a fever in his eyes. He grasped her upper arms and jerked her toward him. His mouth came down suddenly, hard on hers. The kiss felt desperate and verged on painful, but Charlotte's eyes closed as the sensation took her under. She was so deep in the kiss she thought she might drown. She didn't care, feeling only how tightly Jack gripped her skin. How much he wanted her.

Breaking the kiss, Jack leaned his forehead against

Charlotte's. They were both breathing hard, but her thoughts were only of how much she needed Jack's lips to be on hers again.

"Do you love me?" Jack's eyes were closed, and his brow furrowed as though he was in pain.

"Wh-what?" Charlotte stammered, reeling from the question.

"Tell me the truth, Charlotte." Jack was looking at her now. "Do you love me?"

Charlotte reached up to touch his face. Her pulse was drumming so loudly she barely heard herself say, "Yes."

That single word answered many questions that had been nipping at the edges of Charlotte's conscience. Yes. Yes, she loved Jack. That was the only sensible explanation for why she'd been so instantly drawn to Coe. All those pent-up emotions were spilling over, muddying the waters of attraction, and confusing her. That must have been it.

Jack bent to kiss her again. This time his mouth was gentle, seeking rather than demanding. Charlotte slipped one arm around his neck; the other she rested at his waist. Her skin heated as Jack kissed her. She opened her mouth to taste his tongue. Then his hand was in her hair, his other hand pressed between her shoulder blades, and his lips were brushing her cheek, her jawline, her neck.

Charlotte slipped her hand beneath Jack's coat and pulled his shirt free of his trousers. Wanting to know if his skin burned like hers, Charlotte pressed her fingers against his lower back, feeling as his muscles flexed under her touch.

Jack's kisses edged toward her bodice, and Charlotte gasped as sweat beaded on the back of her neck. She moved her hand beneath Jack's shirt from his back to his stomach, her touch tracing the ridges of his abdomen. With a groan, Jack straightened and pulled Charlotte's roaming hands away from his skin.

"Don't." Charlotte's voice was low and thick. "Don't stop."

"I have to," Jack said through gritted teeth. "I won't dishonor you."

"I don't care," Charlotte exclaimed, though she wasn't entirely sure that was true. The fire in her blood had burned away her sense for the moment.

Jack cupped her face in his hands. "I'll do this the right way. Tomorrow I'll speak with Ash. We'll sort everything out."

Charlotte stared at him, numb with shock. Speak with Ash? Did Jack mean to ask for her hand? To marry her? When exactly did he expect all of this to happen?

Not that she was altogether opposed to that idea, but it was so sudden and unexpected. The ground was solid beneath Charlotte's feet, but the room around her seemed to be spinning.

Placing a soft kiss on her mouth, Jack said, "I have to

leave you. But you have my word, we'll speak of this again in the morning."

Charlotte nodded.

Jack kissed her again and murmured into her ear, "I didn't know I could want anything so much as I want you, Charlotte."

His words made her shiver, despite the sheen of sweat that covered her skin, for she knew her feelings mirrored his in intensity. She found that awareness frightening. It was much easier to fight with Jack than to want him like this.

When Jack left, Charlotte stripped out of her gown so her skin would cool. Clad only in her chemise, she walked unsteadily to the bed and lay down. As her shock receded, giddiness spilled through her limbs. She smiled like a fool at the ceiling. She loved Jack.

Athene's mercy, what will Ash say?

Charlotte laughed aloud. She rolled over and hugged a pillow to her chest. Her body felt supple and finer than silk.

When someone knocked at the door, Charlotte sat up. "Come in!"

Charlotte assumed that the knocker would be Meg returning, but hoped it would be Jack throwing reason to the wind and returning to seek her bed, so when Coe stepped into her room, Charlotte shrieked. She dragged the coverlet up to her neck.

Coe quickly pivoted around, giving her his back. "I'm sorry, Charlotte. You did say to come in."

"I thought you were Meg!" Charlotte squirmed beneath the sheets, wrapping herself up like a mummy.

"Are you decent now?" Coe asked.

"Aren't you leaving?" Charlotte replied. Why on earth would he stay when she was half dressed?

Coe glanced over his shoulder, and seeing Charlotte wrapped in bedclothes, he relaxed.

"I'm afraid I have an urgent matter that we must attend to."

"We?" Charlotte frowned at him. That was when she noticed Coe was carrying a gown. Charlotte had never seen a dress so beautiful. Its burgundy silks would have outshone the finest wines. A whisper of black lace edged the gown's neckline and hem.

Coe approached Charlotte and laid the gown along the foot of her bed. "My mother wore this dress at her debut. It seems appropriate that you would wear it tonight."

Nerves pricked at Charlotte. "But I thought the Governor's Ball was at the end of the week?"

"It is, but there's been a change of plans," Coe replied. "We decided it would be appropriate for you to make an appearance for the military ball that's being held tonight. It, too, takes place at the Governor's Palace, but it's a smaller event, something of a preview for the grand gathering to follow in a few days. Since you're being sponsored by the House of Winter, your absence might be conspicuous. I apologize for the short notice, but you'll have to hurry. Put on the gown and meet me at the front gate as soon as you can."

"Are Ash and Meg joining us?" Charlotte frowned at Coe, though she reached a hand out to stroke the extraordinary fabric of the gown.

"Servants don't attend balls," Coe answered. "I'll escort you."

Charlotte looked at him, hesitating. "What about Jack?"

"Jack has a prior commitment," Coe told Charlotte. "But I'm sure you'll see him later tonight."

After the meeting he and Ash have with the Resistance, Charlotte thought. She didn't like the idea of attending some society event while her brother and Jack were risking exposure at a gathering of rebels. But if, as Coe said, the night's plans had changed, and this was part of the new plan, then Charlotte had no reason to object.

"I'll dress as quickly as I can," Charlotte said.

"Good." Coe's smile was rather grim. "I'll await you outside."

To Charlotte's surprise and frustration, Meg didn't return to help her into the evening gown. After a bit of a struggle, Charlotte managed to reach all the buttons and fastenings of the dress. She even styled her hair in an artful twist embellished with a comb of silver and seed pearls.

Charlotte found the house quiet when she exited her room. As promised, Coe was waiting at the iron gate, but he wasn't waiting alone.

A driver and footman stood beside a carriage of blond wood and brass fittings. Harnessed to the front of the carriage was a horse built entirely of metal that Charlotte thought looked more like a trussed-up skeleton than a tinker's mechanical wonder.

"You look beautiful," Coe said, helping Charlotte into the coach.

Charlotte murmured her thanks, but felt uneasy as her senses stirred from Coe's light touch. She loved Jack. She wanted Jack. Charlotte was certain of that. She toyed with the buttons of her gloves as the gears of the horse began to click and whir.

"What do we have to do at this ball?" Charlotte asked Coe.

He laughed. "Most ladies show a bit more enthusiasm about attending a ball."

"I've never been to such an event," Charlotte said. "I don't know what's expected."

"You will be expected to smile and look pretty," Coe replied. "You will curtsey and nod when you are introduced to the lords and ladies of New York."

Charlotte turned to face him. "Is that all? I don't have to give a speech or anything like that?"

Coe waved off her horrified expression. "Please remember when I say this that it's the sentiment of others, not my own: women in the Floating City are meant to be looked upon, not listened to."

Charlotte wanted to curse at that stupidity, but she checked herself, and all that came out was a pathetic, strangled cry. It made sense that Charlotte would attend a military ball because of her connection to the House of Winter, but why wasn't Jack escorting her? Hadn't he claimed that role as his when they concocted this plan?

Leaning back against the carriage seat, Charlotte wished Ash or Meg were there to offer her some comfort.

"It won't be so awful, Charlotte," Coe said, taking her hand. "We can dance as much as you like. The whole night if it pleases you."

Charlotte forced herself to smile at Coe. It wasn't his fault she was here. "Perhaps."

That seemed to satisfy him and they passed the rest of the trip in a not terribly awkward silence and Charlotte tried not to think about how pleasant it was to have Coe's strong hand covering hers.

20.

THE GOVERNOR'S PALACE had been erected at the highest point of the Floating City—its height and girth commandeering an entire platform. Towering over the rest of New York, the building left no doubt as to where the Empire's power resided.

Charlotte peeked out the carriage window when the mechanical horse began to slow. They'd joined a line of similar coaches, though the creature drawing their carriage was the most ordinary of the animals beings operated by drivers. Charlotte spotted a mechanized ostrich, several lions, and even an elephant at the head of a grand coach out of which four couples emerged.

Their coach came to a stop in front of the gilt palace gates. The footman helped Charlotte out of the carriage.

When Coe joined her, she took his arm. Where they walked, heads turned and whispers followed. Charlotte tensed, but Coe whispered to her, "Remember, you belong here."

Forcing her gaze ahead and her back straight, Charlotte tried to fight off an imminent sense of doom. What could Ash have been thinking? She glanced at Coe, tall and trim, with dark hair, a decorated uniform, and a dangerous smile. It dawned on Charlotte that she would be the envy of many a debutante—any girl who claimed Air Commodore Winter as an escort would garner jealousy . . . and gossip.

Charlotte was still mulling over her presence at the ball when they entered the palace. Coe and Charlotte were escorted to a landing at the top of a broad marble staircase.

Coe withdrew a tiny scroll tied with gold ribbon from inside his coat and handed it to a man who awaited them at the edge of the landing. The staircase led to a grand ballroom filled with men and women dressed in their finest. Many of the men wore officer's uniforms while others sported finely tailored jackets and waistcoats.

The man who'd taken the scroll cleared his throat. His voice rang out, sailing down the staircase and through the ballroom.

"The Lady Charlotte Marshall of Bermuda. Escorted by Air Commodore Coe Winter."

The moment their names were announced, the din that

filled the ballroom quieted as curious gazes traveled up the stairs. Charlotte hoped she didn't look as stricken as she felt. Gripping Coe's arm tightly, she tried to keep a placid smile on her lips as they descended toward the ballroom. She could feel hundreds of pairs of eyes boring into her.

Charlotte's heart was racing, and she felt faint in a way she never had before. At that moment, she would gladly have taken the smelling salts she'd been offered on the *Hector*.

But then her feet were on the glossy ballroom floor and the next couple was being announced. Though Charlotte still drew some curious looks, it appeared that the wave of focused attention had passed.

A servant bearing a tray of champagne flutes passed close to them, and Coe lifted two of the slender glasses, handing one to Charlotte.

"This should help," Coe said, taking a swallow. Though he'd been calm enough upon their arrival, now that they'd reached the ballroom floor, he seemed as nervous as Charlotte.

Charlotte sipped champagne, though she was tempted to gulp it down.

"My heavens!" a woman's voice trumpeted at Charlotte. She whirled to find Lady Ott bearing down on her.

"What a delightful surprise this is." Lady Ott beamed at Charlotte. "And that dress! *And* with Commodore Winter! You have been a busy little bee. Good for you." Lady

Ott turned her smile on Coe. "Commodore, it's lovely to see you out in the city for a change. Does this mean the Empire has conquered all her foes?"

"Alas," Coe answered drily, "as long as there is an Empire, she'll have enemies."

"Too true, too true." Lady Ott bobbed her head as she agreed. "But at least you found the time to offer this beautiful girl your attentions. What a fine pair you make—my husband will be *so surprised* when he sees you. Ah, there he is now. Darling! Come see who I've found."

Charlotte didn't know if it was the way Lady Ott said "so surprised" or that Coe flinched when Lord Ott's girth pressed through the crowd, but she instantly knew something was off.

"Miss Marshall." Lord Ott swept his hat off as he bowed. "How lovely to see you again so soon."

"But of course she'd be here, my dearest," Lady Ott said to her husband. "It is her first season, remember?"

"So it is." Lord Ott rounded on Coe. "And though it's her first hunt, she's snared the most elusive prey. I can't remember the last time I saw you at the Governor's Palace, Commodore."

"My command keeps me away," Coe said quickly. "But since Miss Marshall has been sponsored by the House of Winter, I thought it only proper to—"

"Spare me your thoughts, boy." Lord Ott cut him off. Leaning close, Ott growled in a low voice, "What in

Hephaestus's name are you doing here? More to the point, what is she doing here?" Ott jerked his chin at Charlotte.

Charlotte's eyes widened, and she glanced in alarm at Lady Ott, but the plump woman continued to smile beatifically.

"Don't fret, Miss Marshall." Lady Ott didn't drop her smile. "Let the men take care of their business. Oh, careful now—you'll spill your champagne."

Behind Lady Ott's buoyant expression, Charlotte saw an unmistakable sharpness in the woman's gaze. *Lady Ott knew.* She wasn't an ignorant wife—she was a partner to Lord Ott in every way.

Forcing a giggle to continue their act, Charlotte sipped her champagne while watching Coe and Lord Ott out of the corner of her eye.

"The best thing you can do is leave," Lord Ott was saying, though like his wife, he wore an expression of benign amusement. "Leave now."

"We can't," Coe argued. "Not yet."

"Why not?"

Charlotte was about to interrupt and demand to know exactly what the new plan was and how it could be so new that Lord Ott had been excluded from it, but her question was drowned out by the announcement of another couple's arrival.

"The Lady Eleanor Stuart. Escorted by her fiancé, Flight Lieutenant Jack Winter."

Charlotte went as rigid as if she'd stared into the face of Medusa. It was impossible. She could not have just heard what she somehow thought she'd heard.

Coe's voice reached her, as if from a great distance. "I'm sorry, Charlotte."

His hand touched her shoulder, and Charlotte could move again. Without hesitating, she gulped down the rest of her champagne.

"Oh, dear." Lady Ott gave her husband a knowing glance. She snatched the empty champagne glass from Charlotte's hand.

Lord Ott looked up the stairs, then at Charlotte, and then at Coe. "That's what this is all about. Bugger it all, Coe. There are better ways to handle this matter."

Charlotte didn't want to look at the staircase, but her eyes didn't listen to her heart's shrieks of warning. Part of her still couldn't believe this was anything more than a mistake.

But there he was. Jack. Her Jack. He came down the steps with a willowy girl in sky blue silk on his arm. Jack Winter, her fiancé. Spots began to float in Charlotte's vision. She closed her eyes and tried to breathe. When she opened them again, the spots were gone, but she felt sick.

Lord Ott said to Coe, "Get Charlotte out of here before you make things worse."

"No." Coe folded his arms across his chest. "Jack needs to learn a lesson."

"Forget your brother." Lord Ott shook a finger in Coe's face. "Think of the girl."

Lady Ott cleared her throat. "Girls," she corrected him.

"I am thinking of Charlotte," Coe shot back. "Do you think I'd have brought her here, made her see this travesty, if I didn't give a damn about her?"

"And what of Eleanor?" Lady Ott asked. It was amazing to see how the woman could keep a bright smile on her face while throwing daggers with her eyes.

Coe didn't answer her.

"Athene have mercy." Lord Ott pulled a kerchief from his pocket and dabbed at his face.

Somehow, Charlotte found her voice, small and strained though it was. "Please, Coe. I want to leave."

Her words brought doubt into Coe's angry gaze. "Charlotte, I didn't do this to hurt you. I couldn't let Jack shame you with his lies. He would ruin you in ways you can't imagine."

"I want to leave now," Charlotte said again.

Jack and the girl had reached the ballroom floor.

"Take her home, Coe," Lady Ott urged.

Charlotte whispered, "It's too late."

Jack had seen Coe first and frowned, obviously not expecting to find his brother in attendance. When Jack saw Lord Ott, his face grew worried, but then his gaze fell on Charlotte. Jack blanched and took a step backward.

Lady Ott moved to Charlotte's side. "Courage, sweetling," she murmured.

There was nothing to do but wait for Jack and his fiancée to join them. Lord Ott moved to greet the couple first.

"Lieutenant Winter." Ott smiled at Jack. "A pleasure."

"Lord Ott." Jack inclined his head. "I don't believe you've met Lady Eleanor Stuart."

"The pleasure is mine." Lord Ott bowed. "And this is my wife, Lady Margery Ott."

Lady Eleanor's curtsey was the essence of grace. She looked at Coe and smiled.

"Jack didn't say you'd be here, Commodore. What a delight. I've missed you terribly."

"You honor me with kindness, Lady Stuart." Coe gave a quick bow. "I like to keep my brother guessing. Of course, it's lovely to see you again. Good evening, Jack."

Given the fury in Jack's eyes, Charlotte felt certain that if Jack had been holding a knife, he would have stabbed Coe without hesitation.

But what right did Jack have to be angry?

He was the one who had told Charlotte he wanted her. He was the one who had kissed her and made promises to speak to Ash . . . about what? It couldn't have been marriage. Jack was already pledged to someone else. Someone Charlotte had never dreamed could exist.

Not once had he mentioned this Eleanor, his betrothed.

But his mother had.

Have you brought Eleanor to see me?

Waves of anger and disbelief washed over Charlotte.

She forced herself to be very still. She couldn't look at Jack for fear that her poison tongue would prove stronger than her will, so she turned her eyes upon Eleanor. Charlotte searched for anything about the girl she could fault, wanting nothing more than to despise her.

Eleanor had skin like fresh cream. Her honey-gold hair spilled like spun silk over her slender, bare shoulders. Her eyes were the liquid brown of a wide-eyed fawn. And when Eleanor turned her face to smile up at Jack, she glowed with affection.

Charlotte rocked back on her heels, again feeling faint. She dared to glance at Jack. He didn't look happy with Eleanor on his arm, but no doubt his sour face was on account of Coe catching him unawares.

Eleanor looked from Coe to Charlotte. "Will you introduce me to your lovely companion?"

Jack grimaced, but Coe replied, "Forgive me. Lady Eleanor, may I present Lady Charlotte Marshall of Bermuda."

"Bermuda?" Eleanor clapped her hands in delight. "I've never met someone from the islands. How exciting it must be to live there! No wonder you've caught the eye of our dear commodore. Did you meet on one of his missions? How romantic! I often daydream of joining my Jack on his military expeditions, but only nurses are allowed near the front lines."

With every word Eleanor spoke, Jack's expression darkened. "Charlotte's father is a friend of the admiral, so our house has acted as her sponsor for her debut into society. Charlotte and Coe have only just met."

"Ah," Eleanor said. "But what a fine match they make. Don't you think?"

"I'd have to agree," Coe murmured, resting his hand on the small of Charlotte's back. "I never dreamed of claiming a fortune as great as the favor of Lady Charlotte Marshall."

Feeling like a wind-up doll, Charlotte stiffly turned her face to look up at Coe with utter incredulity. By Athene, why would he say such a thing?

"My dear, I must introduce you to some of my friends." Lady Ott snagged Eleanor's arm and pulled her away. "Don't worry, Jack. I'll return her shortly."

When Lady Ott and Eleanor were out of earshot, Jack glared at Coe.

"What kind of monster are you?"

"I'm not the monster here," Coe replied coolly. "I'd wager that Charlotte would agree with me."

Charlotte didn't know what she thought. She had the strangest sensation of having left her body and watching someone else's disastrous life play out before her.

Jack took a menacing step forward, but Lord Ott placed his massive frame between the brothers. "Now, now. Let's remember where we are and how vital it is that you not cause a scene."

Tearing his hateful gaze away from Coe, Jack looked at Charlotte. He took a step toward her, hand outstretched.

His attention forced Charlotte back into the scene. And it was the last place she wanted to be.

"Charlotte—"

"Don't you dare try to touch me." Charlotte drew back, words full of venom.

Coe stepped forward, half shielding Charlotte from Jack.

Jack went still. "You don't understand."

"No, Jack." Charlotte's eyes began to burn. "I don't."

Lord Ott cleared his throat. "I'm painfully aware that I do not have all the facts of this matter, but Charlotte, my dear, your tears will cause as much of a scene as any brawl that should ensue between these gentlemen."

Charlotte blinked rapidly, forcing back teardrops.

"Charlotte, please." Jack's voice was on the verge of breaking. "Just let me talk to you."

Lord Ott frowned at Jack. "Your talking isn't helping."

"Ah, here you are!"

Charlotte almost jumped out of her skin when someone grasped her elbow.

"Startles easily, this one." It took a moment for Charlotte to recognize Linnet. The girl had utterly transformed herself.

Linnet's hair was expertly arranged atop her head, held in place by a fine net of freshwater pearls. Her gown matched the bright blue of her eyes, and a choker of pearls and sapphire embraced her throat.

"What are you doing here?" Lord Ott demanded. "And how much did that getup cost me?"

"The dressmaker is sending you a bill. So is the jeweler," Linnet answered. "I'm here to make my report. I dropped the boy at Winter mansion. You told me to inform you when I'd completed that task. So here I am."

She pointed at Charlotte. "Oh, and that one's brother is worried sick that she's gone missing, so I promised him I'd find her. And now I have. My goodness, I have talent."

"Ash doesn't know I'm here?" Charlotte shot an accusing glare at Coe.

"No," Coe answered. "But if he'd seen everything I have, he would have assented to my plans this evening."

"What did my brother tell you to get you here?" Jack asked Charlotte.

Though she wasn't keen to answer Jack directly, she said, "Coe told me that the plans for this evening had changed. I thought I had to attend the ball for sake of appearances."

Lord Ott snorted. "Not a bad lie. Still a lie, though."

"You did this just to spite me," Jack snarled at Coe.

Coe shook his head. "I did it to remind you of who you are. You're not playing in the woods anymore. This is your life."

Coe's words were like a slap in the face to Charlotte.

Playing in the woods. Pretending. Jack's dalliances were all fiction. Part of his escape from a life he resented. It was never real. How could it have been? Charlotte let her gaze float away from the group to take in the splendor of the ball. This was Jack's world—full of vividly bright silks and gleaming silver. A spectacle of wonders. Charlotte's world was dingy and chaotic, a place of dull brass and cold iron.

Linnet slipped her arm around Charlotte's waist.

"You're unwell, Miss Marshall," Lord Ott said gently. "It's best you get home."

"I'll take her." Jack tried to push past Lord Ott.

"No, you won't." Coe started toward Charlotte. "I'll take her home in my carriage."

"If you so much as touch her—" Jack spat at his brother.

"Don't be idiots," Linnet interrupted, drawing Charlotte back. "I'll see her home."

"Yes," Lord Ott growled. "If you boys would take a moment to remember that we still have *that* matter at hand."

With Lord Ott's words giving Jack and Coe pause, Charlotte seized on the moment to whisper, "Linnet, get me out of here."

Before anyone could intervene, Linnet had turned Charlotte around and they were slipping through the crowd, past dancers and servants and musicians, to the opposite end of the ballroom. Linnet guided Charlotte through glass doors that opened onto a terrace that led to the palace gardens.

They left behind the lights of the palace and ducked into the shadow-filled garden. Linnet stopped beside a bench, reached underneath the hedge just behind it, and pulled out two traveling cloaks.

"Put this on," she told Charlotte. "It'll cover your gown so we can take the trolley without drawing attention."

Charlotte felt numb as she drew the cloak over her shoulders. She followed Linnet along the garden paths, sinking deeper and deeper into melancholy. After a while, Linnet slowed, falling in step beside Charlotte.

"You know, if Jack's that much to your liking, you should just take him to your bed."

Charlotte tripped over her feet. "Excuse me?"

"Why bother with betrothals and marriage?" Linnet shrugged. "I wouldn't. The Raj himself could offer his hand, and I wouldn't give it a second glance. Marriage is a prison for girls like you and me. Nothing more."

"Are you teasing me?" Charlotte asked. Even if the other girl was winding her up, Charlotte was a bit grateful for the distraction.

"Only a bit," Linnet replied. "You wouldn't consider it?"

"Taking a lover rather than a husband?" Charlotte felt scandalous just saying it out loud.

"Yes, that."

"I've never thought about it," Charlotte admitted. She'd flirted with Jack once she'd stopped hating him, but her thoughts hadn't gone further than that. At least not that much further.

"Never?" Linnet sounded skeptical.

"In the Catacombs, you think about the war. About staying hidden," Charlotte argued. "I wasn't worried about . . . that."

"Until Jack."

Linnet took Charlotte's silence for an affirmative reply.

"Sorry, kitten," Linnet said. "It was obvious where you stood with Jack as soon as you got rankled when you thought I might be something other than his sister." A moment later, she added, "Don't be too cross with him."

"You don't know what he did." Charlotte bristled.

Linnet laughed. "I know more than you think. And I knew it before I ever met you. You just sped up the clock is all."

"I don't follow." Charlotte frowned into the darkness.

"Jack set a trap for himself without knowing it," Linnet told her. "And he just sprung it."

They had to crawl through a gap in the outer hedge wall to escape the garden.

"What do you mean?" Charlotte asked as she wriggled through the opening.

"Jack's sole aim in life has been to avoid becoming like his father," Linnet explained. "He despises the admiral."

"So I've heard."

Away from the palace, the streets were quiet; the loudest sound came from their footfalls on the cobblestones.

"Jack knew his parents' marriage was loveless," Linnet said. "Arranged because it was an ideal match between a powerful civil and equally powerful military family. So Jack decided to avoid that doom by finding a wife of his own before his father could make similar arrangements."

"So he found Eleanor." Charlotte's voice was strained. "And he loves her?"

"I'm sure he thought he did," Linnet replied. "She's a very nice girl and all. But I knew that wouldn't be enough. I told him that you don't find love—it finds you."

"What did he say to that?" Charlotte asked.

"He told me to bugger off." Linnet laughed. "Jack never listens to anything I have to say." She cast a sidelong glance at Charlotte. "And now that love has found Jack, he's in a terrible fix."

"You can't know that he loves me." Charlotte drew her cloak more tightly around her body. She didn't want to let hope sneak into her heart. She couldn't bear it.

"You're right," Linnet said. "I can't know. Only you can. But Jack isn't the sort to play games with someone's feelings, not after what he's seen his mother go through."

"I'm surprised you'd defend him," Charlotte admitted.

Linnet's laughter was harsh. "Because he hates me?"

Charlotte cringed. "I don't mean any offense."

"None taken." Linnet was still laughing. "Jack doesn't really hate me. He hates what our father did to his mother. And I'm the living proof of what the admiral did. I understand why Jack resents my presence, but I also don't give him an inch if he tries to blame me for things I'm not responsible for."

When they reached the trolley stop, Linnet turned to Charlotte. "So?"

Charlotte lifted her brows.

Linnet smiled wickedly. "Are you going to give my brother a second chance?"

"I don't know if I can." Charlotte looked down at the trolley tracks.

The trolley bell rang in the distance.

"Well, if you decide you can't, that may be just as well," Linnet told Charlotte. "Because I'm fairly certain Coe didn't bring you to the palace tonight just to torment Jack."

"He said he wanted to teach Jack a lesson," Charlotte said quietly.

Linnet shook her head. "That's not it either."

"What reason would he have?" Charlotte asked as the cable car pulled up.

"Don't you think it's obvious?" Linnet said, stepping into the trolley. "Coe wants you for himself."

21.

THOUGH CHARLOTTE COULD hardly believe it possible, the next morning proved worse than the night before.

For a few blissful moments after she woke, Charlotte didn't remember anything that had transpired at the Governor's Palace. Then the world came crashing down on her. She pulled the sheets over her face and shut her eyes tight. She didn't want to be here. She wanted to wake up and be back in the Catacombs, having never seen the Floating City, met Lord Ott, or entered the House of Winter. And most of all, she wished she'd never admitted that she loved Jack.

When it became clear that no amount of wishing would send her back in time, Charlotte threw off the covers and set about preparing to face the day. She dressed in a clean chemise and soft muslin dress. She wrapped a paisley shawl around her shoulders.

The house was quiet. Charlotte wondered if Ash had yet returned. When she'd arrived at the mansion with Linnet, Charlotte's brother had already departed for his first meeting with the city's contingent of rebels. A little relieved she was spared having to explain the night's events to Ash, Charlotte had bidden Linnet farewell and then collapsed into Meg's arms with a wail. It was for the best. Meg let Charlotte sniffle and weep and condemn Jack to every awful fate she could imagine. Charlotte didn't remember falling asleep, but she knew Meg had stayed with her until she'd cried herself past the point of exhaustion.

If Ash had been witness to Charlotte's heartbreak, he might have challenged Jack to a duel on the spot. While Charlotte didn't ever want to see Jack again, she wasn't sure she wanted him dead. Meg would be able to convey the necessary information to Ashley in a way that might just persuade him to let Jack go on living.

Though it meant risking an encounter with Lady Winter, Charlotte went to the courtyard. Lady Winter wasn't in the garden, but Charlotte found Grave sitting on a marble bench watching the jewel-embellished peacock parade around its home.

Grave looked up when Charlotte approached.

"I'm sorry I ran away," he said. "And for hitting Jack."

"Don't be sorry about Jack," Charlotte said. "And as for running away, I'm just glad you're safe."

Grave nodded and returned to admiring the bird.

"Do you know why you ran?" Charlotte sat beside him. "Did you remember something?"

"I just knew that I'd been that afraid before," Grave answered. "I thought that if I didn't run, I would die."

Charlotte considered that, then asked, "Where did Linnet find you?"

"I wasn't sure where I was," Grave said. "But Linnet said I was walking toward the Hive."

"You were wearing the clothes of a Hive worker when I met you," Charlotte told him. "I think that must be where you came from."

"But the people at the temple will be able to tell me for sure?" Grave sounded neither happy nor sad.

"Meg's mother seemed to think so," Charlotte replied.

"Will we go there today?"

"We have to wait for Ash to tell us." Charlotte rubbed her temples. She hoped they would go to the temple that day, solve the mystery of Grave, and then leave this city and never come back.

"Charlotte!"

Recognizing Jack's voice, Charlotte wanted to crawl under the bench. Instead, she sat up straighter and looked toward the sound of his call.

Jack crossed the lawn, slowing when he saw Charlotte wasn't alone.

"Hello, Jack." Grave stood up. "I'm very sorry I hit you."

"Don't worry about it, mate," Jack said, then added,

"Actually, you can make it up to me by giving me some time alone to speak with Charlotte."

"I don't want to be alone with you," Charlotte snapped, not caring that Grave heard her anger.

Jack came to the bench and dropped to one knee. "Please, Charlotte. Give me a chance to explain."

"Fine." Charlotte hid her trembling hands under her shawl. "But Grave stays."

"I don't think—" Jack began.

"Grave stays, or you can leave," Charlotte interrupted. "I want his opinion on whether what you have to say has merit."

Grave's brow furrowed. "I don't know that I'll be very helpful."

"I'm sure you will." Charlotte patted Grave's hand. In truth, she needed Grave to stay put because she was certain Jack wouldn't try to kiss her with the other boy present. She was equally certain that if Grave left them and Jack did kiss her, she'd be lost.

Turning to Jack, Charlotte told him, "Say what you will."

The annoyed glance Jack threw at Grave gave Charlotte a bit of satisfaction.

Jack lowered his voice. "I was going to break it off."

When Charlotte didn't say anything, Jack added, "The engagement. I was going to end it last night."

"You *were* going to?" Charlotte asked archly. "Does that mean you're still pledged to Lady Eleanor?"

"I don't want to be." Jack sidestepped the question.

"But you are," Charlotte said. "Even now that I know about her, you didn't end it. And that's all that matters."

"That isn't all that matters," Jack insisted. He looked at Grave. "Are you sure he has to be here?"

"Yes." Charlotte stood up. "You should have told me."

"I didn't know how." Jack rose and faced her. "I thought I could end the engagement quietly and you wouldn't have to be bothered with it. I didn't want you to think poorly of me."

"Well, that was bad judgment on your part," Charlotte said. "Because I think very poorly of you now."

"You said you loved me," Jack pressed. "Doesn't that mean anything?"

Grave turned around on the bench and concentrated on the peacock.

"That's not fair." Charlotte's throat tightened. "You lied to me. You never told me that you were tied to your life here. Jack, you're pledged to marry her! Last night, before the ball, I thought you wanted—" She couldn't get the words out, but Jack finished for her.

"You."

Charlotte looked down. The grass beneath her feet pooled and eddied as her vision was blurred by tears.

"I do, Charlotte," she heard Jack say. "I want you more than anything."

"Then why didn't you call off your engagement?" Charlotte didn't lift her face.

There was a long pause before Jack answered, "I needed to talk to you first."

"So you could be certain I'd still want you?" Charlotte turned away from him. "And if I didn't, you could go on with your Eleanor as if none of this ever happened?"

"It's not so simple as that," Jack said. "Eleanor is a sweet girl. We were barely more than children when I asked for her hand. It was foolish—I know that now. But I don't want to disgrace her without cause."

"Without cause?" Charlotte glared at him, no longer caring if he saw her tear-streaked face. "You claim to want me, to love me, but you'll still marry her if I can't forgive you."

Jack shook his head. "You don't understand what it's like here, Charlotte. There are politics and social expectations to consider. It's no easy task to end an engagement without causing a scandal. I'm trying to act with honor."

"I do understand, Jack." Charlotte glowered at him. "You want me, but you don't want to tarnish the perfect future you've been building. You can keep your honor and your pretty fiancée. I want none of it."

"Don't do this." Jack reached for Charlotte, but she drew back.

"I haven't done anything," Charlotte said. "All this was of your making. But your brother put it plainly enough— remember, Jack, you're not playing in the woods anymore."

"Coe never should have said that." Jack's hands balled into fists. "He knows nothing about us."

"I think your brother grasped the truth about us very quickly," Charlotte countered. "What's done is done. Now please leave."

Charlotte returned to her seat on the bench, but didn't look at Jack again. Having confronted him, she knew that it wasn't a matter of wanting Jack as a lover or a husband—before last night she would have welcomed him into her heart either way, but he hadn't responded in kind. Charlotte would have risked everything to love him. When it came to love, Jack had long been hedging his bets. That was something Charlotte wouldn't abide.

Beside Charlotte, Grave stood up and faced Jack. "You should go. She heard what you had to say, and now she wants you to go."

Charlotte listened to Jack's retreating footsteps, and a fresh wave of tears spilled down her cheeks.

Grave sat beside her and frowned. "That was rather awful, wasn't it?"

"Yes." Charlotte sniffled. "Thank you for staying."

He surprised her when he said, "I'll always do what you ask, Charlotte."

"Why?" Charlotte blinked at him through her tears.

"Because you're the one who saved me," Grave replied.

22.

THE TWIN TEMPLES of Hephaestus and Athene stood at opposite ends of the Market Platform.

"These are the Empire's gods?" Grave asked as they moved through the bustling streets. Around them servants went to and fro between the many stores, running errands for their employers.

"Britannia is a Christian nation," Meg told him. "But the Empire's scholars and priests found inspiration in the Greek pantheon and revived its popularity. Athene and Hephaestus represent the most ideal aspects of the one Christian God."

"But if there's a whole pantheon, why these two?" Grave walked between Meg and Charlotte.

Meg said to Grave, "The Empire claims its strength in

industry and craft. Hephaestus is blacksmith to the gods. He is meant to provide inspiration and guidance to the workers of the Foundry, who toil like the god at his anvil. Athene, goddess of wisdom, is also patron of complex craft—weaving, clockwork, machinery. The temples were built at opposite points on the same platform because god and goddess represent the harmony and tension between art and industry. Harmony because both Athene and Hephaestus are servants of war."

"What's the tension?" Grave looked puzzled.

"Hephaestus once attempted to rape Athene," Meg told him. "But she eluded his assault; thus, art must remain free of the corruption of industry, but the Empire requires both to maintain its glory."

"And isn't that why the servants of Athene must be virgins?" Charlotte asked.

Meg nodded, then added wistfully, "Athene is a virgin goddess, and her servants likewise forsake the company of men."

Charlotte's mouth twisted. Maybe the priestesses were onto something. Forsaking the company of men sounded like a fine idea to her.

Coe was leading their small group along the crowded platform while Ash took up the rear. Commodore Winter had offered to escort them through the city, assuring them that his military rank would allow their party access to places where it might otherwise be denied. Ash was happy enough for Coe to join them, but Charlotte regarded his presence with unease. Jack hadn't made an appearance since their exchange in the courtyard, and Charlotte couldn't quite shake off the jarring memories of the Winter brothers and the ball. With Coe along for the hunt after Grave's identity, Charlotte found it all the more difficult to keep her turbulent mood in check. Though she had to admit, having Coe serve as their military escort was far preferable to having Jack volunteer for that role.

Charlotte guessed Jack was avoiding Ashley as much as her. When she had first seen Ash that morning, her brother had been relieved that Charlotte had returned safely to the mansion, but his greeting had been stiff and awkward. Charlotte supposed that Ash was sorry for her heartache, but unsure what he should do about it. And as much as she was certain Ash would have words with Jack, she doubted Ash was eager to talk of love with his little sister. It was just as well. Charlotte preferred not to talk of the matter any more either.

As they neared the temple, the likeness of Athene rose up to greet them. Standing tall before her sacred home, Athene's flowing robes and the spindle in her right hand contrasted with the severity of her helm and the spear she gripped in her left hand.

Supplicants approached the statue and left an eclectic array of offerings: a pocket watch, a bouquet of flowers tied with multicolored ribbon, and a painter's palette accompanied dozens of tiny scrolls that had been placed at the goddess's feet.

Meg paused beside the goddess, looking up at the deity with a sigh. Turning to Coe and Ash, Meg said, "You'll have to stay here. Men aren't welcome inside the temple."

Ash pointed at Grave. "Won't that cause something of a problem?"

"When I explain the reason he's here, I think they'll make an exception," Meg replied.

"It's all right, Ash," Coe said. "You can fill me in on last night's meeting while we wait."

Charlotte looked at Coe in surprise. "You weren't at the meeting?" She'd assumed that Jack, Ash, and Coe had gone to the covert assembly of rebels together in the hours after Linnet had rescued her from the ball.

With a shake of his head, Coe answered, "Jack and I never attend the same meetings. When one of us goes, the other remains in public, keeping an eye out for any signs that the Empire has gotten a whiff of the meeting's time or location."

"That's what happened when you came to warn us about the raid on the fair?" Charlotte asked.

"Exactly."

"Come, Charlotte," Meg prompted. "I want to speak with the Sisters before they begin their midday prayers, or we'll be waiting a long time for an audience."

Taking Grave's hand, Charlotte followed Meg up the steps to Athene's temple. She felt a prickling on her neck and glanced over her shoulder to find Coe watching her.

He wants you for himself.

Charlotte was mostly convinced that Linnet had been teasing her, but ever since the other girl had suggested that Coe had more than a friendly interest in Charlotte, she'd become uncomfortable around him, in addition to remaining angry that he'd lied in order to get her to the military ball.

When they reached the portico at the top of the stairs, Charlotte saw that half a dozen or more men knelt or stood just outside the temple. Some appeared to be praying, others admiring; a few paced anxiously.

Meg stopped and said, "We shouldn't take Grave any farther until we're granted permission. Wait here."

She continued into the pronaos and disappeared from sight.

"Are you nervous?" Charlotte was still holding Grave's hand. She'd always thought that Grave must be near her in age, but today he seemed much younger.

"This is a strange place," Grave replied.

When Meg emerged from the temple a few minutes later, she was accompanied by a priestess.

"My name is Alana," the priestess told them. "Servant of Athene. You are the boy who seeks the goddess's wisdom?"

"Yes," Grave answered, but he sounded uncertain.

"Give me your hands." Alana's command echoed Jedda's from their night at the fair.

Obediently, Grave placed his hands in Alana's open palms. Like Meg's mother, Alana closed her eyes. Soon she was frowning.

Releasing Grave, Alana turned to Meg. "This is troubling."

"May we please bring him inside and receive your aid?" Meg inclined her head to the priestess.

Alana frowned, but after a moment, she nodded and beckoned for the three of them to follow her.

The interior of the temple was cool and airy. They passed through the pronaos into the cella, where Alana knelt before a much smaller statue of the goddess. Meg imitated Alana's reverent action, so Charlotte felt compelled to also. Grave watched them, puzzled.

As Charlotte stood, Grave came to her side and whispered, "Why did you kneel before dead stone?"

Horrified, Charlotte shushed him. "You mustn't say such things here. It's blasphemy."

"What's blasphemy?" Grave asked, eyes wide.

"Something that gives offense to their goddess," Charlotte said quickly. "Don't ask any questions. Just do as they say."

Alana continued through the cella and passed through a door to a smaller chamber. A round reflecting pool was at the center of the room, and six priestesses stood on the opposite side of the pool, waiting for them.

"Is the matter so urgent that you brought a man into the temple?" one of the women asked.

"Not a man, a boy," Alana answered. "So the corruption is less. And yes, I believe his plight merits our aid."

"Step forward, boy," the speaker commanded. "That we may see your face."

Charlotte looked over her shoulder. She hadn't realized that Grave lingered in the doorway, hidden by shadows.

"Do as they say," Charlotte reminded him in a hissing whisper.

Reluctantly, Grave stepped into the room until his pale face was illuminated by torchlight.

One of the priestesses gave a shriek, then dropped to her knees and covered her face. Grave turned as if to bolt, but Charlotte grabbed him before he could flee.

"Rosemary!" Alana knelt beside the stricken priestess. "What have you seen?"

Rosemary lifted her face; her skin had gone whiter than Grave's. She lifted a shaking hand toward Grave.

"He is my son."

Disturbed murmurs flew among the priestesses.

"Are you certain?" Alana pressed.

Rosemary nodded, staring at Grave in disbelief.

Meg tried to smile, but her trepidation showed. "This is a happy occasion, is it not? Mother and son reunited?"

"You don't understand," Alana replied gravely. "Rosemary's son is dead."

Grave had begun to shake, and Charlotte gripped his arm more tightly, knowing that with Grave's strength, if he really decided to run, she wouldn't be able to stop him.

"Then she must be mistaken," Charlotte told Alana. "He isn't her son, because he obviously isn't dead."

Rosemary drew herself up. "He is my son." Her voice didn't quaver.

"Wait, wait," Charlotte protested. "How can he be your son? Priestesses can't have husbands or children."

"Rosemary came to us bereaved," Alana answered. "She left her former life and joined us in service of the goddess, who is the protector of women. Rosemary no longer has a husband."

"Where is Grave's father?" Meg asked Rosemary.

"Who?" Rosemary kept her gaze on Grave.

"That's what we call the boy." Meg groaned in frustration. "Where is his father? Dead as well?"

"He's in the Hive," Charlotte blurted out. Meg looked at her in surprise, but Rosemary nodded.

"How did you know?" Rosemary asked.

"Grave . . . your son . . . keeps trying to go there," Charlotte told her. "And when we found him, he was wearing clothing from the Hive."

"Where was the boy found?" Alana's eyes narrowed at Charlotte.

Charlotte tensed, but Meg quickly spoke up. "Wandering through the city on his own." She turned to Rosemary. "How did your son die?"

Rosemary quailed, but when Alana gave her a nod, she told them, "My son's name was Timothy. From birth he was a sickly child, weak lungs and a failing heart. We used all my husband's income searching for a doctor who could cure him. But we found no one. All they could do was extend his life—but over time, it became clear that all they truly did was prolong his suffering. For thirteen years."

"But he still lived," Charlotte interjected. She glanced at Grave. He might have amnesia, but he didn't seem to be suffering. "Wasn't that enough?"

"Timothy was exhausted by even a short walk," Rosemary replied sadly. "He couldn't run or play. Nor would he ever be able to work. What sort of future did he have?"

"Surely you didn't just let him die?" Meg asked harshly.

Alana cut a sharp look at Meg, but Rosemary held up her hand. "I know how it must sound, but of course that wasn't what happened. We had no more money to pay doctors or healers. The creditors to whom we owed debts began to make threats of violence against my husband. We could do nothing but mourn as Timothy's body shut down. When my son drew his last breath, I told my husband that I had died with Timothy. I came to the temple. I've never left."

"Does your husband know what happened to you?" Charlotte thought it overly cruel that the poor man had lost his son and wife in one stroke.

"We sent a letter informing him that Rosemary had taken her vows," Alana answered. She took Rosemary's hand. "My sister, are you certain this boy is your child?"

"I swear by Athene's wisdom, I know my own son." Rosemary stared at Grave. "And though it be impossible, he stands before me now."

Frustrated by this talk of dead children come back to life, Charlotte snapped, "Obviously you were wrong. Your Timothy wasn't truly dead, and you ran off before you knew that."

Alana shook her head. "We have strict conditions that must be met before a new Sister is admitted to the order. The boy's father wrote to us to confirm the circumstances of the child's death and his hope that Rosemary would find solace in her grief by serving in the temple."

"Maybe he was just angry." Charlotte wasn't ready to believe this strange tale. "Maybe he thought himself well rid of her."

"Charlotte!" Meg's voice was steely. "Remember that we are guests in a sacred place."

Charlotte went silent but folded her arms across her chest. So far this temple seemed more silly than sacred to her. Rosemary was mad, that was the only possibility. This trip had been a complete waste of their time.

"You must find my husband," Rosemary told them, wringing her hands. "I know Timothy died, but perhaps he could offer some explanation. I hate to think it, but if my husband was unfaithful, this boy could be a brother of Timothy's nigh the same age. Timothy's hair was much lighter." She was peering at Grave.

Charlotte cringed. Grave's hair was only dark because

they'd dyed it so he wouldn't be recognized. But hair dye couldn't fool Grave's own mother.

She's not his mother, Charlotte chided herself. *She can't be.*

"Can you tell us where to find him?" Meg asked. "That seems our best course."

"His name is Hackett Bromley," Rosemary said with a note of regret. "He's a member of the Inventors' Guild. You'll find him there."

Charlotte did not like this Rosemary one bit. She had abandoned her penniless husband at the lowest moment in their lives to go hide behind the stone walls of this temple. She might have been a sorrowful mother, but Charlotte judged her to be terribly selfish as well.

"Grave," Meg spoke softly, "do you want to spend some time with Rosemary while we go to the Hive?"

Rosemary awaited Grave's reply with fearful anticipation.

He looked at her trembling frame and said, "I'm sorry, but I don't know you."

Her face remained blank, showing neither relief or disappointment at Grave's answer, and Rosemary said, "Perhaps that is best. I serve the goddess now."

It was all Charlotte could do not to snort in disgust. She was glad of Grave's answer. She didn't want to leave him in this place. Something about the temple and its priestesses unsettled her. Though they'd given Charlotte no cause to distrust them, she had the creeping sense that they were hiding something.

Alana stepped away from the gathered priestesses and gestured to the door. "Return to us after you've found Bromley. I am sorry that we only have questions to give you, not answers."

Meg curtsied to Alana. "Thank you for seeing us."

Charlotte hooked her arm through Grave's and tugged him toward the door. Walking as quickly as she could without breaking into a run, Charlotte pulled Grave back through the cella, past the portico, and down the temple steps. She didn't stop until she reached Ash and Coe.

"Well, boy," Ash said gruffly, speaking to Grave, "did the priestesses unlock that memory of yours?"

Charlotte made a disgusted noise. Ash frowned at her. "What's wrong?"

"Those ninnies couldn't tell us anything helpful."

"What did they tell you?" Coe asked.

Grave answered quietly, "That I'm dead."

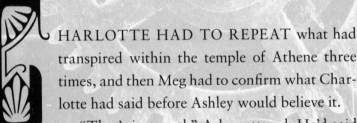

23.

CHARLOTTE HAD TO REPEAT what had transpired within the temple of Athene three times, and then Meg had to confirm what Charlotte had said before Ashley would believe it.

"That's just mad," Ash muttered. He'd said the same thing several minutes ago, and several minutes before that.

Charlotte found no fault in her brother's assessment.

Meg sighed. "Maybe. But it's all we have to work with." She'd been distracted, fidgeting and falling behind in their conversation since leaving the temple.

"So our plan is to find a dead boy's father and show him Grave," Ashley said. "That is a terrible, terrible idea."

Charlotte shrugged. "I agree, but what else can we do?"

"I have another question that no one will like," Coe put in.

They all looked at him, and he continued, "If, as seems likely, this trip leads nowhere, what then?"

An uncomfortable silence fell between them. Charlotte was surprised that it was Grave who finally spoke.

"You won't send me away, will you?"

Ash shifted uneasily on the trolley bench. "What do you mean?"

"I want to stay in the Catacombs," Grave said firmly. "I think that's what's best for me. I like Birch. I'll help him with his work."

"There's more to it than that, Grave," Ash told him. "We don't just live in the Catacombs. We're hiding there."

Grave nodded vigorously. "I won't tell anyone where you are. I promise. Just don't leave me with that woman at the temple."

Charlotte gave an affirmative "hmmpf." She wouldn't want to be sent back to the temple either. Creepy, rude priestesses in their creepy, cold room.

Meg sighed again.

"Are you unwell?" Ash leaned forward to peer at Meg.

"I'm fine. Just tired." She waved him off, but Charlotte agreed with her brother. Meg didn't seem fine at all. Her face was drawn. Her gaze faraway.

Charlotte reached for Meg's hand. "If you need to rest, go back to the mansion. We'll come to you once we've finished this wild-goose chase."

"Have a little faith, Lottie." Meg smiled at Charlotte. "We don't know that it's a wild-goose chase yet."

Meg's words made Charlotte's skin crawl, though she couldn't say why.

"There's the Hive." Coe pointed to the front of the cable car.

True to its namesake, the Hive's tall, cone-shaped structure dominated its platform. Plated in brass interrupted by the rare window and steam vent, the Hive wasn't a welcoming sort of place.

Even before the trolley arrived at its station, Charlotte sensed the distinct change in atmosphere from the rest of the Floating City. The other platforms exuded an ease that bordered on laxity. The Hive, by contrast, was noisy and harried. Passengers, wearing the plain gray garb that signified their status, rushed to exit the car, while others shoved their way onto the trolley. The only thing that curbed their pushy behavior was the sight of Coe's uniform. When Coe walked at the head of their small party, people moved aside to give him a wide berth. As he passed, nervous glances and whispers trailed him.

Coe led them to one of the arched entrances at the Hive's base. Access to the interior was gained through narrow gates that opened and closed at the discretion of an operator.

Coe cleared his throat to gain the attention of the wiry man who sat in the gatehouse. The operator's cap was too big for his weasel-like features and kept sliding over his eyes, making him more inclined to repositioning the cap than opening the gate.

"Excuse me," Coe finally said, rapping on the gatehouse window.

"Lay off or I'll see you fined for disorderly conduct," the operator snarled, but when he looked up and saw Coe, he straightened on his stool so abruptly that he fell right off it.

Scrambling up and readjusting his cap once more, the operator stammered, "M-m-my apologies, s-s-s-sir. How can I be of assistance?"

"We have an appointment with the Inventors' Guild," Coe informed him.

The man's beady eyes narrowed when he looked over Charlotte, Meg, Ash, and Grave. "All of you?" the operator inquired of Coe. "Do you have papers?"

Coe smiled at the little man, but his tone was so cold he might as well have drawn his pistol. "Military business is not subject to your bureaucratic oversight. Let me talk to your superior."

"No, no, no," the operator squeaked. "That's not necessary."

He pulled a chain that dangled from the gatehouse ceiling, and the metal barricade swung open.

When they were past the gate, Ash said to Coe, "He could be talking about that if he heads to the tavern this evening."

"If he talks, Ott will know before anyone else does," Coe replied. "And he'll make sure nothing comes of it."

An amalgam of sound rose from within the Hive's wide base, spiraling toward its pinnacle.

"The workshops occupy the lower levels," Coe told them. "In the middle you'll find a mix of specialty shops and living spaces. The higher tiers are strictly residential."

Charlotte let her head drop back, and she turned in a slow circle, so she could gaze up at ring after ring of the Hive. An elevator bank served as a structural foundation at the center of the Hive, and at each level, bridges extended outward from the elevators like spokes on a wheel.

"Do many artisans choose to live where they work?" Charlotte asked.

"They don't have a choice," Coe answered. "Artisans assigned to one of the Hive guilds are required to live within this structure."

At Charlotte's startled reaction, Coe added, "It's their concession for being allowed to reside in the Floating City rather than with most laborers in the Commons."

The Inventors' Guild occupied a quarter of the Hive's ground levels, its door labeled with a brass plate bearing the guild's crest. But when they passed into the guild itself, Charlotte was certain they were in the wrong place.

Every wall was lined with shelves brimming with stacks of paper. They could barely find space to move through the room due to the easels, drafting boards, and desks—also covered with papers, charts, and sketches—squeezed into every nook and cranny.

Despite the overabundance of inanimate objects in the guild, not a living soul was to be seen.

"Where is everyone?" Ash asked.

"Someone must be here," Coe said, but he sounded uncertain.

Charlotte threw him a questioning glance, at which he shrugged.

"Inventors are notoriously unreliable. Their minds are set to their tinkering, and they make little effort to ensure that the bureaucratic side of the guild runs smoothly."

"Here." Charlotte pushed past Coe to a desk that at first glance seemed to be part of the general clutter, but that Charlotte noted was much larger than the others in the room. Clearing off a layer of papers, Charlotte discovered a button inlaid upon the desktop with the word ASSISTANCE etched above it.

Charlotte pushed the button, and a trumpet fanfare sounded around them. Coe knocked over an easel, and Ash cursed until he was out of breath.

Somewhere behind the dunes of paperwork, a voice piped up. "Is someone there?"

"Yes!" Charlotte called. "We need assistance!" She hoped invoking the official button word would improve her chances of getting help.

A short man whose helmet was twice the height of his head and seemed to boast a built-in telescope, magnifying glass, and astrolabe rolled up to the desk—rolled because he was riding around on a narrow, wheeled plank controlled by two small hand cranks attached to a long metal tube at the center of the plank.

The man arranged the scattered pages on the desk into misshapen stacks, then twirled the ends of his waxed mustache as he peered at Charlotte.

"Guild identification?"

"I'm not a guild member," Charlotte said.

The man snorted in disgust. Rearranging more sheets of paper on the desktop, he pointed to the space above the button Charlotte had pushed. In the newly cleared space, Charlotte read MEMBER ASSISTANCE.

"Oh," Charlotte said. "I'm so sorry, but—"

But the man had already turned his apparatus around and was wheeling away.

"Wait!" Charlotte called after him.

He paid her no mind, disappearing whence he had come.

Shoving all the remaining papers off the desk, Charlotte found another button with the label VISITOR ASSISTANCE. She slammed her hand down on the button.

A moment later, the same man returned on his strange transport.

"May I be of assistance, miss?"

Charlotte stared at him. "But you were just here."

"Yes."

"Why didn't you offer to help me then?"

"I was here to assist on guild matters," the man replied.

"But you're the same person," Charlotte argued.

"I am," he said, returning her stare without blinking.

Charlotte stared so hard that she thought her eyeballs might drop out of her skull.

Coe came to the desk and moved Charlotte aside.

"We need to locate one of your members," Coe told the man.

The man's nose gave a rabbitlike twitch when he took note of Coe's uniform. "Our members spend their time on diverse projects throughout the Hive, sir. The guild hall is simply our repository for member records and idea claims and accident reports."

Coe gave a knowing, but disgusted nod, so Charlotte said, "If we tell you who he is, can you tell us what project he's working on and where we can find him?"

"Of course, miss," the man replied. "What is his guild identification?"

"Hackett Bromley," Charlotte answered.

"That's not an identification."

"That's his name," Coe pointed out.

"Yes. But what is his identification?"

Despite his familiarity with the inner workings of the Inventors' Guild, Coe's patience had run out. "Do I really need to know?" He put his hand on his gun holster, but the man didn't notice.

"Yes. If you don't know the identification, you'll have to look him up." He pointed at a teetering tower of papers in the room's far corner. "All guild registration papers are there. Of course, we haven't had time to alphabetize them yet—"

Coe reached across the desk, grabbed the man's helmet, and lifted him off his feet.

He choked and sputtered as the helmet's chin strap dug into his throat.

"I don't have time to look it up," Coe said calmly.

He let the man kick at the air a few more times before dropping him. The man fell onto his backside.

"It's just the system, sir. I'm only trying to explain how it works!" The man yelped, his mustache quivering.

"You'll change the system as I see fit, or I'll have you hanging in Boston by the end of the day."

Meg must have wanted to put an end to Coe's threats, because she rushed to the desk. "We told you his name: Hackett Bromley. Just tell us where to find him."

The man rubbed at his reddened throat. "He's consulting on weapons development at the Colonial Espionage Bureau: Mechanics Division. Second ring. North sector."

"Thank you," Meg said. She grabbed Coe by the arm and hauled him away from the desk. "We don't need to waste any more time."

Charlotte was more than happy to leave the Inventors' Guild office behind. She would have been even happier to see a torch put to the place. They took the elevator to the Hive's second level and walked the circumference of the ring to its north end. The mustached man hadn't misdirected them. Coe opened a door bearing the plate: CEB: Mechanics Division.

To Charlotte's surprise, Grave went through the door first. Ash and Charlotte hurried after him. The room was full of long worktables. Goggled men wielding tools were hunched over contraptions of all shapes and sizes. They were astoundingly dedicated to their craft. Not a single man looked up when the door banged shut behind Coe.

"It's probably best if I handle this," Coe told them.

Moving to the fore of the room, Coe cleared his throat, then announced in a booming voice, "Gentlemen, your attention, please."

A dozen pairs of eyes, made unnaturally large by their owners' goggles, were suddenly on Coe. No one moved, nor did anyone speak.

"Mr. Hackett Bromley," Coe said, "would you please identify yourself?"

At the fourth table back on the right side, a man slid from his stool and removed his wool cap.

"I'm Bromley, sir." He stepped into the space between the two rows of tables.

Charlotte held her breath. Though his skin was ruddy rather than colorless, there was no mistaking the resemblance to Grave.

Behind Charlotte, Meg whispered, "Not a goose chase."

"If you'd step outside with me, please." Coe returned to the door and opened it.

While his fellows went back to their work, Bromley

came forward, twisting his cap in his hands. He was almost to Coe when he noticed Grave standing beside Ash. Bromley halted, his mouth forming an O of surprise. Then he looked at Coe again. And bolted.

With a shout, Coe dashed after Bromley, leaving the rest of them to scramble behind the pair. Coe chased Bromley along the ring's perimeter, but as they ran, Grave passed Charlotte, Ash, and Meg, gaining steadily on Coe and Bromley. Rushing past Coe, Grave reached out and grabbed the back of Bromley's leather apron.

Grave pulled up suddenly, and Bromley jerked back with a cry.

Coe spoke low and quickly. "Grave, take him into the side passage. We can't have him causing a scene."

Though the boy was half Bromley's size, he had no trouble wrestling the terrified inventor off the main walkway.

They huddled in the narrow corridor. Grave had Bromley pinned to the wall.

"Oh, my boy, my boy." Bromley was trembling. "What have they done to you?"

"Why did you run from me, Father?" Grave asked him.

"Father?" Charlotte edged her way closer to Grave. "Do you remember him?"

"Yes," Grave answered. "He's my father. The Maker."

"What's he talking about?" Ash frowned.

"I have no idea," Charlotte said quietly. "He didn't know Rosemary—and she claimed to be his mother."

Bromley was gazing at Grave as if he didn't know

whether to be relieved or to despair. "What have you told them about me?"

"Nothing," Charlotte answered for Grave. "I have no idea why he recognizes you when he hasn't been able to tell us his own name."

As if seeing for the first time that their party comprised more than Coe and Grave, Bromley gave Charlotte a puzzled look. "Who are you? You can't all be from the CEB."

"None of us are from the CEB, chap," Coe said. "But don't think for an instant that makes us less of a danger to you."

"But you're military," Bromley said to Coe.

"I'm not in research," Coe replied. "And that's all you need to know about me for the time being."

Bromley cringed and looked at Grave. "Can you let me go, boy? You're hurting me."

Grave tilted his head, as if confused by the statement, but released his grip on the older man. Rubbing his upper arms, Bromley stared in wonder at Grave.

"So strong," he murmured. "I suspected that, but there was no way to be sure."

"We have a lot of questions to which you seem to be the only one with answers," Ash said, drawing Bromley out of his musings. "Is there somewhere we can talk privately?"

Bromley hesitated, then relented. "I have a room on the fifth ring. We can go there."

"You live alone?" Ashley asked.

"Yes," Bromley said. "We won't be bothered. I've already

met my quota for the week, so if I don't return to the workshop today, it won't be a problem."

"Good," Coe said. "Let's go, then." He kept his hand on Bromley's shoulder as the inventor led them to the elevator bank.

Charlotte caught Grave's hand, holding him back. When he looked at her, his tawny eyes were sad.

"You remember, don't you?" Charlotte squeezed his fingers. "Seeing Bromley brought your memory back."

"Not all of it," Grave said softly. "But I remember something important."

"What?" Charlotte asked.

"Dying."

24.

HARLOTTE DIDN'T LET go of Grave's hand, though she was afraid to keep holding it. *He must be mistaken. He's been upset because of Bromley, but what he told me can't be true. It can't.*

On the fifth ring, Bromley took them down a long, narrow side corridor until he stopped in front of a metal door identical to ten others on either side of the hall. A tin plate affixed to the door read H. BROMLEY.

The room was cramped and had no windows. A bed crowded against a writing desk and stool. In a narrow alcove, Charlotte spotted a washbasin and toilet.

Bromley made his way to the bed and sat down. Grave left Charlotte's side and sat on the bed with the man he'd called both Father and Maker. Coe took the stool and perched like a watchman near Bromley. Charlotte, Ash, and Meg stood in a cluster near the door.

As their silence filled the small room, Bromley lapsed into staring at Grave.

"I didn't think you'd return," Bromley murmured.

"But you sent him away," Ash said pointedly. "He was wandering alone when we found him."

When I *found him,* Charlotte thought.

Bromley bowed his head. "I had no choice. The boy couldn't stay here."

"Why are you calling him 'the boy'?" Charlotte asked. "Is he your son or not?"

"You think it's a simple question," Bromley replied. "But you're wrong about that."

Meg moved farther into the room and knelt on the floor in front of Bromley. "Your wife, Rosemary, sent us here."

Bromley's head jerked up. "You've seen her?"

"At the temple," Meg said. "She recognized Grave as her son. But she also said her son had died."

"Yes," Bromley said, his expression wan. "Our son died."

"This is ridiculous." Ash ground the heel of his boot into the floor. "We didn't bring a dead boy here."

Bromley's laugh was hollow, but it was Grave who spoke.

"Yes, you did. But you didn't know it."

"It's coming back to you, isn't it, boy?" Bromley asked Grave sadly. "I'm not surprised, given that it all happened here in the Hive."

Grave nodded, then sighed.

"You must be related," Ash snarled. "Because you're clearly both mad."

"Hush, Ashley," Meg chided. "They're telling us the end of a story, but we need to know the beginning."

Ash ground his teeth but held his tongue.

Meg looked up at the inventor. "You're the one who must tell us this tale."

Bromley gazed at Meg's upturned face, and the tension eased from his limbs. His voice took on a dreamy quality.

"The day my son was born, I was the happiest man that ever was," Bromley said. "How could something so perfect as my own child bring a curse upon my life? I never thought it could be so."

"Illness is not a curse. There is something else that caused your sorrow, something hidden. Reveal it to us." Meg spoke in a slow, soothing tone.

Bromley moaned. His jaw clenched as if he was in pain, but he didn't look away from Meg's steady gaze. "I only wanted to save him."

"Your son." Meg nodded. "As any father would."

"But I am not any father," Bromley whispered. "I am an inventor."

"You invented something you hoped would save your child?" Meg asked.

"Yes." Bromley's voice shook. "But I had to let him go before I could bring him back."

"The child died?" Meg inched closer to Bromley.

Bromley's fingers dug into the mattress. "It wasn't his fault. He was born with a body too frail. I wanted to make him stronger."

Meg asked softly, "How?"

"In the mysteries of Athene and the fires of Hephaestus," Bromley said. "That is where I found the answer."

Bromley stood up and reached past Coe toward the writing table. Bromley slid his hand beneath the table. Charlotte heard a click, and something dropped into Bromley's waiting hand. When he sat on the bed again, he was holding a book. The cover was plain; the pages were bound in black leather. Meg took it from him.

When she opened the book and read its opening lines, she drew a hissing breath.

"What is it?" Ashley tried to look over Meg's shoulder, but she closed the cover and tucked it in the folds of her skirt to keep it out of sight.

Meg was looking at Grave, scrutinizing him.

"I know what you're looking for," Bromley said to her. "You won't find it."

"Why not?" Meg snapped, her soothing tone retreated before anger.

"My innovation," Bromley said. "Restructure the body before reviving it."

Meg stood up. "What is he?" She pointed at Grave.

"Flesh and blood," Bromley answered. "But blood is iron, and bone can become steel. The heart and lungs are but machines. If built with skill, they will run perpetually and perfectly."

Charlotte's nails dug into her palms. He couldn't be saying what she thought he was.

"My father." Grave turned his eyes upon Bromley. "The Maker."

Ash had the bridge of his nose pinched between his fingers. "If I'm following this nonsense—and believe me when I say I think it's all nonsense—you're suggesting that your son died, and you rebuilt him with machinery."

"That is precisely what I did," Bromley replied.

"But he's not a machine," Charlotte said, her mind flashing to the mechanical creatures harnessed to carriages outside the Governor's Palace. "He's a person."

"He's the echo of a person," Meg said quietly.

"Yes." Bromley passed a weary hand over his eyes. "I thought I could bring my son back. Stronger. Whole."

Meg shook her head. "That's not how it works. That's why it's forbidden."

"What are you talking about?" Coe snapped at Meg in frustration.

Withdrawing the leather-bound book from where she'd tucked it into her skirts, Meg took a deep breath and said, "This is the Book of the Dead. Not the true book, but transcribed passages from the original."

"Bah!" Ash began to laugh. "That's a child's ghost story."

"I once thought as you," Bromley said in a rough voice. "The book is real."

"What's the Book of the Dead?" Charlotte asked, frowning.

"It's supposed to contain the keys to the art of necromancy," Ash told her bitterly. "It's a fanciful notion, that's all."

"Your mind is closed to the arcane, Ashley," Meg said. "But that doesn't mean others haven't opened doors to those mysteries, or even walked through them."

Coe stood up, towering over Bromley. "If you're goading us with these tales—"

"Look at me, young man," Bromley interrupted. "I am destitute. I lost my wife and my son. What could I gain by lying to you and risking your wrath?"

"He's telling us the truth," Meg said. "But he hasn't yet told us how it was that Grave left the city."

Bromley looked at Meg and nodded. "After the boy died and his mother had gone, I began my work. I had no thoughts, only obsession. On the night I finished, I realized what I had done. The natural laws I had broken. When my invention awoke, he would be something new, something both marvelous and terrible, but not my child. And if he were to be discovered . . ."

"Because it was known that your son had died," Meg offered.

"Yes," Bromley told her. "Before he woke, I secreted him from the city."

"And left him in the wildlands," Charlotte whispered.

Bromley turned a pleading gaze on Charlotte. "I knew he wasn't in danger. That no harm would come to him."

"How could you know that?" Coe glared at Bromley. "He's just a boy."

"No." Bromley faced Coe, his expression grim. "He's a dead boy who cannot die again."

25.

THEY DIDN'T SPEAK of it until they'd returned to the House of Winter.

"I thought you came here to aid the Resistance," Coe said to Ash, pouring himself a brandy. The liquid sloshed over the edge of the glass. "Not assemble a menagerie of the city's lunatics."

"This isn't lunacy," Meg told Coe in a sober voice. She pointed to Grave. "He's the proof that something horrible has come to pass."

Charlotte stepped between Meg and Grave. "Don't talk about him like that. He's done nothing wrong."

Meg looked the floor and whispered, "But he *is* wrong."

"That's not fair," Charlotte countered. "You have no proof that anything Bromley said was true. For all we know, he became a lunatic when his son died. He probably imagined the whole thing. We only went to the Hive because Rosemary told us Grave was her son, Timothy, but she's hardly a reliable source of information. Maybe Grave just looks like this Timothy, and Bromley and Rosemary are nothing more than mad, broken souls."

"Your fear is blinding you, Lottie," Meg chided. "Grave himself is the proof. He called Bromley his Maker." She peered around Charlotte to ask Grave, "Is what Bromley told us true?"

Grave had been silent since they had left the Hive. He had called Bromley Father and Maker, but the appellations didn't seem to extend beyond recognition into affection.

Stretching out his arms, Grave stared at his hands and flexed his fingers. He walked to Coe and took the tumbler of brandy from the startled officer's grasp. Without a word, Grave closed his fist, and the crystal crumpled as if it had been paper.

"Athene have mercy," Ash whispered.

Coe grabbed Grave's wrist. When Grave opened his hand, the pulverized tumbler poured onto the drawing room floor like sand.

Grave didn't object when Coe inspected his palm and fingers.

"Not a scratch." Dropping Grave's hand, Coe muttered, "Hephaestus's hammer. What has that crazy bugger done?"

"You finally believe," Meg noted.

"It's not about belief," Coe replied sharply. "It's about

proof. The proof that this inventor, Bromley, managed what the Empire's been after for years and doesn't even realize it."

"What are you talking about, Coe?" Ashley went to Grave and gave a meaningful glance at the boy's hand. "May I?"

Grave silently offered his palm for Ashley's inspection.

"Can't you see?" Coe was taking agitated turns through the parlor. "This boy—Grave, Timothy, whoever he was or is—isn't just some aberration of nature. He's the perfect weapon."

Ash looked at Coe, his eyes widening.

Charlotte put her fists on her hips, glaring at Coe. "How can you call him a weapon? He's never attacked anyone. He's done everything we've asked of him. He's strong. He can break a glass and take a blow to the head, so what?"

"A blow to the head?" Coe repeated, puzzled.

"My cane," Ash offered. "Charlotte has a point. Grave was built for toughness, but we've no proof that he's indestructible. It may be that a bullet could put him down."

"Maybe we should find out." Coe's hand went to the silver-handed pistol at his waist.

"Stop it!" Charlotte shoved Ashley aside and wrapped her arms around Grave. "How can you all talk about him as if he's not a person? As if he isn't standing right here listening to you?"

Coe shrugged. "We haven't gagged him. If he has something to say, he can speak any time."

Charlotte didn't move, but she frowned at his words. It was true, Grave rarely spoke at all. And even now, when a suggestion to shoot him had been made, he seemed unperturbed.

"I don't think a bullet would hurt me," Grave offered in a soft voice. He sounded not at all worried, and that made Charlotte terribly frightened.

"Do you know that a bullet can't hurt you?" Coe raised an eyebrow.

"No," Grave answered. "It's just what I think."

"If the inventor did find a way to bind necromancy to machinery, then Grave speaks the truth," Meg said. "The stories say that armies of the dead could not simply be slain. They had to be utterly destroyed."

"Destroyed how?" Charlotte asked through clenched teeth. Despite how cold she felt, she wouldn't let go of Grave. No matter what strange revelations had been made, she had been the one who found him in the forest. She knew he *could* be afraid. She had glimpsed the fragments of a lost, lonesome boy in Grave. She refused to concede to any assertion that Grave was merely a machine or a monster.

Meg met Charlotte's hard gaze and looked away guiltily. "Dismemberment."

Coe assessed Grave's body. "That might be a lot of work."

"You're talking about dismemberment as work?" Charlotte shot Coe an accusing look.

"Strategically speaking." Coe offered her an apologetic smile.

"But the risen dead of the old stories did not have bodies rebuilt with metal," Meg said. "Because of that difference, in this case, I don't think dismemberment is feasible. He would have to be obliterated."

"Obliterated?" Coe rubbed his chin while he considered that. "Plenty of weapons can do that. Not a revolver of course, but the bigger guns could."

"It's just a matter of blowing him up," Ash said tartly. "Birch could do that."

"We are not blowing him up!" Charlotte stomped her foot.

"Lottie, we don't actually mean to hurt Grave," Ash told her calmly. "But we need to figure out what to do now that we know—or think we know—who he is."

"What he is," Meg corrected.

"No," Charlotte snapped at Meg. "*Who* he is. I don't care what you say or what your stupid old stories say. Grave is a boy. He is one of us."

Meg started to reply, but turned her face away from Charlotte before she uttered any words.

Charlotte stared at Meg. She couldn't understand how Meg could be so cruel. So unfeeling toward Grave. Meg had always been the most nurturing soul Charlotte knew, but now Meg spoke of killing Grave in a voice cold as stone. The city had changed Meg, and Charlotte didn't know why, only how much it grieved her.

"I would like to be one of you," Grave murmured to Charlotte. Encouraged that her instincts about the boy were right, she hugged him tighter, hoping it gave him some comfort. Grave didn't seem to object to Charlotte's hanging on to him, but holding Grave, whose body was cold and stiff, set off a hollow ache in Charlotte's chest.

I wish Jack were here.

Charlotte wanted to believe Jack would take her side in this. Angry as she was with him, Charlotte trusted Jack to see this situation for what it was, not jump to the extreme conclusions that the others had.

But in truth, Charlotte didn't know what Jack would do. She didn't even know where he was right now. Or if he was ever coming back.

Charlotte's voice shook. "When I brought Grave to the Catacombs, he was running from the Rotpots, just like we would. He hasn't done anything to harm us."

"I don't have a problem with Grave," Coe said. "In fact, I'm damn curious about what else he can do. It doesn't change the threat he is."

With a groan, Charlotte argued, "But I just said—"

"Not him in particular." Coe cut her off. "Not one boy. But he represents the potential."

Meg nodded, her face drawn.

"The potential for more." Ash finished Coe's thought. "For others like him."

"If Bromley did it once, he could do it again," Coe said. "If he's kept that book hidden, I'd wager he didn't burn his notes either. Even if he scared himself half to death with what he accomplished, Bromley's still an inventor—a part of him must be well chuffed at what he's done."

"He's not," Charlotte countered. "We all saw him. Bromley is miserable."

"I agree with Charlotte," Meg said, her affirmation startling Charlotte into finally letting go of Grave. "Hackett Bromley is a pitiful creature, but even the sorriest of beasts can be forced to labor."

Ash was nodding. "If the Empire were to find out what he'd done . . ."

"They'd give him no choice but to replicate the process," Coe said. "And the Empire would have a new army."

Though she wanted to, Charlotte could muster no argument to counter the gravity of Coe's words. Grave she could defend. A thousand faceless reanimated corpses— part flesh, part machine—she could only dread.

"What can we do?" Charlotte whispered. With her last threads of courage, she added, "If you try to kill him, you'll have to kill me first."

"Linnet is right about you." The look Coe gave her bordered on admiring. "Don't worry, Charlotte, we won't make you use your claws. For now, the most important thing is to get Grave out of the city. The longer he's here, the more likely someone else is to recognize him—or for Bromley, Rosemary, or one of the other priestesses to say the wrong thing at the wrong time."

"Will we be able to take the Dragonfly back to the Cat-acombs?" Charlotte asked.

"No," Ash answered. "We'll have to make other arrangements."

"I'll take care of it." Coe buttoned his coat. "With luck, I'll have you out of the city tomorrow."

Before he left the parlor, Coe quirked a half smile at Grave. "Don't break any more of my brandy glasses."

The joke and the wink he spared Charlotte let her breathe a bit easier, and exhaustion poured over her. She sank onto the couch.

"You should go to bed, Lottie." Ash came to sit beside her. "It's been a trying day for all of us."

Charlotte looked into Ashley's worried face.

Where's Jack? If we leave tomorrow, will I see him? Does he even want to say good-bye? The questions were on her tongue, desperate to be asked, but she swallowed the words instead.

Before making up her mind, Charlotte looked up at Grave.

"I'll be all right." Grave smiled at her. "You should go to bed."

Charlotte nodded and kissed her brother on the cheek. She didn't bid Meg good night, though she knew it was a petty thing to do. As she ascended the stairs, Charlotte heard the rustle of skirts and soft footsteps behind her, and was irked that Meg would follow her.

She turned around when she reached her bedroom door

and was unsurprised to find Meg watching her from the top of the staircase.

"I can see myself to bed," Charlotte said coldly as she opened the door.

Meg approached her. "Of course you can. But I would like to speak with you."

"To tell me more about how evil Grave is," Charlotte replied. "No, thank you. I've heard enough of that."

When Charlotte passed into the bedroom, Meg followed her, closing the door behind them.

"I'm sorry to have hurt you . . . or Grave," Meg said. "What's happened has frightened me more than you can know."

"Just because you're frightened doesn't give you leave to be hateful." Charlotte sat on a chair in front of a mirrored dresser. "Grave has done nothing to earn your malice."

"Will you let me try to explain?" Meg asked, coming up behind Charlotte.

When Charlotte didn't say no, Meg picked up a brush from the dresser and began to carefully pull tangles from Charlotte's long tresses.

"You didn't know my ancestors were enslaved," Meg said.

"No." Charlotte rocked slightly with the smooth brushstrokes. "You've never spoken of it."

"When my mother sent me from the city," Meg told her, "she didn't intend for me to find a home in the Catacombs. She wanted me to live in the freetowns."

"Beyond the Mississippi?" Charlotte's curiosity bloomed. "And what about your father? Did he wish you sent away as well?"

"My father believed in the cause of the rebellion," Meg said. "He survived the war, but was one of the founders of the Resistance. He was captured and sent to Boston before I was born. My mother told me stories of him often, of his bravery and his sacrifice. But his fate terrified my mother. She never spoke of her grief or her fear, but I could sense how strong the loss was, a shadow in her blood and bones."

Meg drew a sorrowful breath. "I have aunts, uncles, and cousins in the West. I was to be raised by them, away from New York, beyond the Empire's grasp. Despite the terms of abolition, after the Rebellion, many former slaves feared an attempt by the Empire to return them to forced labor. Rather than take that risk, the freemen and freewomen negotiated a new settlement with the Empire. Those who wished would leave the coast and settle on lands beyond the Mississippi trade zone and the French battlements. In return, the freemen and freewomen pledged to neither raise arms against the Empire, nor to support the Resistance."

"And the Empire agreed to the new settlement?" Charlotte asked.

"They had set a precedent for such an agreement in the negotiations undertaken with their Indian allies after the Seven Years' War and the Rebellion."

"To create the Indian territories in Canada." Charlotte looked to Meg for affirmation, and the older girl smiled.

"That's right."

Setting aside the brush, Meg ran her fingers through Charlotte's knot-free locks. "I was a willful child. I didn't want to leave my mother, much less cross some faraway great river whose currents would mark my separation from her. So I fled the caravan that she'd paid for my passage overland. It was the middle of the night when I stole from the wagons."

"Alone?"

"Yes." Meg laughed softly. "Not only was I willful, I was foolish. At six years old, I was certain I could find my own way back to New York. I was also convinced that when I arrived, my mother would be so impressed that she'd never send me away again."

"What happened?" Charlotte knew the wildlands as well as anyone, and she knew how long a child alone could survive there—not long at all.

Meg began to unbutton Charlotte's gown. "You'll not remember Jonathan. He left to join the fighting before you and Ash came to the Catacombs, but he was to me what Ashley is to the young children in hiding now. A leader, a hero."

Charlotte was tempted to tell Meg about the many un-heroic and annoying qualities her brother had, but kept quiet while Meg continued her story.

"Jonathan was scouting and found me in the woods. I was sick from eating poisonous berries I didn't know to avoid. He brought me back to the Catacombs. When I was well again, I told him I wanted to go back to the city. Jonathan told me that he'd take me to my mother, but only after I'd stayed in the Catacombs for a week to make sure I was well enough for the trip."

With a sigh and wistful smile, Meg continued. "It was a clever ploy. In the Catacombs, I was surrounded by children my own age. Like me, they felt displaced, but they had a purpose: to resist the will of the Empire and, most of all, to survive. I made friends so quickly, felt a camaraderie I'd never experienced. One week became two, and soon I didn't want to leave at all."

"Did your mother find out where you were?" Charlotte asked, thinking of how worried Jedda must have been when her daughter never arrived at the freetowns.

"At Jonathan's urging, I sent her a letter," Meg answered. "I told my mother that I was honoring my father by joining the Resistance."

Having loosened Charlotte's gown, Meg went to the wardrobe to retrieve a sleeping chemise. "When my mother wrote back, she praised my bravery and my choice. I doubt she truly felt such things, but worried that any further attempts to send me to the West would only incite another rebellion from me and lead me to a much more dangerous end than a life with other exile children in the Catacombs."

Charlotte slipped out of her gown and day underclothes and pulled on the chemise Meg offered. "Did you ever see your mother when you were young? Did she visit the Catacombs?"

Though she could remember no such visits from Jedda, Charlotte didn't think that meant they hadn't taken place. But Meg shook her head.

"My mother stayed in the city," Meg said. "I stayed in hiding. This trip is the first time I've returned to New York since my mother sent me off with that caravan. I see now that I waited too long, though. Neglected too many things."

"How can you say that?" Charlotte picked up a shawl she'd draped over a chair, wrapping it around her bare shoulders to ward off the creeping chill in the room. "You do more than anyone in the Catacombs. Even more than Ash. He gives orders and makes decisions, but you *take care* of us."

Meg smiled gently. "I don't mean to deride the role I've played in the Catacombs. But what I learned in the temple and in the Hive made me aware that I've been hiding from truths about who I am. Truths I have to face now."

"Are you talking about magic?" Charlotte didn't intend to snort derisively, but she did. "Do you really believe any of that could be real?"

Despite Meg's strange behavior since she'd visited her mother at the Tinkers' Faire, and her even more unexpected reaction to Bromley's assertions about Grave's identity, Charlotte still had a hard time acknowledging that someone as grounded as Meg could take such wild ideas seriously. Meg obviously did, but Charlotte couldn't bring herself to accept that.

"There have been many moments in the past when you would have believed too, Lottie. No culture is without access to divine mysteries," Meg told Charlotte. "But whether the people in any civilization choose to embrace the arcane is a matter that ebbs and flows with the passing of time. Your Empire chose machines over magic; only the cult of Athene continues to keep the old ways alive."

"It's not my Empire," Charlotte shot back. "I despise everything that the Empire is." Charlotte had always resented the Empire for taking her parents away, for forcing her into a life underground, but the Floating City had inflamed her hatred.

"You may object to the Empire," Meg replied. "But your life is shaped by its power, and its actions dictate your reactions. Thus, it is yours, in a manner of speaking."

When Charlotte fell into a sulky silence, Meg went on. "My anger at my mother made me ignore the fact that I have the same inherent connection to the spirit world that she has. What's happening now has made it clear that I've been selfish and foolish to ignore such a gift when it could aid our cause."

"What are you saying?" The regret Charlotte could hear in Meg's voice made her nervous.

Meg took Charlotte's hands in hers. "I need you to promise me something."

Charlotte waited, her anxiety building with each passing breath.

"Be strong for your brother," Meg said, clasping

Charlotte's fingers in a grip so tight it verged on painful. "He'll need you."

"What does Ashley have to do with this?" Charlotte asked. Ashley had been more than reluctant to accept any magical explanations for Grave's strange origins. She hardly thought he'd be eager to learn of Meg's new interest in exploring her inclinations toward the occult.

"Just promise, Lottie, please," Meg urged. "And remember that you and Ash and everyone in the Catacombs are my family. You always will be."

Charlotte frowned. "Why are you talking like this?"

When Meg just squeezed her fingers again, Charlotte sighed. "I promise."

"Thank you." Meg gave Charlotte a brief hug. When she pulled back, Meg's lips were quirked thoughtfully. "There's one more thing."

"You've already made me promise something I don't understand," Charlotte objected.

"It's about Jack," Meg said, and Charlotte went stiff.

"Things are about to become very difficult for all of us, Lottie," Meg pressed. "Storm clouds build on the horizon. Before long, they'll be upon us. It's not a time to let anger toward those we love fester."

"You know what Jack did." Charlotte flinched at Meg's use of the word *love*. "Why should I be anything other than angry?" *And heartsick.*

"We are all prisoners of circumstance at one point or another," Meg answered sadly. "Consider that when you measure Jack's recent behavior against the weight of his past."

Half of Charlotte wanted to shout at Meg for taking Jack's side; the other half wanted to confess how much she missed him. How much she wished he were here. Holding her. Kissing her again. But then she thought of Coe. How strong and assured he was. How he'd risked Jack's fury to expose her to the truth. Maybe she'd fallen for the wrong brother. What if Coe was like Jack, only better? Guilt and heartache piled up on Charlotte's heart, making her wearier still, as bone-tired as she already was.

"I'll leave you to rest now." Meg went to the door. "Sleep well, Lottie."

Charlotte crawled into bed, pulling the covers up to her chin. Her limbs ached from exhaustion, but she was afraid to fall asleep. This day still weighed heavily on her mind and heart, but somehow she knew the morning would bring worse.

26.

FTER A FEW HOURS of restless sleep,
Charlotte entered the dining room to break
her fast and found Ashley seated with a cup
of tea. Grave sat across from her brother in
his usual quiet repose, but Meg was standing nearby, already dressed for travel.

"Oh, good." Meg's hands fluttered at her sides. "I've
been waiting for you."

Charlotte suddenly wondered if she should have brought
her jacket downstairs. "Are we expected somewhere?"

"No."

At her reply, Ash set down his teacup and looked at
Meg in surprise. Obviously he'd assumed that Meg and
Charlotte had some morning errand to run.

"Then where are you going?" Ash frowned at Meg. "To see your mother and bid her farewell?"

"No." Meg gripped the back of one of the empty dining chairs. "To the temple."

Ashley's frown deepened. "Why are you going back there? It's too risky to reveal more about Grave to Rosemary. She's unpredictable and could give us away."

"I'm not going to see Rosemary," Meg told him softly. "I'm going to join the Sisters of the Temple."

Ash jumped up, knocking over his chair. "You're what?!"

Charlotte's insides twisted into knots. *Be strong for your brother. He'll need you.* This was why Meg had made Charlotte promise. She was leaving them.

"I can't hide from my past, from who I am, any more than Grave can." Meg's chin was lifted, her words confident, though her voice carried a touch of sorrow. "The temple is where I'll have access to books and scrolls that reveal mysteries. It's the only way I can understand the gift I inherited from my mother."

"Bollocks!" Ash slammed his fist down on the table. "It would be a waste for you to stay here, Meg. We need you. The Resistance needs you."

"The Resistance needs me to seek the truth," Meg replied calmly, despite the wildness in Ash's eyes. "There is more danger lurking here than any airship or military commander could ever represent. The Resistance needs someone in the temple to uncover what has been long hidden.

Passages of the Book of the Dead have made their way into the world, and a dead boy lives because of it. The implications of this impossibility make me more frightened than anything I've seen in the war, Ashley. Arcane knowledge possessed by the Sisters might prove as powerful a weapon as any machine the Empire could devise. You ignore that truth at your own peril and the peril of our cause."

Ashley's anger gave way to panic. "It doesn't have to be you, Meg."

"It does," Meg said, backing away when Ash reached for her. "I know what I must do."

"Please, Meg." This time Meg didn't move when Ashley grasped her hand. "There are things I would say to you. But not here. Let's withdraw somewhere and speak privately."

Inwardly, Charlotte cringed. She glanced at Grave, half hoping he'd get up and they could leave the room together and avoid witnessing this now intimate exchange between Meg and her brother. But Grave was watching them calmly, a slightly puzzled expression on his face.

With her free hand, Meg reached up and touched Ash's cheek. "I know what you would say, for the words are in my heart as well. But it cannot be."

"Don't say that," Ash barely whispered. "At least hear me out. There's so much I haven't . . . you don't know—"

"If I let you take me into another room; if I sit with you and listen to your pleas, then I may not have the will to leave you." Meg's eyes were glistening. "And I must."

"If you won't listen to me, then listen to Charlotte."
Ash threw a desperate look at his sister. "Tell her how
wrong this is!"

Though her heart screamed against it, Charlotte met
Meg's steady gaze as she said, "You have to trust Meg,
Ashley."

When that earned Charlotte a glare, Meg said to Ashley, "Don't foist your anger upon Lottie when I'm the one
who has earned it."

Meg pulled her hand from Ash's grasp. The color
drained from his face. "You're leaving right now?"

"I am." Leaning in, Meg planted a gentle kiss on Ashley's cheek before she turned away.

Charlotte saw the first tears escape from beneath Meg's
downcast eyes before she left the dining room.

Ash moved to follow, and Charlotte startled herself by
stepping forward to block his path.

"I have to go after her," Ash said through gritted teeth.

"That would be cruel, and you know it," Charlotte told
him. "You know it just as you know why she's made up her
mind to do this. Her heart is broken too, Ashley. You have
to remember that and hope."

Ash deflated. "Hope for what?"

"That a time will come when she won't be compelled
to live apart from us," Charlotte said. "She needs answers.
We might have learned a little about how Grave came to
be, but you know as well as I do that we don't understand
what it really means. Meg is the one who can find out.

She's making a sacrifice for all of our sakes. For the sake of the Resistance."

Just like her father did.

Ashley held her unwavering gaze for a few moments, then turned around. Righting his chair, he sat heavily and stared into his cup of tea.

"I'm think I'm sad she's gone too." Grave's brow furrowed as he spoke to Ashley. "I like Meg."

Ash's fists clenched and unclenched, but he answered quietly, "Thank you, Grave."

The rest of the morning passed in an uncomfortable silence. Ash suggested that Grave assist Charlotte with packing up her things. Convinced that her brother wouldn't run off to find Meg, Charlotte assented, and they left Ashley to make his own preparations.

It was nigh midday when Charlotte descended the staircase, dressed for travel. Grave followed, bearing her luggage with ease, as if she'd packed trunks full of feathers.

Ashley awaited them in the foyer. Beside him was a young lady whose silk gown and fine hat marked her as a member of the colonial elite. Charlotte bristled, fearing it was Eleanor come to call on Jack or Lady Winter. But when the woman turned and lifted her face, Charlotte blurted out in surprise, "Linnet!"

"Why, hello, Charlotte." Linnet came to meet her at the base of the stairs, kissing Charlotte on both cheeks. "Today I play the part of your dearest friend, a kindred spirit and sole confidante. Feel free to whisper your darkest secrets to me—it's all part of the guise, of course. You can trust me not to share."

Linnet winked at her, and Charlotte couldn't help but laugh.

"Lord Ott has arranged transport up the East River," Ash told her. "Linnet is taking you and Grave to the Great Wheel now. Ott will meet you when you reach the Commons."

"You mean he'll meet *us*," Charlotte said.

"I won't be coming with you, Lottie," Ash said quietly.

For a moment, Charlotte simply stared at her brother. Then she said, "You have to let Meg do this. It's not about you."

Ash shook his head. "This has nothing to do with Meg. I didn't know she would ever consider staying in the city, much less joining the Cult of Athene."

"Then what are you talking about?" Charlotte asked, anxious stones piling up in her stomach.

"The meeting Jack and I had with Lord Ott and the other Resistance leaders in the city," Ash answered. "Lazarus wants us to relay information to the front lines in Louisiana."

"You and Jack," Charlotte said, hardly believing what Ashley had just told her.

"Yes." Ash shoved his hands in his pockets. "We're taking the Dragonfly to New Orleans."

Charlotte spluttered, flailing her hands in frustration

as she spoke. "How can you be such a hypocrite? You were upset with Meg for leaving, when all along you knew you'd be leaving too!"

"This is different," Ash told her, but managed to look somewhat abashed.

"Of course it is," Charlotte huffed. "Because it's you."

"Having Meg in the Catacombs while I was on a mission isn't the same as her staying in the city and joining the Cult of Athene. And I wasn't upset with Meg because of her intentions," Ash said apologetically. "It was . . . you know why—"

"I know, I know," Charlotte said, tamping down her anger. "Just tell me when you're coming back."

He didn't answer.

The implications of his silence frightened Charlotte more than his words. "Ash, you have to come back."

"It's a war, Charlotte," Ashley said. "I don't want to make you promises I can't keep."

"But who will lead us?" Charlotte protested. "What will happen to the Catacombs?"

"There will always be a leader in the Catacombs," Ash replied softly. "When one of us goes to the front, someone else steps into the role."

"Who is there?" Charlotte wanted to stomp her feet and scream, but she wasn't a child anymore. She had to show Ashley she was strong, no matter how scared she felt. Meg had left. Now Ashley and Jack were leaving too.

"There's you."

Charlotte was so startled she gave her head a shake to clear it. "What?"

"You, Lottie." Ash offered her a little smile. "Of course it's you. You're the only one with enough courage and bull-headedness to do it."

If it hadn't meant she was losing her brother to a war, Charlotte might have been thrilled by his praise. Instead she felt a hollow grief followed by a crushing sense of responsibility.

Seeing the bleak expression on her face, Ash put his hands on Charlotte's shoulders. "You were made for this, Lottie, trust me. If I weren't putting you in charge of the Catacombs, I don't think I'd be able to leave in good conscience."

"Can you stay anyway?" Charlotte asked weakly.

Ash pulled her into a hug. "You already know the answer."

When he released Charlotte, Ashley reached into his pocket and withdrew an envelope.

"Jack asked me to give this to you."

"What is it?" Charlotte looked at the envelope, her blood swimming with a mixture of curiosity and trepidation.

"I wouldn't know, Charlotte." Ash offered her a sly smile. "Should I take that question to mean you'd like me to begin reading your private letters?"

That startled Charlotte out of her hesitation. She snatched the envelope from Ashley's fingers and stuffed it into her own pocket.

"Don't get too excited," Linnet huffed. "I don't think my brother has a flair for poetry. Hopefully he spelled all his words correctly."

Charlotte shot Linnet a critical look, but met the other girl's teasing eyes, and her objection vanished before she could speak.

Looping her arm through Charlotte's, Linnet started toward the door. "Come, then. My de facto father doesn't like to be kept waiting. And if we're late, he'll blame me, not you."

"Just a moment." Charlotte pulled free of Linnet and rushed to throw her arms around Ashley. "Be safe."

"You too." Ash held her tight. "And I know you're still too cross with him to ask, but don't worry. I'll keep an eye on Jack."

Charlotte squeezed Ash a little tighter and then returned to Linnet, taking the girl's hand. "I'm ready."

As they rode the trolley to the Great Wheel, Charlotte tried to calm her turbulent spirit. Her hand was in her pocket, clutching Jack's letter. She was afraid of what it would say, or what it wouldn't say. And she didn't know when she'd have the privacy to even look at it.

Grave stayed quiet, and Linnet seemed happy enough to leave Charlotte to her own thoughts. But when they boarded the wheel's carriage and found they had it to themselves, Linnet said to Charlotte, "You can read my brother's letter now."

Charlotte balked. "I don't think—"

"Come, come," Linnet coaxed. "Read it. I won't look over your shoulder. I promise."

"You're hoping I won't be able to hold my tongue," Charlotte said, though she'd already half drawn the envelope from her pocket.

"Your tongue has nothing to do with it." Linnet laughed. "I'll know exactly what's in that letter just from watching your face when you're reading."

"Then why would I read it in front of you!" Charlotte looked to Grave for support, but he was standing in the corner of the carriage, gazing at the gears that turned the massive wheel.

"Because you can't stand to wait any longer," Linnet replied.

"Augh!" Charlotte wanted to prove Linnet and her wicked grin wrong, but she only lasted another minute before stomping her foot in frustration and pulling out the letter.

Linnet smirked, but didn't offer further comment. When she opened the envelope, Charlotte made a show of turning her back on Linnet, but somehow she knew that wouldn't make a difference.

Charlotte's fingers trembled as she opened the folded page.

Charlotte,

I hope you haven't torn this page up and tossed it into the fire before reading it, though I'm all too aware I've given you more than enough cause to do so. On the chance that you have spared me a moment,

I've put down what words I can to plead my cause to you—however insufficient they might be.

I've ended my engagement.

Whether that has any bearing on your judgment of me or not, it was the only honorable course. When I became betrothed to Eleanor, I thought I loved her. I learned much later how wrong I was. I didn't know what love truly was. Not until you.

And with you I've been a coward, hiding behind falsities and all the while convincing myself it was necessary for the mission. But I'm forced to admit now that I used that excuse as a way to escape my past because each day with you filled me with regrets about the choices I'd made.

I wanted to tell you this. To see you. But given all that's happened, forcing you to face me seemed yet another selfish choice when I've already taken too many false steps at your cost.

You know who I was and who I am. I leave it to you to decide whether I merit forgiveness or dismissal. Whatever your judgment, know that I am yours always.

Jack Winter

Charlotte read the letter again. Then a third time. Very carefully she folded the page and slipped it back into her pocket.

Jack's words should have made her jubilant, or at least provided some comfort. But they only made Charlotte feel a cold hollowness beneath her ribs. Jack claimed he wanted to speak to her, to make these professions in person, but had stayed away for her sake.

Those words struck Charlotte as false, cowardly even. She couldn't see the letter as anything other than Jack keeping his distance, hiding behind words until he was assured a safe welcome back into her heart. Charlotte didn't know if she believed the letter, if she believed that Jack actually *had* ended his engagement to Lady Eleanor Stuart. All she could rely on for proof was this letter, and in the balance of time, hadn't Jack offered her more false words than true? Charlotte couldn't bring herself to trust him that much yet . . . She wondered if she'd ever be able to completely trust in him again.

She turned around to face Linnet. "It's not enough." Then Charlotte frowned. "Is that horrible of me to say?"

"Of course not, kitten. From what I've seen, and I've seen quite a lot, men are poor soldiers in love's war. And it is a war—one that never ends." Linnet's gaze was kind. "If my brother isn't a complete dolt, he'll figure that out and do what he must to become your champion." Linnet's smile became sly. "Or someone else will."

27.

LORD OTT STOOD at the edge of the Great Wheel's platform, gazing at his pocket watch.

"We are not late." Linnet scowled, putting her hands on her hips and squaring herself to face him. "Not by one minute."

"Did I say anything?" Ott waggled his bushy eyebrows at her. He turned to Charlotte and gave a slight bow. "Miss Marshall."

Behind Ott was a stumpy wagon to which was harnessed an even stumpier mule. Seated on the driver's bench was Coe Winter. He'd forsaken his military garb for the drab gray clothing of the Hive. He held the reins, but freed one hand to give them a wave. Charlotte's chest burned. A part of her wished it were the younger and not the elder son of the House of Winter here to see them off. But in some ways, it was a relief to see Coe waiting for her.

Without prompting, Grave trundled Charlotte's luggage over to the wagon and climbed in to sit beside the trunks.

Ott noticed Charlotte's wary assessment of their transport.

"Don't worry, my dear," he said. "The sternwheeler's much better looking than the wagon. You'll see when we reach the river."

"I'm not worried," Charlotte replied. "Just wondering about the mule. I haven't seen any mules or horses in the city until now."

"That's because they always panic up on the platforms," Linnet said. "After enough horses had bolted and then fallen to their deaths, the Empire banned work animals from the Floating City."

"Also because they left their shite everywhere." Ott laughed. "And if it doesn't glitter, the Empire doesn't want it in their diamond of a metropolis."

Linnet snorted a laugh and grabbed Charlotte's hand. They climbed into the wagon bed beside Grave. Coe tossed them all heavy traveling cloaks.

"Society folk don't go where we're going."

He tipped his wool cap at Charlotte. For the first time since reading Jack's letter, she smiled and the fist that had been clamped around her heart eased its grip.

The wagon creaked under Lord Ott's weight when he hauled himself onto the bench beside Coe.

Coe shook the reins, and the wagon bumped along the path toward the Iron Forest. Passengers disembarking from the wheel or on their way to the Tinkers' Faire followed the wagon's departure with curious gazes.

"Aren't you afraid we'll be followed?" Charlotte asked Ott.

"Of course we're being followed," Ott told her. "I'm always being followed. But I have people who follow the people following me. And they make certain no one sees or reports anything I wouldn't want to be seen or reported."

Charlotte didn't know whether to smile or shudder.

"You've picked a good time to leave the city," Lord Ott continued. "Things have taken a turn toward the ugly."

"What do you mean?" Charlotte asked.

"Not more than an hour ago, the Enforcers entered the Hive and locked it down," Ott told her. "No one has been allowed in or out since."

Her fingers curled tightly around the edge of the wagon seat. "Why?"

"My sources have yet to tell me," he replied. "But I'll find out soon enough."

Panic made Charlotte's blood icy. She opened her mouth to question Lord Ott further, but Coe spoke first.

"Hive workers are sometimes tempted to chase French gold and Spanish silver by smuggling their crafts out of the city. The Empire frowns upon such habits, of course. These raids happen infrequently, but they do happen. Don't worry too much over it, Miss Marshall."

Coe's tone was calm, but he fixed Charlotte with a hard look. For whatever reason, he didn't want her to reveal anything more to Lord Ott about their visit to the Hive. Charlotte quickly decided his inclination was prudent. Though Ott was their ally, there was no way of knowing how he'd take the news about Grave's unprecedented origins. Coe was right to make sure that the circle of those who knew the truth was as tight and trustworthy as possible. Keeping silent as the wagon lurched on, Charlotte fell to brooding over what might have incited the Imperial raid on the Hive and hoped its timing would prove coincidental to their meeting with Bromley and not its cause.

The smooth stones that paved the pathway near the Great Wheel disappeared when they entered the shadowed Iron Forest, and soon they were traveling on nothing but wheel ruts worn into the soil.

All around them scrap iron had been worked into trees of varying shapes and sizes. Some of the trees featured leaves of beaten steel and copper—it was clear that any crafted of silver and gold had long ago been stolen. Though a forest of metal, it wasn't entirely devoid of wildlife. Some intrepid squirrels had built nests in the higher branches. Birds could be seen flitting between the metal trunks. Even so, the forest felt cold and empty. Sunlight struggled to pierce the dense tangle of heavy, unyielding iron.

Shivering, Charlotte pulled her cloak tight around her and instinctively snuggled up against Linnet. Realizing what she'd done, Charlotte would have been embarrassed had Linnet not cozied right back into her.

"It's why we use the old mules to carry cargo by this path. They're placid and reliable, and most are half blind," Linnet said in a hushed voice. "Horses spook so often you can barely get one to walk in a straight line."

"Isn't Lord Ott worried that someone might give us trouble in here?" Charlotte asked, remembering the sudden attack she and Coe had faced.

"No one bothers Ott." Linnet smiled wryly. "Half of those scoundrels are on his payroll."

"But those brigands attacked Coe and me," Charlotte protested.

"Of course they did," Linnet replied. "I said that they wouldn't bother Ott. But they'd always bother the likes of a rich blueblood silly enough to tramp through their forest. They'd be poor excuses for thieves if they didn't. Wouldn't they, Ott?"

"That sounds like Athene's truth to me," Ott chortled.

Charlotte had nothing to say to that.

The wagon rocked and creaked its way through the forest, and Charlotte was relieved when they finally came to a halt on the riverbank, though she guessed the journey hadn't been half as long as it felt.

Coe jumped down from the driver's bench and came around to help Charlotte out of the wagon bed. She tried to exit delicately, despite her dress. But when Coe tried to assist Linnet, she waved him off, lifted up her skirts, and simply hopped out of the wagon, landing lightly on her booted feet and making Charlotte wish she'd done the same.

"That's where you're headed." Coe pointed to the river. "She's called the *Aphrodite*."

A sternwheeler was moored in the middle of the Hudson. Ott had told the truth—the paddleboat was much better looking than the wagon. The boat was long and slim. The wood that made up its body had been varnished to a glossy sheen, and the pairs of wheels fitted to its stern had been covered in gold leaf.

While Charlotte and Linnet approached the river's edge, Coe and Grave unloaded the wagon. A small boat had been dragged up onto the bank. As Ott descended from the wagon, the man sitting on the bank beside the small craft jumped up and took off his cap.

"All ready, sir," the man piped, ducking his head when Lord Ott joined them on the riverbank. "Captain's holding the ship till we board."

"Very good." Ott nodded to the man and then turned to Charlotte and Linnet. "I'll bid my farewells to you now. Margery especially wanted me to tell you how much she's enjoyed your company and hopes to meet you again."

"Margery?" Charlotte tilted her head at Lord Ott.

"The Lady Ott." He smiled.

"Oh!" Charlotte returned his friendly smile. "Please send her my best regards as well."

"And you'll stay out of trouble." Ott wagged a finger at Linnet.

"If I can," Linnet answered blithely.

"I suppose that's the best I can hope for," he grumbled.

"It is," Linnet said, but she rose on her tiptoes to kiss his cheek before she climbed into the boat.

"Safe journey, Miss Marshall," Lord Ott said to Charlotte. "Should I have any news of your brother, I'll try to get word to you."

"Thank you, Lord Ott."

"Call me Roger, dear child." Ott grinned. "Except in proper company of course."

"Of course." Charlotte dipped into a curtsey.

Lord Ott patted her cheek. "Good girl."

Charlotte was about to follow Linnet into the boat when she heard Coe say, "Are you that eager to get away from us?"

Charlotte *was* eager to get away. Not from her companions, but from this place. She doubted she could ever be at ease in the city. For the sake of courtesy, she turned around.

"Eager to return home," she told Coe.

"What would you say if I told you I shall miss you, Charlotte Marshall?" Coe's hand slipped over hers. "And that I hope it won't be long before I see you again?"

He smiled, and for a moment, Charlotte's heart pattered with anticipation. The brief thrill left her uneasy. Did she welcome Coe's attention because she smarted so from Jack's betrayal? Or was the elder brother's allure something real, possibly more real than anything she'd shared with Jack?

Charlotte gave his hand a gentle squeeze before she pulled her fingers free of his grasp. "I would say you are kind, Commodore Winter."

Coe's smile became wan. "Perhaps someday you'll forgive me for revealing the truth about my brother. And you'll desire more than kindness when we meet again."

With a shake of her head, Charlotte answered, "Don't burden yourself with guilt over showing me ugly things. Though my pride might be injured, you did me honor by believing me strong enough to face the truth and go on."

"And are you," Coe asked softly, "going on?"

Charlotte's throat went dry. She wanted to nod or to say yes, but she wasn't certain enough of her conviction to risk raising Coe's hopes. Unlike Jack, she would not play falsely with another's affection.

Coe leaned down, his voice low. "Forgive me for asking too soon, but I pray that when you are ready, you remember that I asked."

She did manage to nod in reply to that, and the nearness of Coe's face to hers made her breath catch.

Coe spoke again, quieting his voice even more. "I'll

find out what provoked the raid. If Bromley is involved, I'll send word."

"Thank you," Charlotte said.

Conscious of the way heat was creeping up her neck and making her head swim, she did not accept Coe's assistance in boarding the small boat for fear that her body's traitorous response would be noted by onlookers. Lifting her skirts as Linnet had, Charlotte stepped lightly from the bank onto the boat's planked bottom.

Coe lifted his hand in farewell as they rowed away. Charlotte wondered when she would next meet Commodore Winter or his younger brother. Perhaps it would be for the best if she never encountered either of the sons of Winter again. It would certainly make things simpler.

"I wonder if I have ever traveled by boat," Grave said aloud, but he seemed to be speaking to himself.

Charlotte asked, "Are you trying to remember?" She glanced warily at the rowing sailor. He worked for Ott, but that didn't mean she felt comfortable with him knowing too much about Grave.

Fortunately, Grave just nodded and returned to his silent musing.

When they reached the *Aphrodite* and boarded, the captain met them and offered a cursory welcome before returning to his post. The sailor who'd rowed them to the paddleboat told Grave to leave Charlotte's luggage on the main deck.

When Linnet caught Charlotte's puzzled glance, she said, "If we were taking you all the way to the *Mohawk,* I'd put you in a cabin for the night. But we'll be handing you off to your friends at the midway point."

"My friends?" Anticipation bubbled up in Charlotte's veins.

Linnet nodded. "Ott said you have some kind of submersible?"

"The *Pisces*!" Charlotte clapped with delight. Everything in the city had been so strange, felt so wrong. Just the thought of returning to a familiar ship crewed by her longtime companions made her giddy.

"Oh!" Charlotte exclaimed. "I hope they bring Pocky!"

"Who?" Linnet asked.

Slightly abashed, Charlotte said, "Um. She's a gun. My favorite gun."

"Ah." Linnet smiled knowingly. Dipping her hand into her bodice, she withdrew a stiletto not unlike the one Ash had given Charlotte. "This is Brutus."

"Brutus?" Charlotte frowned at such a brawny name for a slender blade.

"You know." Linnet shrugged. "Good for stabbing people in the back."

28.

THOUGH THE CAPTAIN'S butler offered to prepare a lunch for them, Charlotte was much too restless to sit below-decks and eat. She and Linnet took apples from the ship's store and munched on the crisp, tart fruit while leaning over the railing at the fore of the paddleboat. Grave had demurred when Charlotte invited him to join them. He wanted to stay near the stern and watch the turning of the boat's four wheels.

There was no denying that the boy, with his cold, colorless skin and strange manner, was an odd duck. But Charlotte couldn't bring herself to condemn him as her friends had. To Charlotte, Grave was neither monster nor machine. Though he was a puzzle, she believed him still a person. And as a refugee in the Catacombs, Grave was under Charlotte's protection. *An orphan for now. Like the rest of us.*

It was mid-afternoon when a bell began to clang. The *Aphrodite*'s paddles slowed as its steam engines were shut down. Sailors hustled about the deck, dropping anchors at the fore and stern of the boat.

"There!" Linnet shouted, pointing ahead at what had been an empty patch of river.

The surface of the water roiled, then parted, as a gleaming, monstrous shape rose from the Hudson's depths.

"The *Pisces*!" Charlotte spun around and jumped up and down, unable to contain her excitement.

The massive fish glittered and gleamed under the afternoon sun, and Charlotte judged the submersible lovelier than any gilded sight of the Floating City. The ship glided toward the *Aphrodite,* slowing until it was floating alongside the sternwheeler.

When a pair of green pigtails peeked out of the hatch, Charlotte cried out in delight. "Pip! Pip, here!" She waved wildly, smiling so hard her cheeks hurt, but she couldn't stop.

"Prepare to be boarded!" Pip shouted back with a salute. She scrambled out of the *Pisces*'s hatch and shimmied her way down its metal scales.

One of Ott's sailors tossed her a line, and Pip tied the *Pisces* onto the merchant vessel. In the distance, thunder rumbled. Charlotte didn't take her eyes off Pip and the shimmering submersible, but in the back of her mind, she thought the sound odd. It was a clear day with no sign of rain that she'd noticed.

"What's that?" Linnet put her hand up to shade her eyes from the bright sun. "A fire?"

Charlotte followed Linnet's line of sight to the northwest, where she saw oily plumes of smoke billowing into the cloudless sky. She gazed at the thick smoke erupting from a concentrated site like ash spewn from a volcano. *How far off was that spot?*

A flurry of approximated calculations of time and distance and space swept through Charlotte's mind. She swayed on her feet, feeling as though a fist had been thrust beneath her ribs to squeeze the life from her heart.

No. No. No.

Falling forward, Charlotte caught the edge of the deck rail and vomited over the side.

No. No. No.

"Charlotte!" Linnet rushed to Charlotte's side, rubbing her back until the wave of sickness passed. "Are you ill? Surely you're not seasick—there's barely a ripple on this river."

Shaking and scarely able to force words from her throat, Charlotte said, "You don't understand. The fire . . ."

Linnet's eyes narrowed, then went wide. "Hephaestus's hammer. You think that's the Catacombs."

Feeling another wave of nausea rising, Charlotte could only nod. The smoke was too black, too greasy to be natural. As if to confirm Charlotte's thought, an explosion boomed through the air, its force rattling the ship. Grave came running up from the stern.

"What is that?" He looked as fearful as the first time Charlotte had seen him running from the Rotpots.

Then Charlotte heard Pip shrieking.

"Get her onboard!" Linnet's voice cracked like a whip, and sailors scrambled to follow the order.

Not a minute later, Pip appeared kicking and screaming as four sailors struggled to drag her aboard the *Aphrodite.*

"Athene, no!" Pip screeched. "We have to go back. Let me go! We have to go back!"

A sailor swore and dropped one of Pip's legs when she turned her head and gave his arm a vicious bite. The sailor pivoted. His fist shot out toward Pip's jaw, but Grave caught the man's wrist mid-strike.

"Don't," Grave said, closing his fingers tighter. The sailor's eyes went very wide, and his forearm began to shake. Images of the Enforcers' steel fists smashing faces and crushing limbs flashed through Charlotte's mind.

He's the perfect weapon, Coe had said.

Charlotte knew she couldn't let Grave become that. Once he crossed that line, if he killed easily and without remorse while others witnessed it, he would be deemed a monstrosity. If that happened, Charlotte doubted she'd be able to shield him from the designs of friend or enemy. Grave would cease to be a person; he'd simply become a priceless implement of war for one side or the other.

"Grave, let him go, and, Pip, stop struggling!" Charlotte was on her feet. "These men aren't your enemies."

You're the only one with enough courage and bull-headedness to do it.

Grave immediately released the sailor, who swore, shaking his bruised fist.

Pip continued to struggle until Charlotte yelled, "Pip, that's enough!"

The green-haired girl went still and then began to sob.

"Let her go," Linnet told the men.

The bitten man stomped away cursing, while the others set Pip down on the deck. Charlotte went to the crying girl.

I have to be strong. I can't falter. They are my responsibility now.

She forced herself to ignore the tiny voice that whispered, *Whoever's left, that is.*

"Go to the submersible and get Scoff," Charlotte told Grave. "Bring him up here."

Grave nodded and hurried to the edge of the deck.

"There's so much smoke." Pip sniffled. She blinked at Charlotte through her tears. "Birch's explosions never make that much smoke. Never."

"I know," Charlotte said. "But we can't be sure what's happened."

"So much smoke." Pip's voice trailed away. She drew her knees up to her chest and curled up into a ball.

Linnet's mouth set in a thin line as another boom shook the boards beneath their feet.

Grave reappeared on the deck leading Scoff, who moved along in a stupor.

"I'm pretty sure that was my laboratory," Scoff muttered to himself. He glanced over his shoulder at the smoke. "If the smoke starts to change colors, I'll be sure."

"Hello, Scoff," Charlotte said, trying to keep her tone light. "It's good to see you."

Scoff nodded, and dropped into a cross-legged position next to Pip, who didn't uncurl from her ball but inched over until she could lean against him. Grave stood over the boy and girl with their odd-colored hair, watching them like a sentinel.

"What happened to the Catacombs?" Scoff asked Charlotte.

"We don't know," she answered, watching the black smoke fill with ribbons of green and violet. She decided not to tell Scoff. "Not yet."

Linnet scrutinized the new arrivals. "Did you notice anything unusual near the Catacombs today? Anything odd at all?"

"No," Scoff answered. "Everything was exactly like it always is when we left. I mean, except that Ash, Meg, Jack, and Charlotte were gone. But that's been odd for a while."

"You didn't see anything?" Linnet pressed. "Like a strange bird that stays at its perch too long or a stiff-moving rabbit?"

Pip lifted her head long enough to give Linnet a scornful look. "We know about crowscopes and rabbit moles. We're not idiots."

Linnet let that pass.

"Was Birch going to try anything particularly dangerous in his workshop?" Charlotte asked. It wasn't hard to imagine that without Ash around to curb the tinker's enthusiasm for experiments, he might have taken on some inadvisable project.

But Scoff frowned. "Not that I know of. I thought he was just building more mice. Those can blow up, of course, but not like . . ." He craned his neck to gaze at the smoke. "Not like that."

"Do you want me to tell the captain to turn us around?" Linnet asked Charlotte. "We can take your submersible to Lord Ott's dockyard. There's an underwater entrance you could use to access the port without being seen."

"No." Charlotte already knew where she had to go. "We have procedures in place. A location we're to meet at."

"We have to go back!" Pip glared at Charlotte.

"We can't, Pip," Charlotte told her firmly. "Not until we know what really happened. The others will go to the rendezvous point. We'll meet them there."

If anyone survived, the tiny voice whispered, and Charlotte briefly closed her eyes against a sharp sting of pain.

"I should report this to Ott," Linnet said. "He'll probably want to pass it along to Jack and your brother."

"Ask him to wait until he hears from me," Charlotte

told her. "Ash and Jack wouldn't have stayed away from the Catacombs unless this task they're undertaking is truly vital. I don't want them to come running back here until I'm certain they should."

"Are you sure?"

Charlotte clenched her teeth, but nodded. This was what Ash would do.

Reaching into her pocket, Linnet withdrew a wooden egg and handed it to Charlotte.

"Is this what I think it is?" Charlotte asked, flipping open the clasp to reveal the hollow case.

"I don't know." Linnet half smiled. "Do you think it's a homingbird?"

Ignoring Linnet's grin, Charlotte peered at the tiny metal bird inside the egg.

"It's already set to the latitude and longitude where Ott receives his envoys," Linnet told her. "When you're ready to send us news of what happened, use that bird." She eyed Charlotte pointedly. "And if that little flyer doesn't show up by tomorrow night, we're coming out to look for you."

"Deal." Charlotte held out her hand. She was somewhat surprised when Linnet suddenly embraced her.

"Keep those claws sharp, kitten. I hope we'll meet again soon."

Hugging the girl tightly, Charlotte felt her throat closing and her eyes pricking with heat. "I hope so too."

Turning away from Linnet, Charlotte took Pip's hands and helped the girl to her feet.

"Come on," she said to Pip and Scoff. "We need to get to the rendezvous point."

Pip looked at Grave, her gaze speculative. "You were very brave to stop that man from hitting me. I know I shouldn't have bit him, but I still don't think I would have liked to be hit."

"I'm not brave," Grave told her. He glanced at his hand, flexing his fingers. "I just know that I'm strong."

Taking Grave's hand, Pip said, "I think you can be both."

With her other hand, Pip grabbed Scoff's arm, and the trio set off toward the *Pisces* together.

"Interesting little troupe you've got here," Linnet said to Charlotte.

Charlotte smiled at the other girl, who gave a brief nod. "Safe journey."

"And you."

Charlotte went to the fore of the ship, climbing the rope ladder down the front of the *Aphrodite* and onto the slippery surface of the *Pisces*. When she scrambled into the submersible, she closed and locked the hatch behind her.

Pip was waiting for Charlotte in the corridor that linked the cargo bay and the bridge. Charlotte laughed when Pip handed over the POC.

"Thought you probably missed her," Pip said wistfully. "Though I was hoping this would be the kind of trip where we wouldn't need guns."

Nodding regretfully, Charlotte said, "So was I."

"I'm going to ride in the cargo bay with Grave," Pip told her. "You should copilot for Scoff."

Pip spun and went running off toward the rear of the *Pisces*. Moving in the opposite direction, Charlotte ducked through the doorway that opened into the bridge. Scoff was already strapped into his chair.

"I see Pip made sure you and Pocky were reunited," he said.

"She did." Charlotte took the chair beside Scoff. She buckled her harness and held Pocky on her lap. The weight of the gun was reassuring.

"We won't reach the rendezvous point until after dark," Scoff told Charlotte, flipping controls. The *Pisces* began to sink into the river.

"I know," Charlotte said. "It can't be helped."

Scoff steered the ship upstream. Beyond the glass, the Hudson's waters were dim and murky.

He fell silent for a few minutes, then asked, "Do you think anyone else will be there?"

Charlotte hesitated, and Scoff quickly said, "Never mind. That's not a question to be asked."

When they were fully submerged, he reached forward and pulled a brass lever. The *Pisces* shot forward. Scoff leaned forward, fully absorbed in piloting the ship. As they sped along, Charlotte's temple began to throb with anxiety and exhaustion. She leaned her head back and let her eyes close.

In the darkness behind her heavy eyelids, she heard

Meg's voice. *Storm clouds build on the horizon. Before long, they'll be upon us.*

The darkness of her vision gave way to a blue sky where greasy smoke boiled above the treetops. *They're already here.*

Charlotte slipped her hand into her pocket, fingers tracing the outline of Jack's letter. The storm had come, but Charlotte wouldn't cower at its force. She would keep fighting. For Ash and Meg, for Grave, for the Resistance. Charlotte silently swore a pledge to all of them, and most of all to herself—she'd keep fighting.

AUTHOR'S NOTE

IN THE MIDDLE OF AN eye exam, when my optometrist was peering at me from behind a mask of glass, gears, levers, and dials, I realized I wanted to write a steampunk series. While visits to the doctor and dentist seem to reflect advances in medical technology, the tools of an optometrist remain decidedly nineteenth century–esque. The idea of inventing a world filled with fantastic and frightening devices, machines, and weapons proved irresistible.

The allure of steampunk lay not only in its abundance of mad scientists and quirky gadgets, but also in the opportunity to create an alternate historical narrative. While most steampunk novels are set in the late nineteenth to early twentieth centuries and, more often than not, in Europe, the history I wanted to reinvent was much earlier, exploring a period of American history very near and dear to my heart. Prior to becoming a full-time novelist, I was a history professor at Macalester College in St. Paul, Minnesota. My research specialization focused on the intersection of religion, gender, and violence in the British colonies, and I've long held an interest in the transition from colonial rule to republic in early America.

The Inventor's Secret posits the question: What would North American society have looked like if the American Revolution failed? As a nation and society, the United States locates the beginnings of our highest values— freedom, equality, the pursuit of happiness—as a result of a successful eighteenth-century revolution. What, then, would be the fate of those values and that society if the Revolutionary War had been won by the British?

The central characters of *The Inventor's Secret,* a band of teenagers who are the children of men and women still resisting British rule, are struggling to survive in this alternate reality: Having failed to secure the aid of France in the war, George Washington and the Continental Army are unable to defeat British forces. The revolution is quelled, its ringleaders hanged as traitors, and the United States never born.

The year is 1816, just after the Napoleonic Wars conclude in Europe, and the British Empire is on the verge of achieving dominance in the Western Hemisphere. As the novel's protagonists uncover nefarious secrets and confront the violent tyranny of the Empire, they come to grips with the very questions that remain at the heart of American identity. What is the value of liberty? At what cost must it be won?

ACKNOWLEDGMENTS

THE INVENTOR'S SECRET has a special place in my heart because it brings together two of my passions: history and fantasy. My amazing agenting trio at InkWell Management, Richard Pine, Charlie Olsen, and Lyndsey Blessing, are always my first and best advocates as I begin to nurture a new creative project. I'm indebted to Penguin Young Readers for traveling into an alternate past and a new world so this book could come to life. Thank you to Don Weisberg and Jen Loja for letting me forge a new path. The enthusiasm of the sales, marketing, publicity, and school and library teams fuel my writing more than the strongest cups of coffee ever could. Thanks especially to Shanta, Emily R., Erin, Elyse, Laura, Lisa, Elizabeth, Marisa, Jessica, Kristina, Molly, Courtney, Anna, Scottie, and Felicia.

Thank you to Michael Green for that first conversation

about steampunk and the amazing history of New York. Jill Santopolo, my amazing editor, helps me strike the right balance between action and romance and never lets me neglect the swoony boys—which I love. Thanks to Kiffin and Brian for all their work.

I soldier on with the support of wonderful, creative friends: David Levithan, Eliot Schrefer, and Sandy London help me laugh and sing. Beth Revis, Marie Lu, and Jessica Spotswood are my sisters forever. Elizabeth Eulberg, Michelle Hodkin, and Casey Jarrin inspire me with their talent, spirit, and love. Thanks to Conor Anderson, Rachel Noggle, and Eric Otremba for keeping me excited about this project.

I am ever grateful for my exceptional family. Thanks to my mom and dad for all their love. Thank you to Garth and Sharon for being such amazing people and for making me the happiest Auntie Annie.